ALWAYS A BRIDESMAID

ALWAYS A BRIDESMAID

Renea Overstreet

iUniverse, Inc.
New York Lincoln Shanghai

Always a Bridesmaid

iUniverse, Inc.

For information address:
iUniverse, Inc.
2021 Pine Lake Road, Suite 100
Lincoln, NE 68512
www.iuniverse.com

ISBN: 0-595-32067-8

Printed in the United States of America

Acknowledgements

I am so thankful for my number one fan, my mom, Helen Fisher Coffee. Thank you for always reminding me that I can do anything I set my mind to. Thank you, Kim Prince, my best friend. As iron sharpens iron, you make me a better person. Thank you Stephanie Bankett, a true gem. Your faith helped me finish. Thank you Sharon Berry-Brown, my sister-friend. Your loving support is priceless. Thank you Desharon Venson, my creative friend and intellectual muse. Your diligent editing and honest evaluation got me to the last phase. Thank you Heart to Heart readers, especially Gwend Larry. Your seeds of encouragement spawned this work. Thanks to my internet writing buddies, especially Linda Beed. Let's all keep writing! Thank you to my Pastor, Dr. Dana Carson, an extraordinary man of God. Your teaching and preaching laid the foundation and your life's example is still showing me how the impossible can become reality.

Lastly, thank you to my wonderful, loving husband, Morris and my sweet little girl, Marrissa for allowing me the time to write.

CHAPTER 1

As Gail Hardy pulled up to the hotel on the San Antonio Riverwalk at six-thirty on a Thursday evening, she concluded her musings, deciding this, indeed, was the craziest thing she had ever agreed to do. She had already vowed not to be in any more weddings unless she was the bride. Between her sisters, other relatives and high school and college friends, Gail had been a bridesmaid in ten weddings in six years. The last one was four months ago. She didn't mind wearing magenta taffeta for her best friend, Shawn who moved to San Diego right after the nuptials. But, this would be her eleventh wedding, and the crazy thing about this time was she didn't even know the bride. Apparently, she and the bride, Nina, attended the University of Texas around the same time, but she could not place the girl. The only reason Gail agreed to be in this wedding was because her new friend Sara Martin had begged her, assuring her everything would be paid for, including gas to get to San Antonio from Austin. This was the first wedding Gail had been in that was all expenses paid so she decided to be a good sport and look at it as a free trip to San Antonio.

Gail and Sara had been working together for about two months since the reorganization of the accounting department in the state transportation division. They became fast friends the first week they worked together and Sara began inviting Gail to her church. Sara was the kind of woman who was everybody's friend. She was born and raised in Beaumont, but her parents were from Louisiana. Her jovial attitude and quick smile were enhanced by a baby face with cute, fat cheeks and big brown eyes.

After three weeks of Sara's inviting, including a glossy, full-color invitation card from her church, Gail finally gave in and visited the church. Gail was accustomed to a quiet, terse, Methodist service. The Living Word Christian

Fellowship was neither quiet nor terse. Gail felt like she was at some kind of stage production because the first service she went to included a short children's play about the importance of being involved in their children's church, a dance routine by some teenagers, a rap routine in a choir song and then the preacher used a skit in his sermon which was about relationships. That's not to mention the opening praise service with everyone singing and dancing, making her feel like she was at a concert. It turned out that she had gone to a special service for family and friends who had never been to the church. She had to admit she did enjoy it; however, she was not Pentecostal and she was not about to give up her lazy Sunday mornings of lounging around her apartment.

Gail smiled as the valet opened her door and assisted her from her red Honda Accord. She chuckled to herself thinking, "Sara is something else. I guess I would do anything she asked me to do."

Sara had taken off work Wednesday through Friday to help with the wedding in San Antonio, and late Wednesday afternoon, just when Gail was beginning to miss her new friend, Sara called her at the office and asked her for "a great big favor." One of the bridesmaids had gotten sick and couldn't be in the wedding, and the bride was getting even more hysterical. Sara offered to find a replacement and immediately called Gail to see if she would fill in.

"But we don't even know each other. Why would she want me in her wedding?" Gail asked.

"She trusts me to find a good replacement. You'll be great. The dress is your size, and all we have to do is get your shoes and stockings from Niemans. Everything is already paid for so all you have to do is come up tomorrow after work."

"Why don't they just have one less? This doesn't make much sense to me," Gail tried to argue with Sara, but she did think about that free pair of shoes from Niemans. "Why don't you fill in? Isn't this a good friend of yours?"

"You don't understand. You're a perfect fit, and everything is set already for eight girls because there are eight guys. We can't kick any of the guys out and a guy can't walk down the aisle by himself. Look, they'll pay for everything—the shoes and whatever else you need. The dress is waiting for you at the bridal shop. You get your own hotel room. They'll give you gas money. They'll—"

"Okay, okay. I'll do it. I just hope I don't have a problem getting off work with such short notice. I need time to run some errands tomorrow. I can't work a full day."

"Girl, please. You know Jim will give you the time off. He never says no."

Sara was referring to their boss. He had always granted her requests for time off when she asked, even when she just wanted an afternoon off to go to the spa or get her hair done.

So that's how Gail found herself in this predicament, getting ready to walk into a room full of strangers to be a bridesmaid in the wedding of a bride and groom she had never met. Well, she did pride herself on being the adventurous type.

The Grand Pavilion lobby was a huge atrium of real trees and beautiful tropical, blooming plants. After checking in, Gail went to her room on the fourth floor. She felt better about deciding to be in the wedding when she found a nice fruit basket and a note from the bride in her room. "Classy," she thought. She looked forward to meeting the bride. It was obviously a five-star hotel and the balcony of her room overlooked a scenic section of the River-walk. Sara had told her there was a greeting reception for the wedding party and families that began at 6:00 p.m. They had given her the same information at the front desk when she checked in, so she decided she'd better hurry and get to the party.

From the first floor, she was directed around a corner, down a wide staircase to one of the meeting rooms. When she got halfway down the stairs, thankfully she spotted Sara.

"Hey, girl, I'm so glad you could make it!" Sara said as she excitedly rushed her into the room to meet everyone. The spacious room was packed with people including members of both families, the wedding party and a good number of children running around. Sara introduced her to all of the other brides-maids and four of the groomsmen. Two of the bridesmaids were familiar faces from UT. Gail remembered Thelma from a history class she had taken, and she remembered seeing Crystal around campus. They told her they had both pledged a Christian sorority, Alpha Chi Delta, with Sara and Nina, the bride. Gail started to sit at the table with Thelma and Crystal, but Sara tugged on her arm.

"Come on girl. Let me introduce you to Nina before you get comfortable."

She led her to the back of the room toward two women who were seated at a small table looking over some papers. The younger was a prettier replica of the older. They both had smooth dark skin with high cheekbones. The mother reminded Gail of the late actress Madge Sinclair who played James Earl Jones' wife in *Coming to America*.

"Excuse me, Nina, Mrs. Nelson. This is Gail," Sara said.

Both women stood and greeted Gail so cheerfully she felt like she was a relative. They were both almost two inches taller than Gail's five-seven height.

"Oh, Gail!" Nina said and gave her a hug. "Thank you so much for coming. Girl, you are a life saver!"

"We really appreciate your being a part on such short notice, Gail," Mrs. Nelson said also giving her a quick hug. "Let me know if you need anything." She turned to her daughter and said, "All right, Nina, I'm going to discuss those final changes with the coordinator."

"Thanks, Mom."

"Nice meeting you, Gail." Mrs. Nelson excused herself and began making her way through the crowd toward the door.

"So, did Sara fill you in on the details?" Nina asked. "You get your hair done early in the morning. Then you pick up your shoes and other accessories and meet us at the bridal shop by one-thirty."

"Slow down, Nina, I told you I've taken care of everything," Sara said.

"I know you have, Sara. That's why I love you so much, girl." Tears welled up in her eyes and threatened to spill over. Gail had seen enough brides a couple of days before their weddings to know that this was typical behavior.

Suddenly Nina's face brightened as she looked beyond Sara and Gail toward the door. "Oh, here comes my groom. Gail, have you met him yet?"

"No, so far I've only met the other bridesmaids and some of the groomsmen."

"Well here he is," Nina gushed. "Mario Lewis, meet Gail Hardy, the wonderful woman who agreed to fill in for Shannon at the last minute."

A tall, dark and very handsome man had joined Nina at her side and when Gail looked up at him, she could not believe her eyes. Yes, she knew this groom, and she knew him very well. Or at least she used to know him. She saw the same shock she was experiencing reflected in Mario's eyes.

"Hey, do you guys know each other? Mario graduated from UT, too," Sara said.

"We might have met at a party on campus," Mario jumped in before Gail could say anything. She was staring at him with her mouth hanging open.

"Oh, yeah, maybe so," Gail said trying to recover. "I did go to a bunch of parties during my UT days."

"Well, we didn't hang out with the party crowd," Nina said pointedly. "Sara and I were in the Black Voices Gospel Choir and our Christian sorority."

"Yeah, I *was* in the party crowd in my B.C. days," Mario said.

"What's B.C?" Gail asked finally taking her eyes off Mario and looking at Sara. She couldn't bring herself to look at Nina. She was afraid she had that "I've been with your man" look in her eyes.

"That means 'before Christ.' Mario has been a preacher for some years now," Sara explained.

Now Gail was really shocked. She could not believe that the Mario she knew could be a preacher. He was the ultimate player when she knew him. She'd had a hot, short affair with him the summer after her sophomore year. That had to be eight years ago, but as she looked at Mario now, it seemed like just yesterday. She had been taking summer classes and working part-time on campus. He was a tutor for a youth summer program at UT and had a lot of free time on his hands. Much of that time was spent with her in his apartment just West of the campus. Gail had flash backs of that summer and pictured their naked bodies intertwined on his bed, in his bath tub, on the kitchen counter, on his balcony, even in the hot tub at his complex around 3 a.m. on a sultry summer morning. She remembered that he took great pleasure in setting the atmosphere for sex. He would do simple things like lighting scented candles all over the bedroom or complex things like transforming her small apartment into a spa. He had given her the full treatment and had even washed her hair. The final touch was when he lavished her with the best sex she had ever had. She had thought it was just a sex thing and didn't even bother getting to know him very well. He was leaving Austin after that summer anyway. He had finished his business degree and was auditing a graduate course while working with the youth program. That's about all she knew about him outside of what he liked sexually.

And now here she was speechless, trying not to stare at him. She had a million questions to ask him, but she knew this was neither the time nor place. Nina was giving him instructions about picking up more relatives from the airport later that evening. He said he needed to make some calls and excused himself, which was a good thing for Gail. She had started thinking about the night they had spent with the chocolate syrup, whipped cream and cherries. That was not a vision she needed to have while standing next to the man's fiancée. And of all things, he was a preacher now!

Nina and Sara began discussing the schedule for Friday afternoon and had seemed to forget about her. She needed to get out of that room which had suddenly become quite stuffy.

"Hey you guys, I'll be back. I'm going to the lady's room right quick," she said.

"Okay, hurry back though. I want you to meet the rest of my family," Nina said.

Gail made her way out of the room, went up the grand staircase and back through the front lobby where she found a lady's lounge down a secluded hall-way on the other side of the hotel. She sat on a plush sofa in the sitting area of the rest room and thought about her predicament. What was she going to do? Maybe she needed to tell Sara that she couldn't be in the wedding after all. But she was already here and Nina seemed nice enough.

What she needed to do was calm down and just make it through the week-end. Everything would be over by Saturday evening and she could go back to Austin, resume her life and forget about Mario and his new wife, Nina. Her relationship or fling with Mario didn't mean anything anyway. She had been on the rebound after breaking up with Calvin, her boyfriend of almost two years. He had dropped out of UT after his freshman year and was becoming a bum in Gail's opinion. For her the final straw was when he asked to move into her efficiency apartment east of campus. Gail had met Calvin when they were bright-eyed freshmen and he seemed to have such potential as an engineering major. He was from Dallas and had graduated as the valedictorian of his class, but UT was quite a challenge for him. They called it "Spring cleaning" or "weeding out" the students who couldn't handle the system of a serious four-year university. She had felt for Calvin, but he was bringing her down with his slacker ways.

She met Mario while eating lunch at the student union a week before the first summer session started. He took a very direct approach and asked her if he could join her for lunch. She recognized him from some fraternity parties she had been to during the school year. He was 6'3" with a muscular build, but not too bulky. His smooth dark skin was accented by a nicely groomed mus-tache and a low fade hair cut. He had full lips and a strong chin and jaw line. For Gail, what attracted her the most were his expressive eyes. His eyebrows were a little bushy, but for her that only added to his allure. He could speak volumes by just looking at her with those eyes and not saying a word. Gail had a good time reading Mario's eyes that summer.

As he talked to her at the student union that first day, he told her to call him "Rio." They exchanged basic student information and he asked her out to a movie that night. He picked a rather erotic film at the Dobie Theater just off campus and that pretty much set the tone for their relationship. She didn't sleep with him the first night, but she gave him a long, juicy kiss at her door-step. He lingered at her door but didn't ask to come in. Instead he went home and called her. He explained that she had left him in quite a state, and he needed her to take care of him. Before she knew it, she found herself experiencing phone sex for the first time with Rio. She had a lot of sexual "firsts" with Rio that summer. In fact, she hadn't done many of those things with any other man since being with him. She'd had some pretty good sex with other guys, but no other man could really compare to Rio.

Well, now he was getting married. Lucky Nina. If Gail were going to get through the weekend with her sanity intact, she would need to avoid the memories of how good his body felt. Surely this kind of thing happened to people all the time. She had been in one wedding where the bride had slept with the best man *and* one of the groom's cousins. But this was different. No one knew about her and Mario except the two of them, and Mario seemed determined to act like they had only been casual acquaintances at UT. That was fine with her. She used the bathroom, washed her hands, primped a little in the mirror and headed back to the reception.

As soon as she walked out of the lounge, there he was, looking sexier than he ever had.

"Hey Gail. I wanted to talk to you," he said as if he had been waiting for her.

"What, so you followed me?" She was surprised, but didn't mean to sound so irritated.

"Well, no." He hesitated, put his hands in his pocket and looked down sheepishly. "Yes, I followed you, but I just wanted to apologize for acting like I didn't really know you," he explained. He looked directly into her eyes, and Gail realized that she would need strength that she did not have to get through the wedding without lusting for this man in a major way. He would definitely be the main character in her dreams that night.

"Oh, it's okay. I understand. Really." The first thing she had to do was get out of that dimly lit, secluded hallway with him.

"I hope you're not upset."

"I'm not upset, Rio. I'm just surprised. It's been so long since I've seen you. And I find out all at once that you're getting married and that you're a minister," Gail said. "It's actually good to see you again. The circumstances are just weird."

Mario smiled and she melted a little more. "It's good to see you, too." He softened his voice and stepped closer to her. "I love the way you call me that."

"What?" Gail asked, subconsciously licking her lips.

"My nickname. No one calls me Rio anymore, but I love it when you say it."

Gail knew it was dangerous for her to continue staring into his eyes, so she lowered her gaze to his chest and arms. The soft material of his black shirt fit his biceps just so, and her mind again drifted back to that summer.

"So, how long has it been?" he drawled even more softly and took another step closer. She was engulfed by the smell of his cologne. She remembered his easy way of switching from his usual business-like manner to his smooth, sexy mode.

"Years. About eight years," she answered. She thought she should run back to the party and find Sara, but she was paralyzed by the memories of the past. Then he touched her. The tips of his fingers moved gently across her cheek. She looked up at him and saw that he was also flooded with memories of that summer. Their mutual lust had them suspended in a fateful moment. After about ten seconds of staring into each others eyes, one of them gave in to the temptation and they became locked in such a hungry embrace and kiss that Gail felt as if she was his bride.

Mario took his time exploring Gail's mouth with his strong but soft, imploring lips. She felt other parts of his body responding to hers, and she thought she was going to lose her mind as she was transported back to one of those hot summer nights. Why had she let this one get away?

She began to feel a tinge of guilt, but she couldn't bring herself to pull away from his embrace. It felt so good. But it was only a tease. He's getting married Saturday to a very nice girl, she reminded herself. Instead of pulling completely away, she placed her hands on his chest, pulled away from the kiss and looked into his face. His eyes were closed and he was breathing heavily.

"I really should be ashamed of myself. I was overcome," he said quietly, but still didn't release her from his embrace. She knew she had to do something quickly or they would end up having wild sex in her hotel room or in that dark hallway. She pulled away from him.

"We should stop before someone catches us and asks for an explanation." She tried to laugh it off.

"You're right." He held his hands up. "This is wrong. I'm really sorry. I shouldn't have done that. I don't know what's going on with me. I guess I'm getting those last-minute wedding jitters or something."

"Mario, don't apologize. I was wrong, too."

"Please, call me Rio," he said, lapsing back into that shady mood of memories.

"Mario, Rio, whatever," she joked. "You're getting married on Saturday, and I'm happy for you." She was trying hard to lighten the moment. "You're getting married and I'm a bridesmaid. How about that!" She moved past him down the hall toward the lobby area. "I'd better be getting back to the reception, and you have people to pick up from the airport."

"You're right. I'm getting married," he said in a melancholy monotone.

The tone of his voice made her stop. She turned back toward him. "Are you okay? Everything's cool?"

"Yeah, it's cool. I'm okay. You go on back. I'll see you later."

CHAPTER 2

Back at the reception, Gail met more of the wedding party, including a guy from Sara's church, Jason Tucker whom she vaguely remembered. She ended up sitting with Jason at one of the small tables after getting some food and punch from the buffet.

"Sara didn't tell me you were one of the groomsmen."

"She didn't tell me you were one of the bridesmaids," Jason said. Gail explained how she ended up being a part of the wedding.

"Well, Praise the Lord! It's really nice of you to help out like this," Jason said. Gail looked sheepish and thought, *You wouldn't be praising the Lord if you knew what I had just been up to.*

"Sara is so sweet, I couldn't say no to her, so here I am." It didn't seem like she could say "no" to anyone these days. She tried to carry on the conversation with Jason, but she was just too distracted by her predicament. Jason was still talking but she wasn't listening. Maybe she could find Sara and confess everything to her. She looked around the room for Sara.

"So when will you be back?" Jason asked.

"Umm hmm," Gail mumbled still looking around.

"I said when are you going to visit The Word again?"

"What? I'm sorry Jason. I'm looking for Sara. Do you see her anywhere?"

"No, I don't see her. She's probably tending to wedding stuff. Is something wrong?"

"Actually, no. Nothing's wrong. What were you saying again?"

"For the third time, when will you be visiting the church again? I haven't seen you lately."

"Oh, I don't know. Maybe I'll come this Sunday."

Just then, Sara rushed up to their table.

"Change of plans. All the dresses are here including yours. You have to come up and try yours on so it can be altered if needed. Go get you some church shoes and meet us in room ten twenty-five," Sara said and rushed off to tell the other bridesmaids.

"And that's an order, missy," Jason joked. Gail saw that Sara could be bossy when she wanted to. She hadn't seen this side of her at work.

"I guess I'd better get to stepping, then," Gail said. "I'll see you later."

Gail went to her room to grab her heels. She figured that's what Sara meant when she said "church shoes." On her way out of her room she paused to check herself in the dresser mirror. Since she had blossomed at fifteen, she had been dealing with guys and their attraction for her. She was the female version of her handsome father. "Baby, you look like your daddy just spit you out," her relatives would say at family events. She shook her head in the mirror, thinking about the curse his goods looks had been for him. He'd had a problem saying "no" to the women who were so attracted to him and his smooth caramel skin and wavy coal-black hair. She had inherited all of that, including his almond-shaped eyes and thick lashes. She smiled at herself in the mirror and decided that whatever Mario was attracted to, she was not going to let her good looks turn into a curse for her.

When she got to room ten twenty-five, Thelma, one of the bridesmaids, answered the door and led her into a large, beautifully decorated living room area. The long room, which included a dining area, had a wall of windows overlooking the river. All of the bridesmaids were in various stages of trying on dresses with about five other women in the room who were probably supposed to be helping, but most of them were just talking. Two of them must have been seamstresses because they were the only ones working.

"I think Sara has your dress. The seamstress will make some adjustments if you need any," Thelma said. She was wearing a fitted, floor-length navy blue dress. It was strapless with a sexy slit on the side.

"That dress looks great on you. Is it an Alfred Angelo?" Gail knew all the wedding and bridesmaids dress designers by now.

"Yes, it is! I'm glad you like it because yours is exactly like mine," Thelma joked. "There's a little jacket that goes with it."

"So where is Sara?" Gail asked.

"I think she's in the bedroom with Nina," Thelma said. "You can go check if you'd like. It's right through there." Thelma directed her to the right of the entrance area.

Gail tapped politely on the slightly opened door and stuck her head through.

"Hey, Gail. Come on in," Nina said. She was reclining on the king-size bed while Sara perched in a chair near the bed. They looked like they were involved in some serious girl talk. "Maybe you can give me some advice."

"About what," Gail asked, curious.

"Come on in here and sit down," Nina seemed excited about including Gail in on the discussion. Nina sat up and Gail sat on the bed next to her.

"So what are you guys talking about?" She asked again.

"Sex, girl. We're talking about the honeymoon," Nina said.

"Oh, so where are you going?" Gail asked.

"We're going to Jamaica, but the important part is what we're going to do," Nina said. Gail squashed a thought about what *she* would do with Mario in Jamaica.

"You are going to have a wonderful time! That is exciting Nina. There'll be all kinds of stuff to do." Gail was trying to ignore the "s" word Nina had mentioned.

"Nina is a virgin," Sara said matter-of-factly. "I've been trying to get her not to be afraid of having sex." Here was another shocker for Gail.

"You're a virgin for real? You've never done it at all?" Gail didn't know anyone her age who was still a virgin.

"No, I haven't. Neither has Miss Sara here, and she's trying to give me all this advice," Nina said. Gail looked over at Sara and just couldn't believe what she was hearing.

"You've never had sex either?" She asked.

"Nope," Sara said as if it were the most natural thing in the world.

"Don't you have a boyfriend?"

"Yes. You met him at church."

"Girl, you are twenty-seven years old and you have NEVER had sex?"

Sara looked like she had a lot to say, but didn't answer. Nina said, "No neither of us has had sex. Now since you obviously have, tell me how to avoid screaming in pain the first time?" Gail felt like she was talking to girls who were in junior high school. This was just too much for her.

"First of all, tell me how you both have avoided having sex for all these years. Have your boyfriends even tried?" Gail asked, watching them as Nina and Sara glanced shyly at each other. Sara was the first to speak up.

"Anthony hasn't really tried. I only had one other serious relationship before him when I was in high school," Sara said. "We try to keep things holy by avoiding late nights together."

"Holy?" Gail threw her head back and laughed. She quickly sobered when the other girls didn't join her. "Surely it's not that simple."

"It is for us," Nina interjected. "I simply avoid being with Mario when we're both really tired or it's late at night."

"But why? Why not have sex? Don't you all love your men?"

"We love our men, but it's actually better not to have sex before marriage," Sara said.

"Girl, I have never heard of anything like this in my life. I don't know if I could marry someone I haven't had sex with. What about compatibility?"

"What about disease and pregnancy? Abstinence is not a foreign concept," Sara said.

"Look, we can talk about the moral and spiritual ramifications about sex before marriage later. But right now, I need some questions answered," Nina said.

"Didn't your mother and cousin tell you everything you need to know?" Sara asked.

"They told me mechanical stuff. I need to know some other stuff."

"Like what?" Gail asked reluctantly.

"Okay. Now Mario is not a virgin right?" She didn't have to tell Gail that. "So I'm sure he knows what to do, but what if I turn him off?"

"How do you mean?"

"Because I won't know what I'm doing. Will that make him not want to do it?"

"That won't stop him at all. More than likely he'll be concerned about making sure you feel good," Gail said, quenching the urge to scream and run out of the room. She was definitely overqualified for the job of telling Nina about Mario's adeptness and attentiveness in the bedroom.

"Oh, Lord," Nina moaned and started shaking her hands in front of her. "I'm going to be so nervous. I'll probably just freeze up."

"No, girl, you won't freeze up. He'll make sure you are as relaxed as you need to be." Gail couldn't believe she was coaching the fiancée of a former lover about having sex. "Mario is probably a great lover—I mean he seems like a nice person. I'm sure he'll know what to do," Gail said.

"Well, he is very kind and considerate. My mom said that a man who is gentle with you outside of the bedroom will be gentle with you in the bedroom," Nina said.

"I think your mom is right. Don't you, Sara?" Gail asked.

"I guess. But I'm not exactly an expert witness. Nina has polled all the other bridesmaids and everyone has tried to reassure her," Sara said.

"Yeah, I talked to some of my bridesmaids. Actually, I've talked to all of them. I have been kind of taking a poll, I guess."

"Are they virgins, too?"

Nina and Sara laughed. "No, four of them are married, Elaine is engaged and Thelma and Crystal aren't virgins, but they're celibate," Nina said.

"Why are they celibate?"

"For the same reasons we're virgins. We're serious about our relationships with the Lord, Gail. Being sexually abstinent is a part of that relationship," Sara said.

"I know it's important to have safe sex, but I don't know about not having sex at all. I mean that seems like a lot for the Lord to ask for. You're not nuns," Gail said seriously. Sara and Nina laughed again.

"Girl, you are something else. So what's going to keep me from freezing up?" Nina said getting back to what was most important to her at the moment.

"Well, you've at least kissed him before haven't you?" Gail wasn't sure if kissing was forbidden as well.

"Yes, I've even French kissed him."

"So how did it feel?"

"That's what I'm saying. At first it would feel good. I'd start feeling all melted inside, and then boom! I'd freeze up and make him stop."

"He'll have plenty of time to make you melt on your honeymoon," Gail said. "How long have you been together?"

"About a year and a half. We've been engaged for nine months," Nina said. "But we've known each other since we were kids. We grew up in the same church."

"What made you decide to get married?"

"Well, I've always had a crush on Mario, even when we were at UT together. But he was into his thing, and I was into my thing, so we didn't really associate at school," Nina explained. "We would see each other more at church when we came home for weekends and holidays. That is, when he would come home or when he would come to church. He kind of went astray for a while there."

Gail thought about her part in his time of being "astray."

"I was kind of groomed to be a preachers wife, but I didn't know that preacher would be Mario," Nina continued. "Once he got saved and serious about his call to ministry, he began talking to me and we started dating. I didn't let him know about my crush immediately because I didn't want him to get the big head. When I finally told him, he claimed that he knew all along."

"Look, do you have any more questions, Ms. Nina? Because Gail needs to try on this dress," Sara said, moving back into her drill sergeant role. She got up and went to the closet and pulled out the bridesmaid dress. Gail caught a glimpse of a white wedding dress in the closet. Nina would certainly be wearing that color honestly. She wondered what color she would wear at her own wedding. Probably white.

"I think I'll just take Gail's advice and relax. I mean, how bad could it be right?" Nina said, shrugging her shoulders. Gail could tell she was still nervous about the whole thing. Her guilt about Mario compelled Gail to help Nina somehow.

"You can take your time too. I mean, who says you have to do it right away? My best friend didn't have sex the first night. Of course she wasn't a virgin, and they had sex before they got married. They were just too tired that night so they slept," Gail said.

"Are you serious? Well, that's something to think about. Maybe Mario will just give me time to get used to the idea of sleeping in the same bed before we even do it."

Gail couldn't imagine being able to do that herself, but to each her own. Maybe getting to know Nina better would be a good way to stop her from obsessing over Mario.

"All right ladies, I'm going to check on things with everyone else. Gail, you try on the dress and come on out, and Nina, you just relax. We've got everything under control," Sara said as she headed into the living room.

"I've only known Sara for two months and I'm just finding out how bossy she can be," Gail said once Sara left the room.

"Yeah, that's why I asked her to help with the wedding. She's a doll, but when it comes down to taking care of business, she'll have everybody in the room jumping to her orders. She was even able to find the right person to fill in. You are exactly the right size and type to be in my wedding."

"Because I fit the dress?"

"That too. But you know what I mean. I wanted everyone to, well, look a certain way, you know." Nina was reluctant. Gail was silent. She had been in enough weddings to know what Nina was talking about. She had noticed that all the bridesmaids were thin and nice-looking with shoulder length hair like hers. She guessed that Sara was too short and a little too much on the chubby side to actually be in Nina's wedding, but then maybe Sara didn't want to be in the wedding. Whatever the case, Gail got a weird feeling about Nina after that comment.

"Yeah, I know," she mumbled as she went into the bathroom to try on the dress. She looked fabulous in the dress and was glad that Nina had good taste even if she was a little superficial. She wondered if any of the other brides had picked her to be in their weddings based on how she looked. She liked to think that it was because they considered her a good friend or close relative. When she joined the others in the living room, the crowd had thinned out, but Thelma and Crystal were still there. Sara introduced Gail to the two seamstresses and Nina's cousin, Sharon. Thelma commented on how good she looked in the dress and Gail complimented Nina on her good taste in choosing such a nice Alfred Angelo. Gail needed very little alteration on her dress. It was a size seven and almost a perfect fit. After changing back into her own clothes, Gail got an update on Friday's schedule and escaped to her room.

It was almost 10 p.m. when Gail got back to her room, and she decided to prepare herself a relaxing bubble bath. She needed something to ease her mind about this strange situation she was in. After preparing the bath, she found San Antonio's smooth jazz station and turned the radio up before she slipped into the tub filled with bubbles.

Now that she had gotten to know Nina a little, she felt even more awkward and guilty about kissing Mario. Maybe she should tell someone. But, what good would that do? The only person she could tell was Sara who seemed too wrapped up in the wedding preparations to have time for Gail's little soap opera. If someone knew what had happened, would that stop the wedding? She certainly didn't want to be a part of that kind of drama. No, it would be better if she kept this to herself, did her bridesmaids duties and went back to Austin as soon as she could. It had been over between her and Mario a long time ago anyway. He just had the last minute jitters like he said.

She had to get her mind off of that man! Gail willed herself to relax and think of a quiet stream as she soaked for ten more minutes. She got out of the tub, once her fingers started looking like prunes. As she was drying off, the phone rang. It was probably Sara with some more changes to the schedule, she thought.

"Hello," she said as she wrapped the towel around her and sat on the bed.

"Hey, it's me, Rio."

"Mario? This is Gail. Did you call the wrong room?" She was really hoping this would be a very short conversation.

"No, I meant to call you," he said. "Actually, I wanted to apologize for what happened between us earlier this evening."

"You know this is the third time you have apologized to me today," Gail quipped.

"So do you forgive me?"

"For which sin?"

"Hmm. I guess for all of them, past, present and future." Mario chuckled, and Gail felt a flutter in her stomach. It seemed as if everything about the man was sexy to her. Her mind was spinning as she sat there with only a towel wrapped around her body. She didn't trust herself to speak for fear of what she would say to him.

"Really, I was thinking about the relationship we had and I wanted to talk to you," Mario said.

"Well, if you could call it that. It was more like a fling," Gail said.

"A fling? It was more than that to me. That was one of the nicest summers I've ever had." Mario seemed hurt by her description of their time together.

"All we did was have sex," Gail said bluntly. But it *was* nice, she said to herself.

"Gail, come on now. We did more than just have sex. We went to that film festival. You took me on a tour of every museum in Austin. I took you to all the good restaurants. You made me take those Latin dance lessons—"

"No, you made me take dance lessons once you decided I didn't know how to dance," she said, laughing.

"You didn't know how to dance, but you had rhythm when I got finished with you," he said pointedly. Gail stopped laughing.

"Yeah, you gave me plenty of rhythm and plenty of surprises," she said quietly, remembering how romantic he had seemed. At the time, she'd thought it was just a part of his player role.

"It was a really nice summer, Gail. We had some great times together," he said in a mellow tone.

"Well, I guess I missed out. We've both gone on with our lives. What did you do after that summer," Gail said trying to change the mood.

"I went to seminary in Dallas, and then I came back to San Antonio," he said.

"Did you end up working in your father's business?" She began to remember more things about him besides his favorite positions in the bedroom.

"I did, and I'm still working with the business. I travel a lot across the state checking on the different cleaners," Mario said. His father was one of those black men who actually lived the American dream. He became independently wealthy in the dry-cleaning business by strategically placing his stores in wealthy white neighborhoods. He ensured his position in the market by following the trend in the industry and opening up low-price stores in other neighborhoods under a different name.

"So what did you end up doing?" Mario asked her.

"I finished my accounting degree and started working in Austin right after I graduated. I worked for a small company that ended up going bust, and then I started working for the state. I figured that was more secure," Gail said.

"What are you doing now?"

"Still working for the state."

"No, I mean now in your room." Mario steered the conversation in the other direction again. She decided to humor him. What harm could there be in playing along a little?

"I was drying off from a long bubble bath when you called, so I'm sitting on the bed with a towel wrapped around me," she said remembering their first telephone conversation years ago.

"I wish I was that towel," Mario said.

"Now, that's corny," Gail said, laughing.

"It may be, but I'm serious. I want to see you."

"Do you realize that in less than thirty-six hours you are getting married?"

"Nonetheless, I want to see you. Why don't you come over right now?"

"Come to where? Your hotel room? Yeah, right."

"No, I'm at home. I live here by myself. No one would know."

"Are you serious?" She kind of wanted to see him, too. But it seemed like there was a lot at stake. Actually, she was free, single and didn't have to answer to anyone. He was the one who had something to lose. "You have a lot of obligations right now, Mario. What are you thinking about?"

"At the moment, I'm thinking about you. Your hair. Your eyes. Your smile. Your body." He sighed. "I just didn't expect to see you today. I'm flooded with memories of you. I told you earlier, I was overcome." He did sound genuinely taken aback and helpless.

"Well, I don't know what you have in mind, but I didn't come up here to stop a wedding. I was just as surprised as you were. Probably more so than you," Gail said.

"It was a lovely surprise for me. You're even more attractive now than when you were in school," Mario flirted.

"If I was all of that, why didn't you contact me after you left?" Gail asked.

"I did contact you. I called you several times and I emailed you. You stopped answering my emails. You act like you don't remember anything at all about our relationship," Mario said. He sounded annoyed at her.

She was surprised that he thought so much of the relationship. She had always thought of it as a fling because they were so sensual and sexual all the time, but maybe it had been something more. She had heard that he was a player so when he approached her that summer she just didn't have very high expectations for the relationship. Once the fall semester started, she got wrapped up in her studies and didn't take his emails seriously. She thought it was all part of his game, that he just wanted to keep her warm for him in case he came back through Austin.

"I remember, Mario. And right now, that's a problem. Neither one of us needs to be remembering that stuff right now."

"Remember, the fourth of July and that American flag?"

"I'm about to hang up."

"No, don't hang up, Gail. I'll stop. But just answer one question truthfully for me."

"What?" Gail asked impatiently.

"Do you *want* to come over to see me?"

Gail breathed a deep sigh and decided to call his bluff. "Baby, if I came to see you right now, you would absolutely not be able to get married to another woman on Saturday."

"You didn't answer my question," he said, unfazed by her brazenness.

"It really doesn't matter because I'm not coming over," Gail said. She had to put an end to the conversation before he tried to convince her. She was close to getting in her car and driving to his home, so she didn't want to allow him to tip the scale any further. "I have a busy schedule tomorrow. You should let me get off the phone now."

"I know why you want to get off the phone. You want to come over. But I'm going to let you go," he said abruptly.

"Bye," she said.

"Sweet dreams," he said.

She hung up before he could say anything else. She was absolutely floored! There was no way she would be able to get any sleep now, but she put on her nightgown and got in the bed anyway. What was Mario thinking, flirting with her like that two days before his wedding? She thought about what Nina had said about being "groomed" for a preacher. Maybe this was some kind of arranged marriage and Mario's heart wasn't in it. According to Nina, they hadn't even slept together. So maybe that's why he came on to her so strongly. He'd been celibate for too long. See, she knew that celibacy thing caused problems. Here this man was so hard up, he's hitting on an old girlfriend because he can't get any from his fiancée. If he had been having sex with Nina, maybe he wouldn't have been so moved by Gail after all these years.

It suddenly occurred to her that he might say something about her to Nina. She felt panicked for a second and then calmed down when she thought about the kind of man Mario was. He wouldn't want to cause a scene like that. He liked his stuff to be on the down low. She would just make sure she didn't get caught alone with him again. Even though she doubted he would take it any further than that kiss earlier, she would be on guard just in case. Fortunately, he wouldn't have any more chances to approach her beyond calling her again. Friday's schedule was full of activities, including his bachelor party that night. As an extra precaution, she would keep herself busy Friday evening by offering to help Sara with whatever she may need after the rehearsal dinner.

CHAPTER 3

Gail was impressed with how smoothly things were going with the wedding. It was easily the most expensive wedding she had been in, and she was certainly glad she didn't have to spend a dime herself. She knew Mario's family was rich, and she suspected that Nina's family was also well off. Gail went shopping at Nieman-Marcus with Thelma, Crystal and Sharon, Nina's first cousin. Sharon explained that everything would be charged to Mr. Nelson's account at the store, and whenever a sales clerk found out they were bridesmaids in the Nelson-Lewis wedding, they were given the royal treatment. Gail ended up with a new pair of shoes, three pair of panty hose and some blue lingerie.

"Why not?" Sharon said about the lingerie. "Besides, it's a part of the outfit. It matches the dress."

After they shopped and grabbed a bite to eat in the mall, Sharon hustled them across town to a beauty salon and spa. They got shampoos and touch-ups if needed. Gail found out that they would be wearing almost identical hairstyles, but no one complained, probably because of the generosity of the bride's family. Nina's family undoubtedly knew how to assure a smoothly run wedding with no problems from the wedding party. Money has its benefits. They were also offered the full spa treatment—manicures, pedicures and massages. Gail took advantage of everything without feeling guilty. She saw it as payback for the hundreds, probably thousands of dollars she had spent being in weddings over the years.

Gail didn't see Nina or Sara again until they got to the church at 6 p.m. for the wedding rehearsal. The nicely decorated church seated 750 people with a balcony that featured two spiral staircases in each back corner leading down to the main floor. The rest of the architecture was more traditional: stained glass windows, dark wooden pews with maroon cushions and a picture of a black Jesus painted on a mural behind the baptismal pool.

Gail had spotted Nina and Mario in a front corner of the church, but the main attraction that evening was the wedding coordinator, Xavier, a tall, slim man wearing all black. He came on the scene with a flourish and let everyone know who was boss. He controlled everyone with ease, including both sets of parents, the little flower girl and ring bearer and even the cackling women relatives who sat in the back of the church commenting on everything.

Another guy whom Xavier introduced as his partner, Kyle, held a clipboard and looked generally bored. Gail wasn't sure if he meant business partner or otherwise or both.

In any event, Gail was thoroughly impressed by Xavier. A good wedding coordinator couldn't be shy or disorganized. He knew what he was doing and was able to command silence with two sharp claps the few times people dared to get loud or out of order. Somehow he knew everyone's name, showered the older people with attention and respect and charmed the children into walking at the right time and pace.

Xavier kept to his tight schedule and completed everything in one hour and fifteen minutes. He had the bridesmaids on one side and the groomsmen on the other side in the balcony at the back of the church. After the parents were seated, the bridal party would descend on each side of the spiral staircase, and each couple would meet and walk down the middle aisle. Gail was glad Xavier kept her attention. It kept her from worrying about Mario and what he was doing. Although she did notice Mario staring at her at one point while Xavier was working with the mothers on the lighting of the candles.

Xavier dismissed everyone at 7:15 sharp, and they headed back to the hotel for the rehearsal dinner.

In the wedding, Gail was paired with Jason so they sat next to each other at the rehearsal dinner. The room had six round tables with ten settings at each. There were 20 people in the wedding party including the bride and groom, and the rest of the room was filled with relatives and close friends.

"You seem distracted again. What's up?" Jason asked after they had settled at a table with four other couples from the wedding party.

"I'm fine," she lied. She was extremely distracted because Mario kept stealing glances at her. Nina was completely occupied with being the center of attention as people came up to her gushing congratulations and looking at her ring. That left Mario free to torment Gail as he wandered around the room pretending to listen to well-wishers. Once the bride and groom were seated at their elevated head table with their parents, Gail shifted her chair and turned as far away from Mario as she could. She figured Jason could further distract her, and she knew what topic would interest him most.

"So tell me more about your church," she said giving him her full attention.

"What do you want to know? Do you have any specific questions?"

"I did have a question about the Pentecostal thing. I'm Methodist and don't know much about your beliefs."

"So what church do you attend normally?"

"I actually haven't found a church, but I've visited a few." That was stretching the truth a bit. Gail had only been to one Methodist church in all the years she had been away from home. The only other time she had attended any church services was when she went with Sara.

"Well, we basically believe the same things about God and Jesus," Jason said. "What really sets us apart is how our service is conducted and that we speak in tongues regularly."

"You seem to be very knowledgeable." Gail thought she would give a compliment since she didn't know what else to say.

"I'm actually a teacher for our Sunday school. Maybe you'll come to a class this week," Jason said excitedly. Gail knew that he was really into his church just as Sara was, but she wasn't ready to give up her Sundays on a regular basis. She decided to try to change the subject.

"Wasn't that Xavier something else?"

"Yeah, I guess you could say that," Jason said ruefully.

"Uh oh, don't tell me you're homophobic."

"It's not that at all. I've known Xavier since we were kids. I'm just disappointed about some of the choices he made in his life."

"It's been proven that homosexuality is not a choice. People are actually born that way," Gail said emphatically.

"Like I said, I've known him for a long time, and I know his history. I'm talking about his responsibilities as a man."

"He is a man. He just prefers other men relationally. I believe that gay people have the same rights as everyone else," Gail said.

"I'm not talking about rights. I'm talking about his responsibilities and purpose."

"Well, doesn't God love all his children?"

"Yes, he does, but he doesn't love the fact that many of us choose to live only to satisfy ourselves. That's not living according to God's purpose."

"I know gay people who have more love and compassion than many straight people. What if their purpose is to go through being gay and suffering prejudice in order to help other people express themselves and be who they really are?"

"Now that's ridiculous," Jason said.

"Okay, now I feel insulted," Gail said.

"I'm sorry," Jason said quickly, looking around to see if anyone at the table was listening in. Thankfully, everyone was involved in other conversations. "I shouldn't have said that. Do you accept my apology?"

"Apology accepted. Maybe we just need to agree to disagree, but we of all people should understand the discrimination suffered by gay people. They deserve civil rights just as much as everyone else," Gail said.

"I think you're missing my point. I don't know how we ended up all in Xavier's business, but the fact is he was married and had children, and then he decided one day that he wanted to live a totally different lifestyle."

"Oh," Gail said, feeling foolish. "I see what you mean."

Jason munched on his salad, piercing each bite with much more force than needed. They sat in awkward silence and Gail daintily picked at her salad, glancing sideways at Jason. Even though the discussion had gotten a little heated, Gail enjoyed talking to Jason. He seemed confident, and she liked men with confidence. She decided to make up with him by returning to his favorite subject. She struggled to find something related to his church to talk about.

"So you're a teacher at your church? I'll bet that's interesting," she said, knowing she didn't sound genuine.

"Good try, Gail," he said, flashing her a smile. She smiled back at him and the tension between them seemed to resolve. They ended up joining in other conversations around the table for the rest of the meal. After some toasts by the parents, people began to disperse. Sara had a short meeting with the brides-maids about the next day's schedule and encouraged everyone to get a good night's sleep. Gail overheard some of the bridesmaids talking about going out on the Riverwalk, but she didn't want to risk running into Mario. She didn't know if the guys were going to be holed up in a room or wandering around on the Riverwalk for his bachelor party. To be on the safe side, she decided to enjoy the rest of her evening in her room. After showering, she lay in bed thinking about her conversation with Jason. For some reason she began comparing Jason to Mario and wondered how Jason ended up being in Mario's wedding. Jason wasn't a party guy. Then she remembered that lately Mario wasn't either. He was a preacher now. On this night, she fell asleep thinking about Jason's serious eyes rather than Mario's dark, sexy ones.

Even though the wedding was one of the most beautiful she had been in, Gail struggled to get through the ceremony and pictures. Mario stared at her like she was the bride as she walked down the aisle with Jason. And then she got annoyed at how similar all the bridesmaids looked. She remembered what Nina had said about her being the right size and type and was so turned off, she felt like walking straight out of the church door instead of down the aisle. When she had first met all the bridesmaids on Thursday, she had not noticed all the similarities; however, once they were dressed and standing next too each other it became obvious to Gail that Nina was overly concerned with looks. They were all basically pretty girls, but they were also the same height. Nina had even said Gail was the right "size" and "type" to be in the wedding. If only Nina knew. Gail was the right size and type all right. The right type for Mario to have a summer tryst with and then claim it was a real relationship. She had to keep herself from shaking her head during the entire ceremony as she stood with the other bridesmaids.

When Nina came down the aisle, Gail smiled as a song started going through her head, "Congratulations, it should have been me." She chided herself, knowing that her relationship with Mario was not that deep, even if he thought it was something more. She pictured herself walking down the aisle, looking even happier and glowing even more than Nina was at that moment. That got her through the ceremony and then the pictures started.

She was doing fine until Mario slipped her a note while Nina was taking a picture with her parents. Gail had been standing with three other bridesmaids who were telling Nina how beautiful she looked, and he came up behind them and pressed a note into her hand. He remained behind them and pretended to join them in praises to his new wife, but Gail could feel how closely he leaned over her shoulder. "Isn't this lovely?" he said directly into Gail's ear. She felt his warm breath on her neck and knew that he wasn't aiming his compliment to Nina. Gail was tempted to make a scene, but she knew she would be the only one looking like a fool. The photographer was finishing up and everyone was being herded out into cars and back to the hotel for the reception. In the limousine with some of the bridesmaids, she stole a peek at the note. It was his cell number. She crumpled it up but decided not to leave it on the limo floor. She would throw it away once they got back to the hotel.

At the reception, the guests were served lunch in the grand ballroom. Gail was able to avoid Mario's stares and advances because the wedding party was seated at the head table with the bride and groom. She took her place next to Jason and they managed to keep the conversation pleasant and away from controversial subjects. Gail was actually able to enjoy the reception festivities. Nina was the typical happy bride, and Mario appeared to be the doting groom as they cut the cake and drank their first glass of wine together as a married couple. Gail had been in so many weddings she had read about what each activity meant. She wondered how serious Mario was about the covenant he was making on that day.

Later, Gail stood at the back of the crowd when the single women gathered for Nina to throw the wedding bouquet. It was a good thing because a couple of women got into a little shoving match, fighting over the flowers. When it was time to remove the garter from Nina's thigh, Mario appeared to be reserved and proper, but suddenly, he lifted her dress and dipped his head under the folds of material, removing the garter with his teeth. Nina was mortified, but the crowd loved the show Mario put on.

They were preparing to say good-bye to the bride and groom when Mario and Nina started hugging all the bridesmaids and groomsmen. Gail was trying to figure out a way to avoid hugging Mario, but they had formed an impromptu line and she couldn't move without looking conspicuous. Nina came to her and gave her a genuine hug.

"All right, girl. Here I go. I'll take your advice and just relax and see what happens," Nina said as she hugged her.

"Congratulations. You're going to have a great time," Gail said. Mario hugged her next and she was unable to determine whether his hug was genuine or if he was still trying to flirt with her. He decided to leave no doubt in her mind.

"I hope to see you soon," he whispered as he gave her an extra squeeze. He moved on to the next person and Gail went through the motions of seeing the happy couple off with everyone else. She couldn't wait to get back to Austin so she could call Shawn, her best friend who had moved to San Diego.

CHAPTER 4

Gail had called Shawn as soon as she could on Sunday morning. She called at 11 a.m. her time hoping that Shawn would be up by 9 a.m. California time. Shawn said she was still lounging around but her energetic husband was out doing some work in the yard.

"So what are you going to do?" Shawn asked after Gail told her the whole story about Mario.

"I don't know what I'm going to do. I'm finding it hard to resist him right now."

"But he just got married, and he's a preacher. Doesn't that help you resist him?" Shawn asked.

"Maybe he didn't want to get married. Maybe he was forced into it somehow."

"Is she pregnant?"

"No, she was a virgin."

"Girl, I know you don't believe that."

"She told me herself. I do believe her."

"It sounds like you're too involved to get involved. I mean, you became friends with her during the course of the wedding, so that ought to keep you from getting involved with Mario."

"I wouldn't say we're friends. I don't know if I would even like her as a friend. I probably won't even see her again since she lives in San Antonio."

"Well, you don't have to see Mario again either."

"I just have a feeling that I will see him. He travels to Austin a lot for his father's business."

"So it sounds like you want to see him. Why would you want to be involved with a married preacher?"

"I don't know. On one hand, I think it's wrong to have a relationship with him because he's married now. On the other hand, he is a very fine brother and I wouldn't mind being with him again. What if he doesn't even want to be with Nina? He acted like he wants to be with me."

"But nobody forced him to marry the girl."

"Well, look at your situation."

"This doesn't have anything to do with my situation."

"David was married when you met him."

"Yeah, but he was separated and preparing to file for divorce. I didn't break up his marriage."

"You're right, but I have a feeling that Mario doesn't want to be with Nina."

"Well, the only advice I can give you is to be careful. He may just want to have his wedding cake and eat it, too." They laughed at Shawn's joke, but Gail was thinking that she might want the same thing.

"And you say these people are Baptist?" Shawn asked.

"Yeah, Mario and Nina are in a Baptist church, but Sara is a part of a non-denominational church."

"I don't know about the non-denominational church, but you have to watch those Baptists."

"Now come on, Shawn. Your grandfather was a Baptist pastor wasn't he?"

"Yes, but my grandfather was different. He spoke in tongues and stuff. I'm talking about these other kinds of Baptist folk. They have that church covenant on the wall that says they won't drink, cuss or smoke and then as soon as they get out the church door, they cuss somebody out, light up a cigarette and pull their whiskey out from under the seat in their car."

Gail didn't want to get Shawn started down the road of religion bashing. They'd had this conversation too many times before. That was one of the reasons Gail avoided church. Shawn was so negative about people in the church that she insisted that people she met in clubs were much easier to deal with. Gail tended to agree. At least you were clear on their motives.

"Back to Mario. If he's off limits, then I need to have a game plan if he tries to approach me again," Gail said.

"I think you'd better be prepared to deal with him straight up. If he's crazy enough to flirt with you and kiss you during his wedding festivities, then he probably *will* try to see you again. By the way, what did you end up doing with his cell phone number?"

"Oh, I threw it away," Gail cringed as she lied to Shawn. She had slipped the number into her strapless bra, thinking that if it fell out somehow, then she was meant to lose it. When she changed clothes after the reception, the paper drifted onto the hotel room bed like a dying leaf. She had quickly put it in her purse.

"Well good. There are plenty other men for you to get with. Mario has too many attachments. What about the guy you walked with in the wedding. What was his name?"

"You mean Jason? He's a church boy. He would drive me crazy. He's all right, but not really my type."

"Just try to keep busy so you won't be sitting at home waiting for Mario to call."

"That's good advice."

Gail felt better after talking to Shawn, but that night she dreamed that she was on her honeymoon in Jamaica with Mario.

Gail was thinking about asking Sara some probing questions about Mario, but when they returned to work Monday, they were swamped with work that had piled up the previous week. Part of their mundane duties included accounts payables for several different divisions, so there were a number of checks that had to be processed. After working through their lunches for three days straight, Gail insisted they break for lunch on Thursday. They ate in the cafeteria in their building so they wouldn't get too far away from the office.

Gail and Sara sat down by a window in the corner of the cafeteria after getting their food.

"I just want to thank you again for being such a good sport. You saved the day!" Sara said.

"I actually had a good time. It was a free weekend in one of the best hotels on the Riverwalk."

"Everything was moving so quickly at the wedding that I didn't get to talk to you like I wanted to," Sara said.

"What did you want to talk to me about?"

"Well remember that conversation we had with Nina about celibacy? I wanted to give you a better explanation than I did on Thursday night," Sara said earnestly.

"Oh, yeah. You're serious about being celibate?"

"I am, and I wanted you to know that it's not just because of diseases or a fear of getting pregnant," Sara said.

"You guys made it pretty clear that night that you're celibate because you think God wants you to be," Gail said. "I think that's admirable, but it's not for me." Gail didn't want to argue, but she didn't mind being frank about the celibacy issue.

Sara was quiet for a moment and then said, "I'll bet Nina and Mario are having the time of their lives right about now!"

"Humph," Gail said raising her eyebrows. "I guess."

"What do you mean by that?"

"I don't know if Nina is really enjoying herself. To tell you the truth, she seemed like she might be frigid the way she was talking last week."

"But you said that Mario would know how to relax her and make things go smoothly," Sara said.

"I hope he was able to, but it's important for a woman to be excited about her sex life with her man. I mean, you can't be running scared when it's time to get your groove on."

"You certainly had me convinced that everything was going to be all right the way you were reassuring her."

"Well what could I say two days before the girl's big night? Just between me and you, Sara, I think that it's okay for you guys to be celibate before marriage, but you can't have these outdated views about sex."

"My views on sex aren't outdated."

"Maybe yours are not, but the way Nina was talking was just plain juvenile to me. I don't mean to be insulting, but we are living in a new day, post women's lib. Even if you aren't sexually active, it's important to be educated about sex for your own good and safety. It's actually a women's health issue."

"You know, Gail, you may be right about that, and I think that celibacy is the best way for a woman to be healthy and fully protect herself in this day and time," Sara said, giving Gail a half smile.

"Touché. We'll just have to agree to disagree on that one," Gail said. "You didn't tell me before hand that Jason was going to be there."

"Yeah, we all run in the same crowd."

"Well, I wouldn't mind hanging out with your crowd, but I have to watch my big mouth around Jason."

"Oh Lord. What did you guys get into it about? Not celibacy!"

"No, not exactly. I was going on and on about gay rights issues, not knowing about Xavier's leaving his wife and kids."

"As far as I'm concerned that girl should have known that Xavier was gay in the first place."

"Was it that obvious?"

"It was obvious to me, but you know, we see what we want to see, especially when it comes to love and marriage."

"Yeah, you're right about that," Gail said. "Jason seems even more involved in your church than you are. I didn't know that was possible," Gail teased.

"It hasn't always been that way. You know he used to run with Mario. They were a part of the same fraternity, but he went to A&M. He and Mario were always running up and down the highways of Texas and Louisiana looking for the biggest party. It's a wonder that either of them graduated."

"Oh really? I thought Jason looked familiar when I first met him at your church."

"Well we'd better head back to work before things get out of hand up there."

CHAPTER 5

After such a hard week of working, Gail planned to spend her weekend loung-ing around doing absolutely nothing. When Sara asked her if she was going to come to church on Sunday, she promised she would attend the next Sunday because she already had plans for the weekend. Sara didn't press the issue and Gail was grateful for that because she needed the weekend to recuperate from the shock of seeing Mario and dealing with their past. After day dreaming about him all Saturday morning, she promised she would not think about him again. She went to the gym and afterwards resumed her usual weekend sched-ule of cleaning, shopping and relaxing.

Things were back to normal the next week at work, and Gail was even look-ing forward to attending church with Sara as she had promised. They made plans to meet in the vestibule on Sunday morning so they could sit together.

That Saturday afternoon Joanna, one of Gail's party buddies, called to see if she wanted to check out a new jazz club. Preferring the live music scene over the dance clubs in Austin, Gail looked forward to meeting her group of friends at the club. They weren't close friends, just girls she hung out with when she wasn't dating anyone seriously. The group could be as large as six women, Gail, Joanna, Tish, Karra, Catherine and Marsha. They enjoyed each other's com-pany and used each other to shield unwanted male advances at the clubs. They cheered each other on when one spotted a man she wanted to go after, and served as the pity party and sounding board when a relationship didn't work out.

Once she got to the club and met the girls, she enjoyed the live jazz band and had a couple of drinks, but found herself thinking about Mario and became distracted. She knew she needed to call it a night when she couldn't keep focus on the very handsome man who was trying to talk to her. She was also thinking about going to Sara's church the next morning and didn't want to be too tired. On the drive home, she was still thinking about Mario and some of the things they had done together that summer years ago. She kept thinking about him once she got home, took a shower and got in bed. She was dozing off with the television on when her phone rang.

"Hey old friend." It was Mario. It was as if she had conjured him up with her obsessive thoughts. She couldn't believe it.

"Is this Mario?"

"In the flesh."

"So, umm, what can I do for you?" She thought she sounded stupid, but she didn't know what else to say.

"I'm in Austin, and I called to see if you would meet me for lunch tomorrow."

"For lunch? Where is your wife?"

"In San Antonio. What does that have to do with anything?" Mario asked. "Anyway, meet me around two o'clock at the Omni North."

"You want me to meet you at a hotel? You must be kidding."

"I just like their pasta bar, that's all."

"I don't know about this Mario. Why do you want me to meet you?"

"I just want to see you and talk. Can I see you?"

"You just got married."

"And? Can I see you? Tomorrow? Two o'clock?"

Gail really did want to see him, but she felt like something was wrong with seeing him now that he was married. Maybe she was being influenced by all of Sara's ideas. She decided to think for herself and go with her feelings.

"Sure Mario. I'll meet you," she said. "But Mario, if you wanted to see me so bad, why didn't you ask to come over tonight?"

"Tonight? Isn't it kind of late?"

"Well I guess that depends on what you want to do."

"Right now I want to get some sleep. I've had a hard week. I'll see you tomorrow."

After hanging up, Gail stayed awake another hour wondering about Mario. Why had he had a hard week? Why did he want to see her? Hadn't he just returned from his honeymoon? She had a list of questions for him the next day.

"You look mighty nice," Mario said as he kissed Gail on the cheek. When she first saw him standing in the lobby of the hotel, she felt a fluttering in her stomach, and then when he kissed her cheek, she felt a flip-flop. He looked extremely handsome as usual in a tailored brown suit complimented with a crisp white shirt and a gold tie. He wore dark brown square-toed leather shoes that looked brand new. She got a nice whiff of his cologne and identified it as one of the more exclusive designer brands.

"You look good yourself. Are you coming from church?" she asked him.

"Actually, I preached at St. Peter's this morning. A guy I went to seminary with is the pastor there," he said as they headed for the restaurant.

"What? You didn't tell me that. Wow, if I had known that maybe I could have come to hear you."

"It was a bit of a surprise for me. I went to the early service, and Mike just asked me if I wanted to preach. I guess I should have invited you last night, but don't you go to Sara's church, The Word?"

"Is that what they call it? No, I didn't go this morning."

"So you're not a member there?"

"No, I'm not a member of any church. Sara goes to church every day it seems. I'm not ready for anything like that," Gail said.

Mario chuckled. "I'm sure she doesn't go every day, but I understand what you're saying."

They entered the restaurant and were seated at a small table. Gail noted how intimate the restaurant was and speculated as to why Mario had asked her to meet him there. After giving their drink orders to the waiter, they watched a chef make their pasta to order at the pasta bar and went back to their table. Mario had bow-tie pasta with sausage and Gail kept it simple with chicken fettuccini Alfredo.

"So what did you want to talk to me about?" Gail asked abruptly as soon as they sat down. Mario didn't answer immediately and apparently decided to avoid the question for now.

"Do you like your pasta?" he asked.

"Yes. It's wonderful, actually," Gail said, trying to be as casual as he was about the whole thing. She managed to get through the meal exchanging small talk with him as if they were just old friends meeting for lunch. It was Father's Day and they joked about how dads get a bad rap compared with the popularity of Mother's Day. He had a good relationship with his father and had bought him some kind of golf club. Gail had only sent her father and stepfather cards. She thought maybe she should call them both later.

By the time they were finished eating, she felt more comfortable with Mario. He was still very attractive to her, and she enjoyed his company as well as his good looks. However, she knew he hadn't asked her to meet him for just lunch and small talk.

"Now, Mario, why did you want me to meet you here?"

"Maybe I just wanted to see you again," he said looking at her with his teasing eyes.

"Well, did you want to tell me something? I don't get it."

"I don't know Gail. Maybe I made a mistake," he said quietly and seriously, looking away from her.

"A mistake? You mean by asking me here for lunch?"

"No, not that. It's just that sometimes I think I should never have gotten married."

"I must say I was quite surprised myself. I mean you hadn't even had sex with the girl." Mario looked shocked, and Gail immediately regretted what she had said.

"Now who told you that?"

"You mean she wasn't a virgin?"

"Well, yes she is, but how do you know?" he asked.

"You know how girls talk."

"Oh, so I guess Nina knows about me and you then."

"No, I don't talk that much. Nina was very nervous about her wedding night, so she talked about it with the bridesmaids. But why do you think it was a mistake to marry her?"

"You know there's so much pressure to be married when you're a preacher. I probably would have waited a while if I'd really had my choice."

"I can see where you're coming from. People have a lot of expectations of you. It's almost like you're just an actor in someone else's play, and all you can do is say the lines they've given you."

"That's a good analogy of how I feel," he said looking at her with interest, ignoring the hint of sarcasm in Gail's tone. "How did you know?"

"I kind of felt that way when I was in your wedding. I mean, everything was so planned out and pre-arranged. They even picked my hairstyle. It was just weird. I can't imagine how it was for you as the groom."

Mario had begun laughing when she mentioned the hairstyles.

"I'm not even going to tell you how it was for me. I'm just glad it's over. But it really was like I was just a pawn in someone's game," Mario said.

"Actually I think all grooms feel that way," Gail said. "I've been in enough weddings to know." She actually went down the list of weddings she had been in and she had him laughing again with her bridesmaid stories.

"I'm really glad you agreed to meet me. This was just what I needed. You're like a breath of fresh air," Mario said looking genuinely happy. But Gail couldn't shake the feeling that there was something more he wanted from her.

She had a mixture of relief, surprise and disappointment when she drove out of the Omni parking lot and headed to her apartment. He had walked her to her car and said he was heading back to San Antonio. He hadn't tried to kiss her good-bye or make any other kind of pass at her. But what did she expect? He was a newlywed and probably wanted to get back to his wife even though he thought it was a mistake to marry her. Gail was just confused by the whole thing and felt a headache coming on.

She got to her apartment and settled in for a nap. Just as she was dozing off, the phone rang.

"You thought I was going to seduce you, didn't you." It was Mario calling from his cell phone, and Gail's body immediately responded to his ultra sexy phone voice.

"No, I believe you *are* seducing me. You're just taking your own sweet time."

"Is that what you think?" he drawled.

"Mario, I really don't know what to think about you."

"I was just calling to make sure you got home all right."

"Yes, well, I'm here."

"Okay. You have a good night."

"I will."

"Bye," he said softly.

"Good-bye Mario." She hung up and pressed her face into the pillow, screaming in frustration. She needed to make some decisions about Mario before he drove her crazy. If he was actually trying to seduce her, she didn't have the strength to resist if he turned up the heat. She probably would have gone up to a room with him at the hotel if he had asked. Gail knew she would have sex with him at least one time for old times sake. If he didn't have a problem with his new marriage, she certainly didn't. On the other hand, if Mario really wanted her, why had he allowed himself to get caught up with Nina? He said it was the pressure, but Mario was a grown man who ought to have the courage to run his own life. Whatever his reasons, he certainly was pursuing some kind of relationship with her, and she admitted to herself that she enjoyed his company and the attention he was giving her.

Because Gail felt like Mario was just playing games with her, she decided to maximize the moment while she could. She would turn the tables on him and enjoy the pleasure of his company and body if he let her, and then she'd see if he would go running scared back to his wife. It wasn't like she was trying to break up his home. She didn't want Mario for anything more than sex for old times sake, and if she knew Mario, that was all he wanted as well. Although there was a slim chance Mario may be reluctant because he had become a preacher, she wasn't interested in that part of his life. She drifted off to sleep thinking about another hot summer night she had spent with Mario.

CHAPTER 6

Two weeks later, Gail still hadn't heard from Mario, but she knew he would call eventually. She had been dodging Sara's invitations to church, partially because she thought Mario would call on the weekends and want to see her and partially because she just didn't want to go. But when Sara invited her to a night of bowling that Friday, Gail couldn't resist. She was a great bowler, having taken lessons and joined a league in high school at a time when bowling became the "in thing" among teenagers at her school. Some of her crazy friends even stole the shoes from the bowling alleys and wore them as their regular shoes. It was just a fad for some of them, but she actually liked bowling and was serious about her game.

When she met Sara at the bowling alley, she saw that a lot of the people from Sara's church were there. It turned out to be a singles' ministry outing. Sara noticed that Gail was a serious bowler because she had her own bag, ball and shoes.

"Girl, you need to go down there with the real bowlers."

"Well, I thought I would be bowling with you."

"I'll be in the group next to you, but I'm not that good. If you have your own ball, you must be pretty good."

"It doesn't really matter to me. But who would I be bowling with?"

"I know Jason is down there, but I'm not sure who else. Go on down to lane seven, and I'll be down in a minute. We'll need to switch to a lane closer to you."

Gail went down to her assigned lane looking for Jason. She saw a lot of familiar faces, but she didn't know anyone. A nicely built guy with well fitted black jeans and a red polo shirt caught her eye. Actually she could only admire him from the back and she wondered if he looked as good from the front. When he turned around it was Jason. She raised her brows in surprise.

"Hey, Jason. Sara told me I would find you down here."

He looked at her bag and said, "A woman after my own heart. You must be a serious bowler if you've invested in the tools of the game."

"I guess I'm all right, but I haven't practiced in a while. I might be a little rusty."

"We'll see about that."

Gail and Jason played against two other guys, Will and Jared. Their opponents were pretty good, but not as good as Gail and Jason. At least that's what Jason whispered in her ear at one point. Since they were all pretty serious bowlers, it was decided at the beginning that they would compete and not just fool around like some of the other people were doing on other lanes. The teams formed an instant rapport and naturally, the men were very competitive. It had gotten to the point where each team had won two games and they decided that whoever won the next game would be the winners.

Many of the other bowlers in the singles' group had just played three games and people were crowding behind their lanes to check out the competition with the "real bowlers" as they called them. Gail had been holding back on her game because she was better than all the guys except Jason, but in the last game she got caught up in the competition and bowled so many strikes that people started cheering her on. Before she realized it, she had bowled a near perfect game and the spectators were yelling her name and doing cheers for her. After their victory celebration and hand shakes with their opponents, Gail remembered Sara and started looking for her in the crowd.

"Wow, you are the hit of the bowling alley. Girl, I didn't know you were that good."

"I used to play in a league but it's been quite a while," Gail said. She looked at the guy standing next to Sara. "Oh, hi Anthony. It's good to see you again."

"Hey, you were really great. You ought to get on a team."

"I don't really have the time to put into it anymore, but I do enjoy the game."

Just then she felt an arm go around her shoulders. "Isn't she just terrific!" It was Jason still basking in victory. He pulled her closer to his side and she was surprised by the tightness of his muscles. She had noticed how fit he was when they were bowling, and she had felt his biceps when he would hug her during the game, but at the time, her mind was on the sport. Now her mind was on other things, and she began to see Jason in an entirely different light.

"So where do we go from here?" he asked Sara and Anthony.

"I'm starvin' like Marvin," Anthony said. "Let's go to TGI Friday's in the Arboretum."

"Just us four?" Jason asked.

"Yeah, I'm tired of this big crowd," Sara said.

They decided to go in one car and Anthony volunteered to drive. Gail secured her bag in the trunk of her car and looked around the parking lot for Sara. She saw her standing next to a black Lexus near the entrance.

"This is Anthony's car? He's driving mighty nice," Gail said to Sara.

"He does all right."

Gail made a mental note to get more information about Anthony and his job status from Sara next week at work. Right now she had other things on her mind. She hopped into the back seat and bumped into Jason's shoulder. He was leaning on the armrest, holding some CDs.

"Excuse me Jason. I guess I'm still pumped from bowling."

"No, it was me, I was leaning over trying to read this CD cover in this dim light."

"Is everyone in? Are we ready to roll?" Anthony asked.

"Let's get out of here," Sara said.

Gail was enjoying the jazzy music of Kirk Whalum and wondering why she was just now noticing how fine Jason was. She couldn't hear the conversation that Anthony and Sara were having in the front seat because of the music. Jason leaned toward her and she turned to him.

"You like jazz?" he asked.

"Oh, I love jazz, mainly classic jazz. The newer stuff is okay, but you can't beat Dizzy, Miles, Monk, The Bird—"

"Oh, you are really a woman after my own heart. We're two for two so far. I might have to marry you if we have anything else in common," he said excitedly, but not loud enough for the people in the front seat to hear him.

Gail was glad that it was dark because she was blushing big time under her caramel skin. "We have a common friend, but I don't know if I'm ready for marriage, Mr. Tucker. I'm thinking about pursuing my professional bowling career, and I won't have time for the relationship."

"If you pursue a professional bowling career, I'll travel with you and be your ball boy."

They both fell out laughing, drawing curious looks from the front seat.

"What's so funny back there?" Sara asked.

"Oh, we were just discussing Gail's career options," Jason said between laughs.

At the restaurant, Gail started to suspect a set up. After they placed their orders, she did the classic girl move and excused herself, inviting Sara to the restroom.

"Now, Sara, tell me the truth. Are you trying to set me up with Jason?"

"Set you up? I don't think you guys need to be set up. You all were having a blast in the back seat. We won't even mention the bowling show ya'll put on. If I *were* trying to set you up, you made my job very easy."

"So what's the deal?"

"Jason was the one who suggested we go out to dinner. I mean I had plans for us to eat afterwards, but I didn't know who would go. I didn't even know that you were such a good bowler. It just ended up this way, I guess."

"Well, I feel like I'm in high school with the question I'm about to ask you," Gail said.

"What, girl? What is it?"

"Does he like me or what?"

"I don't know. Do you like him?"

"I asked first."

"And I told you, I don't know. Believe me, Gail. I didn't plan this. After what you told me about you and Jason at the wedding, I wouldn't have tried to set you up anyway. You acted like ya'll didn't get along."

"It's not that we didn't get along. We just had a few debates. Things are certainly different tonight. We're finding out all the things we have in common now."

"So you do like him?"

"I didn't say that. We'd better get back to our table before they think something's wrong."

Once Gail and Sara were settled back at the table, Anthony said, "You two were the hit of the bowling alley." He was looking from Gail to Jason with a big grin on his face.

"It was mostly Jason's skills," Gail said. And at the same time, Jason said, "Yeah, Gail is a great bowler."

"I don't know that much about bowling, but it looked like Gail could out-bowl everybody in the place," Sara said.

"So how did you learn to bowl so well?" Anthony asked.

"I was in a league when I was in high school and I just played for fun in col-lege mostly. I've entered some tournaments and gotten in some summer leagues, but it's just something I picked up and really like."

"Do you have trophies?" Sara asked.

"Yeah, I have a few."

"I'll bet you have more than a few," Jason said.

"Enough about me. Anthony, what do you do for a living?"

"I'm in real estate."

"Are you an agent?"

"No, he's a land baron. Anthony probably owns the land under this restau-rant," Jason said.

"One day I will," Anthony said. Gail knew that he must own more than a house or two but she would remember to get the full scoop from Sara later.

"Are you going to ask me what I do for a living?" Jason asked playfully.

"From what I hear, nobody understands your job, but I know you're an engineer and you deal with circuitry design, whatever that means," Gail said.

"Very good." Jason said.

"I have a good memory. You told me this while we were bowling."

"Well, that's just my day job," Jason said. Gail took the bait.

"And what is your other job?"

"My brother and I started a software company, but I'm really a silent part-ner. He does all the work."

"What kind of software?" Gail asked.

"Various kinds, but I don't want to bore you guys with technical stuff."

"Jason and his brother are real brainiacs, as you can see," Sara said, winking at Gail.

"I'll bet you guys are on your way to being millionaires. Let me know when you go public so I can invest. How can I get on this train to millions?" Gail asked.

"You get on the train by discovering your purpose in life. When you're doing what you were created to do, you'll have unlimited success," Jason said. He sounded like an infomercial to Gail, but she was interested in hearing more nevertheless.

Just then, the waiter brought their food. Gail knew enough about this crowd to wait for someone to bless the food. Jason did a brief prayer, and then she asked, "So how do you discover your purpose in life?"

"You ask the One who made you," Jason said.

"That sounds kind of simple. It seems to me that a person would discover their purpose by exploring their interests and abilities. I mean how much control does God actually have in your life?" Gail asked. You would have thought she had something hanging out of her nose the way everyone looked at her. "I mean, it's not like God gives you some kind of owner's manual when you're born."

"That's exactly what the Bible is. It's like an owner's manual for our lives," Jason said.

"Yeah, but it's not specific to my life. Besides, what about the other books of wisdom out there?"

"There are all kinds of books out there. But upon close scrutiny, I've found the Bible to be the most convincing when it comes to being in a relationship with God," Jason said matter-of-factly.

"So back to my original question. You asked God what your purpose was, and then what? Did he send you an email?" No one could resist laughing at that remark.

"Girl, you are something else," Sara said.

"I'm just kidding. I guess I know what you're talking about. I just enjoy grilling you guys about your religion—I mean relationship. Sara always tells me that Christianity is more than a religion. It's a relationship," Gail said. "But sometimes it just seems too simple. Life is really more complicated than that."

"I know what you mean, Gail. Maybe one day I can share my testimony with you. God had to do some awesome stuff in my life to get me to become a Christian. I am very analytical and doubtful of things that can't be proven with empirical data. The Lord didn't just send me any old email. He sent a virus into my computer that destroyed all my files and then rebuilt them based on a totally different operating system," Jason said with intensity.

The depth of his statement wasn't lost on Gail, but she still had her doubts about becoming a Christian. She couldn't understand how people so young and with so much going for them could just give everything up and put all their eggs in one basket. It just made more sense to her to keep her options open and explore spirituality in a more general sense. She did look forward to hearing Jason's testimony, though. That meant she would get to spend more time with him.

Anthony drove them back to the bowling alley, and Jason insisted on escorting Gail to her car even though Anthony had stopped right by it.

"Will I see you at church Sunday?" Jason asked.

"I plan to be there," Gail said as she unlocked her car door.

"Here, let me get that for you," Jason said opening her door.

"Thank you," she said, but she didn't get in. She wanted her final moments with Jason to last as long as possible. "So when will I hear your testimony?"

"I don't know," Jason said. He had anticipated her getting into the car, so he was standing kind of close to her looking straight down into her face. "Just keep hanging around and I'm sure we'll find the right time and place."

Although Gail knew she should get into the car, she also wanted the moment to linger. Her body began to respond to his closeness, but he seemed unfazed and as if he were just waiting for her to get in the car so he could close the door. She couldn't think of anything else to say so she said good-bye and finally sat in the car.

Gail drove home thinking about Jason and how much they actually had in common. She wanted to see him again so she would probably have to go to church with Sara. It wasn't like he would frequent any of her regular hangouts. Besides, The Word was a nice place. She enjoyed the singing, and the preaching was down to earth and understandable. Their Pastor, Rev. Kline, didn't do a lot of hollering, but he would do that sing-song thing called "hooping" every now and then at the end of his sermons.

CHAPTER 7

Upon entering her condo, Gail noticed the message light blinking on her answering machine. The first message was from her mom asking how she was and why she hadn't called home. The next message was from Mario. She dropped down on her couch when she heard the sexy drawl.

"Hey, I have something I need to ask you. Call me on my cell phone. You have the number."

Gail sat basking in the warm feeling brought on by Mario's voice. She contrasted this feeling with the warmth of Jason's closeness. Mario catered to the secretive, seductive side of her sexuality and Jason brought out a different side to her that she was still discovering. She didn't exactly know how to read Jason, but she knew with certainty where she could end up with Mario.

That Sunday morning found Gail sitting in a pew at The Living Word Christian Fellowship pastored by Rev. Nathaniel D. Kline. Every service she had attended was upbeat, but this service was different, maybe because it was the Fourth of July, Gail thought. Before Rev. Kline began his sermon, he gave some encouraging words about victory and, for reasons unknown to Gail, people started becoming ecstatic, standing to their feet and responding to him with amens and hallelujahs. The church was filled with raised hands and all kinds of excitement.

"I'm not into my sermon yet, but you must remember that when the enemy is caught, he must restore to you seven times what he has stolen. The devil may have power, but you have the authority, and ultimately you have the victory. It may look like defeat when you don't have enough money to make two ends, let alone make the ends meet. But you have to tell yourself that you have the victory! It may look like defeat when your marriage seems on the brink of failure. But you have to know that you have the victory! It may look like defeat when you get a bad report from the doctors. But you have the victory!

"It looked like I was defeated when my youngest son was diagnosed with leukemia, but God said not so, and we have the victory!" Rev. Kline stepped back from the podium and started dancing. The men on the stage behind him started dancing. The choir behind them was dancing. Gail stood up looking for Jason and Sara. She caught glimpses of them through the crowd, and they were dancing. She had heard about holy rollers, but she had never seen anything like this before. Gail recognized the fast beat they were dancing to from a cut off her Maxwell CD. She figured Maxwell must have been raised in this kind of church.

Once she stood up, the beat became contagious and she started tapping her feet and clapping to the beat. There was an older man on her right who was doing his own version of the dance and the woman on her left was in the aisle spinning around and doing some serious dancing. As things started to calm down, Gail wondered if Rev. Kline's youngest son was all right.

"The doctors were so astounded and confounded that they just decided that it was a misdiagnoses. I told them that the diagnoses was healed!" Rev. Kline wiped sweat from his brow and continued, "They told me they wanted to continue doing follow-up testing and I told them to go right ahead so they could observe the wondrous miracle working power of God in my son's body!" That set off another round of dancing, but Rev. Kline stayed at the podium and opened his Bible, preparing to preach. As things calmed down, he sang slowly,

"There is power, power, wonder-working power
In the blood of the lamb
There is power, power, wonder-working power
In the precious blood of the lamb."

He sang the song one more time, substituting the word "healing" for "power." Gail noticed the tears streaming down his face right before he wiped them away with his handkerchief. He finished the song and everyone was seated, intently waiting to hear his sermon. Gail didn't have a Bible, but she had remembered to bring a notebook to take notes like so many other people did at The Word. If she was going to remember anything from the sermon, she needed to take some notes. She also wanted to have something to talk about with Jason when she saw him again. She was surprised when the man beside her pulled out a laptop and opened a new Word document. At first she thought he was going to play solitaire or some other computer game while Rev. Kline preached.

The lady next to her shared her Bible with Gail when the preacher gave his text. She noticed that Mr. Laptop had a Bible on his computer. They followed along as Rev. Kline read from II Corinthians 2:10-11, "If you forgive anyone, I also forgive him. And what I have forgiven—if there was anything to forgive—I have forgiven in the sight of Christ for your sake, in order that Satan might not outwit us. For we are not unaware of his schemes.

"The King James Version says, 'his devices.' Today the title of my sermon is The Devil's Devices." The man beside her saved his file accordingly and typed the words again at the top of the document. Gail wrote the title in her notebook. Rev. Kline gave a brief history of the Corinthians and explained that the author, Apostle Paul, was speaking of forgiving someone in their church who had opposed Paul. The guy had been disciplined by the church and Paul was instructing the church to forgive and restore the man. Rev. Kline also explained that it had been traditionally thought that the man was the same one who had committed incest, but that line of reasoning was just speculation. Gail was intrigued by this story and wondered what happened to the incestuous guy. She couldn't believe that such things happened in the church, especially back in the Bible days.

Rev. Kline discussed the relationship between Paul and the church in Corinth and explained that if Paul and the church were to become estranged because of what happened with the man who opposed him, then the devil would have gained an advantage over them. As he crafted his sermon, Gail saw a neat pattern emerging in her notes. She had a list of some of the devil's devices: discord, division and disbelief. And, she had concise explanations under each word. Rev. Kline gave graphic examples of how discord or lack of agreement leads to division, which then leads to believers losing faith and the unbelievers' continued doubt in Christianity.

The last part of the sermon was more animated as Rev. Kline preached about the weapons of warfare against the devil. Although she didn't really understand them, Gail managed to jot down the weapons: the word of God, the blood of Jesus, the name of Jesus and the word of our testimony.

After church, Gail discovered that her bowling expertise had brought her a little celebrity status at The Word. Several people spoke to her and acted like they'd known her for years. She was disappointed, though, because Jason was nowhere in sight. She kept looking around for him but didn't want to ask anyone where he was. She did see Sara who invited her to lunch, but when it was clear that it would just be the two of them, Gail begged off, claiming that she was going to her mother's house.

Driving home, she felt a tinge of guilt for lying to Sara. She wasn't about to go to her mother's house because she didn't feel like putting up with her family. Her parents had divorced shortly after she was born and they had both remarried. Gail grew up feeling like she didn't fit into either of the complex blended families. Gail's father had gotten her mother and another woman pregnant around the same time. Gail's mother, Annette, was only five months older than her half sister, Lisa. Gail's father, Phillip Adams, married Lillian, the woman he had gotten pregnant, and three years later they had another daughter, Leslie. Annette got married to a widower, Matthew Hardy. (They wisely decided to give Gail the last name of Hardy rather than Adams.) Matthew was an okay stepfather, but he already had a daughter, Denise, who was two years older than Gail.

Growing up, Gail always felt like a middle child, lost in the shuffle. In her pre-teen years, she tried competing for the attention of both her father and stepfather. She got good grades, did her chores around the house, kept her room clean and never got into trouble. Her attempts proved futile. Denise seemed to get special treatment because her mother had died. And Gail's biological father, Phillip, always seemed preoccupied with trying to prove his loyalty to Lillian and their two daughters, even though Gail knew without a doubt that he cheated on Lillian just like he cheated on her mother. She knew of one other child he had fathered outside of his second marriage.

Gail's mother surprised everyone and got pregnant when Gail and Denise were in high school. The birth of her brother, Kenny, was the final blow for Gail because her stepfather was so excited about having a boy that the little attention he did give Gail was gone the instant Kenny came into the world. She didn't blame Kenny though. She really did love her little brother. He was born a happy, bouncing baby, and now at eleven years old, he knew how to brighten up a room and make people laugh. Everyone loved Kenny. Thinking about her brother almost made Gail want to make the drive out to far Northwest Austin to see her family, but she knew she wasn't in the mood for all the questions about her not being married yet. Denise had gotten married at twenty-five and already had two children. Her stepsister Lisa was married and Leslie was engaged. Of course, she had been a bridesmaid in Denise and Lisa's weddings, and she was thinking about simply refusing to be in Leslie's wedding. Thankfully her father and stepmother lived in the Dallas area so she didn't feel any pressure to visit them more than once a year.

When Gail got home, there was a message on her machine from Joanna reminding her about the Fourth of July party that afternoon. Gail had almost gotten depressed thinking about her family, and Joanna's message gave her a burst of energy. She changed into some blue jean shorts and a sleeveless red shirt and headed to Joanna's house. Joanna was an attorney who worked for the state as well. She had a nice house in Round Rock, and she sure knew how to throw a party. She had rounded up her brother and his crew to barbeque the meat and had hired a D.J. Gail didn't drink much, but the alcohol was flowing in abundance. All the regulars were there, including a bunch of flirtatious men Gail didn't know. She was approached and eyed many times, but she wasn't interested in forming a new relationship. Her life was already complicated enough without adding to the mix. And just like the time she had met her friends at the jazz club, she became preoccupied thinking about Mario and decided to go home to see if he had left another message on her machine.

There was no message, and she was tempted to grant his last request and call him on his cell phone. She decided to eat some Blue Bell ice cream and channel surf instead. She spent the evening trying to catch the funny comedians on BET's Comicview and flipped through the other cable channels during the dud comedians and commercials for black psychics and phone sex lines.

The next week at work went smoothly as Sara and Gail worked with no supervision. So many people had taken vacation during the first two weeks in July that they were the only ones in their suite of offices. By Friday, Gail and Sara found themselves wondering why they were still at work. Sara dared Gail to leave before noon since all the work they could do was done by Thursday morning. Instead of leaving, they lounged around the office all afternoon. That way they would be in the office if a phone call came in from a manager or someone else from another department checking up on them.

"So have you decided if you like Jason or not?" Sara asked. Gail was getting used to her direct approach.

"He's a great guy. I wouldn't mind spending more time with him," Gail said. "To tell you the truth, I might even be interested in a closer relationship with him."

"You're moving mighty quickly. How do you know you would be compatible?"

"Well, after Friday night, it's pretty obvious we have a lot in common, but there's also enough differences to keep an interesting tension in the relationship," Gail said sounding only half serious.

"There are more than a few differences if you ask me," Sara said matter-of-factly with her eyebrows raised.

"What do you mean?"

"Well, for one thing, you're not saved—yet."

"Oh, so if I'm not a member of your church, I'm not good enough for Jason?"

"No, that's not what I'm saying. I mean Jason probably wouldn't date someone who is not a Christian."

"And how do you know that?"

"Well, because he's serious about his relationship with God and I've known him for a long time," Sara said.

"Now let me tell you something, Sara. I consider myself to be a spiritual person. I treat people like I want to be treated. And I can't believe you're telling me that I'm not good enough for Jason."

"But, see, that's not what I'm saying." Sara began making analogies that only made Gail feel more alienated.

When Sara said that darkness and light couldn't fellowship, Gail countered and said she wasn't in darkness. Sara talked about being equally yoked and Gail argued that her and Jason had plenty of things in common. They ended up going their separate directions around three in the afternoon. Gail knew that church was important to Sara, but she was quite surprised by her strong opinions. How did Sara know what Jason thought or felt about Gail and her church attendance or lack thereof?

CHAPTER 8

As she drove home that afternoon, Gail grew more pissed off at Sara partially because she knew Sara was probably right, and it didn't help that Jason had not called her. It was time to stop worrying about Jason and Sara and pursue more exciting things in her life anyway. While she was watching the Friday evening news, she decided to finally return Mario's call. Now where was the paper with his number on it? She looked in her purse and dumped the contents out on the couch looking for the little piece of paper. She even got her luggage out and went through the bags she had taken to San Antonio searching for the number. Finally she decided to replay the messages to see if he had left the number on her machine. She had been careful not to erase any of his messages, but he had never left the number. She even checked the caller ID but she had gotten into the habit of erasing the numbers immediately after a call came through, so there were no numbers stored.

Oh well, she thought, maybe he would call again. After a boring Friday night she took a steaming, hot shower to ease her frustration and settled into bed for a restless sleep.

She was in her car stuck on the upper deck of Interstate Highway 35 going the wrong way, but it was okay because she knew it was a dream. She was try-ing to relax as the cars honked at her and tried to get her to turn around as she laughed at them and increased her speed. They needed to get out of her way because she was trying to get to work downtown. One of the car horns grabbed her attention because it sounded like a phone ringing. She turned to look at the car ringing it's horn as it passed her, but she didn't recognize the car and couldn't see the driver. When she turned back around, she was about to crash head-on into an eighteen-wheeler. That's when she decided to wake up and answer the phone.

"Gail, why haven't you called me?" Mario sounded irritated.

"Who is this calling me so early on a Saturday morning?" Gail matched his irritation, but was trying to affect a sexy, sleepy tone even though she was wide-awake the moment she heard his voice.

"You know who this is," he said playfully. "I wish you had called me. I'm in town now and I really need to see you. If this is too short a notice, it's your own fault."

"Why didn't you call me again if it was so important?"

"I've just been so busy, and I was counting on you calling me on my cell phone."

"Well, I guess I'm sorry to say that I lost the number. What can I do to make it up to you?"

"Can I see you tonight?"

"How about dinner at my place around seven."

"That would be perfect," Mario said.

After hanging up, Gail began plotting out her morning and afternoon. She was going to make special preparations for Mario's visit. She already had an appointment to get her hair done at a new salon. She had received a post card in the mail announcing the opening of the Isis Spa and Salon. Her former hair stylist had partnered with two of his friends, one from Los Angeles and one from Atlanta, to open a black-owned spa in Austin. Gail had made an appointment as soon as she had received the post card. There was a buzz in the air about the new salon, and she wanted to be one of the first people to try it.

When Gail arrived at the salon, she was offered lemonade and teacakes, and then she was led to her new hair stylist for a consultation. Kenneth didn't do hair anymore and she didn't mind. She was impressed by the attentiveness of her new stylist, Lanelle. Apparently, they were trying to revolutionize the black hair care industry with the quickness of their service. She had arrived at the salon at 10:30 a.m. and her hair was relaxed and beautifully styled by 11:30 a.m. Kenneth stopped by to chat and ensure she was pleased with Lanelle's work. He told her about the spa services and ended up talking her into getting a facial, massage, manicure and pedicure. After paying her bill and heading out the door, she decided it was well worth the money because she felt like a new woman.

Gail then went to Victoria's Secret in the mall to buy a new teddy. She found a sexy, black piece that she knew Mario would love. After buying groceries for the meal, she went home and made sure her whole apartment was ready. She kept her home meticulously clean, so she didn't have much work to do.

She prepared pasta with grilled chicken and vegetables. She was tossing the salad and enjoying the smell of garlic bread cooking in the oven and soft jazz playing on her stereo when the doorbell rang.

Gail opened the door and felt her heart leap in her chest. The look in his eyes, the warm, lingering hug he gave her and the wine he brought for dinner let her know how the night was going to end. They didn't talk much. They didn't eat much. They just kind of grazed over the meal and had foreplay with their eyes. When Mario reached across the table and gently ran his index finger over the back of Gail's hand, she felt a shock of electricity run from her hand, up her arm and then down through her chest. As he stroked back and forth with his finger, every pore on her skin opened to receive him, and she remembered why she had never returned his phone calls or email after that summer.

Mario's sensuality was again about to consume her, and she would be unable to concentrate on anything else in her life. But what else was there?

He took her hand, pulled her up from her seat and began dancing with her. For a moment, Gail thought about asking this married man why he was here with her, but then he kissed her. Her questions faded away as her body responded to his every move. Mario danced her into the bedroom and made love to her intensely. So intensely that she almost believed that he must love her.

After three rounds, her body was tired and her mind slowly began to think again. They were both on their backs recovering slowly. As her heart rate dropped, she tried to frame a question or a statement in her mind, but her thoughts were muddy and she knew that if she opened her mouth she would babble as if she were speaking in tongues like someone from Sara's church. Then he began to talk.

"I guess you're wondering why I came back to you," he said softly. "I'm going to tell you the truth. After that summer, I couldn't find anyone else like you. I was really disappointed when you didn't stay in touch with me." He turned toward her and propped his head up on his elbow.

It was a moment before she replied. "If you wanted me like that, then why did you marry someone else?"

"That's what I asked myself when I saw you again."

"And what was your answer?"

"I don't know the answer, but I know that it feels good being here with you." He stroked the side of her face and kissed her gently on the lips. "I know I have to go, but please let me stay the night. In fact, anytime I come to see you, I want to stay over because I don't know if I could stand to leave you after making love to you."

Gail looked into his eyes, speechless. His sincerity caused her heart to open to him and she felt energized once more. She rubbed a questioning hand down his torso, and Mario's body answered. They had sex again, slowly and tenderly.

As soon as Mario left the next morning, Gail phoned her best friend Shawn in California.

"Well, we did it," Gail said.

"Who did what?"

"Me and Mario."

Shawn shrieked. "Girl, no! You did it with Mario? When?"

"Last night. He just left."

"Mm, mm, mm. So is he out of your system now?"

"I don't know. He was so sweet."

"Don't tell me you're going to see him again. Are you going to have an affair with this man?"

"I think I'm going to let him call the shots until I sort out how I really feel about all of this."

"Well, tell me how you feel right now."

Gail threw her head back and closed her eyes. "I feel languid and guilty, but I know that if he came back in here right now, I would be with him again. A part of me is sort of happy that he wants me."

"I guess that *is* flattering, seeing that the guy has a new wife at home."

"I think I missed my chance to be that wife. He said that he wanted me back in college, but I wouldn't return his calls or emails."

"Why didn't you?"

"I don't know. I guess I was young and scared. Mario is an intense kind of guy. He totally possesses me when I'm with him. It's like my mind and body don't belong to me when he's in the room. There's some kind of connection that makes him irresistible for me."

"Sounds like you're playing with fire, Gail. You might get burned."

"I might."

"What about the guilty feelings."

"I feel a little guilty, but on the other hand, I feel like if Nina were doing her job, Mario wouldn't have come to me. I didn't chase him and force him to have sex with me."

"Well like I told you last time, just be careful. I also hope you can find the strength to resist him and find you someone else. You are an attractive woman and there is no reason that you have to be involved with a married man."

Gail thought about Jason, but she didn't want to tell Shawn about him and how Sara implied that she wasn't good enough for him. Shawn's views about church people were negative enough, and Gail didn't want to give her more ammunition. Gail was surprised that Shawn wasn't harping on the fact that Mario was a preacher in the Baptist church, and if she had forgotten, Gail wasn't about to remind her.

After the conversation ended, Gail thought about going to church, but it was already close to noon. Instead she cleaned up her kitchen and changed her sheets. As she moved around the condo, she remembered the different ways Mario had touched her and the tenderness of his voice. By the time she was finished cleaning up, she had gotten so worked up thinking about Mario that she decided to go to the gym and have a vigorous work out. She worked out for two and a half hours, forcing herself to think of anything else but Mario.

CHAPTER 9

On the way to work Monday morning, Gail resolved that she couldn't stay mad at Sara. Gail really didn't hold grudges against people anyway, and Sara was way too nice for Gail to be mad at her. As soon as she got to work she went to Sara's cubicle.

"How are you this morning?" Gail asked, greeting her with a hug.

Sara seemed surprised. "I'm fine, Gail. I hope we're still friends."

"Of course we are."

"I missed you at church. I thought maybe you were mad at me so you didn't come."

"Actually I thought about coming, but I spent too much time on the phone with my friend Shawn in California. They're two hours behind us, so I have to wait kind of late to call her. We have a tradition of talking on Sundays."

"Well, remember we have a 7 p.m. service you can come to if you miss the morning service."

"All right, Ms. Church Lady, I'll remember that next time," Gail said and headed to her work area to begin her day.

Gail was deep into analyzing some numbers when a deliveryman came to her cubicle.

"Delivery for Gail Hardy." He held a colorful burst of beautiful wild flowers arranged in a large vase. She signed for the flowers and looked up at all the women, including Sara. They had gathered at her cubicle admiring the flowers and asking her who sent them. She couldn't read the card with Sara standing there. To make it worse, Sara hung around after the other women drifted back to their desks talking about how their husbands and boyfriends never sent them flowers.

"So, who are they from?"

"Oh, just an old boyfriend. He's trying to get me back, but it's not going to work." At least she was able to tell half the truth.

Once it was clear that Gail wasn't giving any more information, Sara went back to her cubicle as well. Gail was finally able to read the card.

It said, "You drive me wild!—M."

She felt a hot flash coming on and wondered how she was going to get through the day without thinking about him constantly. She moved the huge arrangement into a corner on her desk and tried to get back to work.

Monday night, Gail was not surprised when Mario called.

"Did you like the flowers?" he asked.

"They are beautiful, but you know I work in the same office as Sara," Gail said as she gazed at the beautiful flowers. She had brought them home so they wouldn't cause any more questions at the office.

"No, I didn't know that. I'll be more discreet from now on."

"So how long is this going to last? Are we just going to keep sneaking around until we get caught?"

"Oh, it won't be like that. When the time is right, I'm going to tell Nina about us." Mario said matter-of-factly.

"Whoa, I don't think that's a good idea. A bunch of Nina's friends live here in Austin. I work with Sara, and I see Jason and other people in that circle at church."

"So what are you saying? Are you ashamed of me?"

"No, but there are things we need to think about. For instance, you are a preacher and here you are having an affair weeks after getting married."

"I'm also a man, and I make mistakes. I don't have a problem being honest about that."

"Okay, but you can't tell your wife about us right now. This is just not a good time."

"So are you more concerned about your reputation than being with me?"

"I don't know about that. But I have to see these people who are connected to both you and Nina. I don't want them to think I'm a home-wrecker."

"Okay, I guess I understand where you're coming from. Now, I have a special request," he said, playfully changing the mood of the conversation. "How about spending a fun-filled, sunny weekend with me in Corpus Christi next month. You don't have to answer right now. Just think about it."

"I don't think that would be such a good idea."

"It'll give us a chance to talk about what we should do. I promise I won't tell Nina anything until after the trip, even if you don't go with me."

"Okay, that's fair."

"You have a good night. Sweet dreams, my love."

"Bye, Mario."

Mario called her again Tuesday night and Wednesday night around 10:30 each time, right when she was about to go to bed. He would talk to her until she was about to fall asleep. Then she would have dreams about him all night.

Thursday at work, Gail was surprised by a phone call from Jason.

"I'm calling you at work because I don't have your home number," he said. "I missed you at church Sunday and I just wanted to invite you to the next service."

"Oh." Gail had previously planned to get to know Jason better, but now she was totally distracted by Mario. Did she even want to go to The Word while she was seeing Mario?

"So can you make it this Sunday?"

"Well, I umm. Sure, I'll be there. I'll see you there."

"Great! I'll look for you. Have a blessed day."

About thirty minutes later, Sara came to her cubicle and sat down.

"I need a break from the numbers," Sara said slumping in the chair.

"I know what you mean."

"Hey are you coming to church Sunday?"

"Between you and Jason, I guess I don't have a choice."

"You always have a choice," Sara said. "I also wanted to invite you to my house for lunch after the service. So Jason called you?"

"You know he called. You probably transferred him or gave him my extension."

"Okay, I admit it. So are you going to come for lunch after church Sunday?"

"That sounds good. How many people will be there?"

"Just a small group. Are you trying to ask if Jason will be there?"

"No, I would just ask you straight up if I wanted to know. So, is Jason going to be there?"

They chuckled together and Sara answered, "Yes, he'll be there."

"Oh, then I'll definitely be there," Gail joked.

"Well, I don't know if Jason can compete with Mr. Wild Flowers."

Gail was thrown off guard, but she quickly recovered, knowing that Sara had no way of knowing the real identity of Mr. Wild Flowers. Sara was just trying to fish for information about who sent the flowers.

"According to you, Jason won't date me unless I'm a member of The Word."

"You know, there's a difference between being a member of a church and being a Christian. Some people go to church every week but don't have a relationship with God."

"So why do they waste their time in church?"

"Many reasons. Some people go because of a religious duty or because they were raised to go to church. Some people are seeking answers like you are. I want to help you find what you're looking for. That's why I was disappointed that we had the misunderstanding about Jason. I don't want to be a hindrance to your seeking the Lord."

"Well, right now, I'm just investigating what you all believe. I think it will take some time before I can commit to anything. Plus I have some things to work out first. And honestly, I'm not really interested in Jason romantically. I just think he's fun to be around," Gail said.

"Well I think he enjoys your company, too. And who knows what may happen in the future?" Sara asked, raising her eyebrows playfully.

CHAPTER 10

Mario called Gail again that Thursday night and again Friday night. Each time he asked her if she had decided to go on the Corpus Christi trip with him and each time she told him that she was still thinking about it. Gail spent Saturday browsing antique furniture stores and shopping for new lingerie with Mario in mind. Even though it didn't stay on long, she knew that Mario, like most men, liked the way the skimpy lace and sheer fabric looked on women. Gail also knew that her slim, shapely body looked especially good in anything with a thong. Mario called Saturday night and talked very briefly. He said he would be in town on Thursday for only one night.

"What about the weekend? I'm already spending this weekend alone," Gail pouted, surprising herself with how eager she was to see him again.

"I'll make it up to you. We can be together all weekend at the end of the month."

"Let me look at a calendar." Gail walked into her kitchen and glanced at a small calendar on her refrigerator. "The whole weekend?"

"Yes, the whole time. And we'll spend it at a nice hotel in Austin for a change of pace."

"Sounds good to me. I can't wait to see you Thursday."

"Sweet dreams," Mario said in a soft, mesmerizing voice that followed Gail into blissful sleep.

This time Gail was looking forward to all the dancing and singing that she had come to expect at The Word. She was not disappointed. Things were just as exciting as the last time she was there. People were dancing during the praise service and then the choir songs had everyone up, clapping to the beat. Gail enjoyed the musical part of the service, but she found herself anxious to hear Rev. Kline speak. During the last choir song, which was slow and meditative, Gail was pleasantly surprised when Sara came to sit next to her.

When Rev. Kline finally got up to speak, Gail was ready with her notebook. She still didn't have a Bible, but she knew Sara would share with her. Before his sermon, Rev. Kline did his usual exhortation.

"I don't know if you really understand what God meant when he told Moses, 'I am that I am.' I don't know if you comprehend what God means when He says, 'I'll be with you always, even unto the end of the earth.' You see, God is what you need when you need Him. He doesn't have to send a doctor. He is a doctor. He doesn't have to send a lawyer. He is a lawyer."

The organist and drummer responded to Rev. Kline each time he took a breath, and the people responded to every phrase with "amen," "that's right," and other colorful responses. As the congregation became more excited with every word spoken, Gail smiled and thought about how animated black folks were. Whether they were in the club or in church, they knew how to have a good time.

"God doesn't send strength. He *is* strength and He is present with you even now. All you have to do is tap into Him. He does not just send love. He is love. He doesn't send joy. He is joy. In fact, He is everything you need."

By this time, everyone in the church was standing up and excited. Gail even found herself excited about God's ability to be everything she needed. She had never heard anything like this before in her life.

"Ya'll sit down. I'm not preaching yet. Just know that God is. Yes. He is. He is everything you need." Gail sat down and wrote it at the top of a blank page: God Is.

The music slowed and Rev. Kline began talking in a calming, soothing voice. He explained that his sermon was about sanctification and read from II Thessalonians 2:13-17. As the sermon progressed, Gail took notes and was reminded of her college years when she sat in classes and diligently took notes. She was always a good student and enjoyed learning. The sermon was easy to follow along, but she had so many questions that she just began to write question marks in the margins. At one point, she became so interested in what Rev. Kline was saying that she just stopped taking notes and listened.

"As we go through the process of sanctification, we find ourselves having to really deal with the things we've done in the past. For instance, our past sexual immorality causes us to form soul ties with each and every individual we have sex with. God meant for one man and one woman to be connected with each other for life, and when we violate this principle, we pay the consequences," the preacher said to the quiet congregation. "You can squirm in your seats if you want to, but you know it's the truth."

Gail was shocked at his frankness, but she was eager to hear more.

"Every time you have sex with a person, you leave a deposit. You exchange something with them. The essence of your being is involved when you have sex. Oh, it's quiet in here." Only a few brave souls ventured to say amen now, but Gail was intensely interested in what he was saying. She made a mental note to ask Sara about soul ties later. Rev. Kline went on to talk about other aspects of sanctification, but Gail didn't take any more notes. Her mind was still on soul ties. She couldn't wait to get to Sara's house after church.

"So explain more about this soul ties thing the pastor was talking about today," Gail said. She had waited as long as she could before asking about the topic. The festive, family atmosphere at Sara's house made Gail feel comfortable even though there were people there that she didn't really know. Besides Jason and Sara's boyfriend, Anthony, the other six people there were familiar to her from the single's group at the church. She had directed her question to Sara, but the many conversations that were going around the table stopped when she spoke. She looked around the table at some curious faces. Jason and Anthony, were both at the table along with Gail and Sara. Melinda and Angela, two girls Gail had met at the bowling outing, were also seated at the table. Gail looked at them all, but still no one spoke. "So what's the big deal?" Gail asked, breaking the silence.

"It's no big deal. I just didn't know who you were asking," Jason said.

"So what's your point of view on soul ties?" She turned to Jason.

"Basically, I agree with what Rev. Kline said. When you have sex with someone, you form a connection with them that you have to deal with for the rest of your life," Jason answered in his usual matter-of-fact tone.

"To me, it makes sense if you're still attracted to someone. But if you are completely over a person, I don't think they can still have any influence over you."

"That may only be possible with the help of the Holy Spirit. If that person catches you at the right moment, you may find yourself under their influence even though you thought you were over them," Jason said.

Sara finally spoke up, "The world has such a messed up view about sex. It was meant to be a special thing shared between a man and a woman in the union of marriage. But according to the world, any two people can have sex, regardless of their marital status, with no real consequences."

"Yeah, and right now the only thing they say is that it's better to have safe sex," Jason said.

"They're not even promoting that as much as they used to. It's like people think that if they get AIDS, they'll just take some drugs that will help them live until a cure is found," Sara said.

"But I think the safe sex message is important, especially for young people who are going to do it anyway. You might as well be safe," Gail said.

"That may be true. But the message of abstinence is the safest thing to teach to our young people," Jason countered.

"Well what about people our age? What if you've been dating for a while or you're engaged. What's wrong with forming a soul tie then?" Gail looked at Sara and Anthony. She remembered that Sara was a virgin and proud of it, but she was curious about Anthony's point of view. Gail thought he looked a bit uncomfortable.

"The Bible says that the marriage bed is undefiled, meaning that sex is only right between a couple when they are married," Sara said.

"But if you're engaged, you're practically married. So what's wrong with having sex then?" Gail pushed.

"Haven't we had this conversation?" Sara asked, exasperated. Gail glanced at Anthony. Although he was silent, Gail thought he may agree more with her than with Sara. Angela and Melinda were looking from person to person like they were watching a final tennis match between the Williams sisters.

"Gail, actually that's a very good question," Jason said. "It all goes back to what the sermon was about. Sanctification is the process of putting off the things of the flesh and taking on spiritual attributes. There are certain things that we just shouldn't do as a matter of moral and spiritual discipline. Before we even look at the spiritual effects of premarital sex, let's look at the moral and social issues. Premarital sex can cause rampant disease. It also causes many children to be born without a stable family. The majority of the poor in today's society are women and children.

"Spiritually, when you become a Christian, every aspect of you becomes God's property. You become a place where the Holy Spirit dwells. Your body should then be used to honor God. Put simply, having sex outside of marriage does not honor God."

Gail didn't have a response to that explanation, and neither did anyone else. Everyone at the table was silent. The other four people who were eating in the living room glanced over at the dining area wondering what was going on.

Sara pushed her chair back and got up from the table. "Does anyone want dessert?" She quickly began clearing the dinner plates.

Later that afternoon as everyone was leaving Sara's apartment, Jason pulled Gail aside and asked if he could walk her to her car.

"Actually I need to get something out of my car first. And then I'd like to walk you to your car if you don't mind walking with me."

At his car, Jason pulled a maroon Bible out of his back seat and handed it to Gail. It had her name engraved on the lower part of the front cover.

"Wow, thanks," Gail said. "This is so thoughtful, and my name is on it." She instinctively reached to give him a hug and he leaned forward and gave her a warm, friendly hug back. "How did you know I needed a Bible?"

"I just guessed. Most people who are seeking the Lord could use a new Bible. Either they don't have one or they have the old King James Version. This is the New King James Version, much easier to read."

"I didn't even know there were different versions," Gail said.

"There's an explanation of versions in the preface. It's still God's word. When you read, start with Matthew, Mark, Luke or John, and then read the shorter books after that. That's all in the New Testament. Whenever you have questions, jot them down in a notebook and ask Sara or me when you get a chance."

"I feel like I'm about to take a class at UT or something." Gail joked.

"I think that would be a good approach to take. I might even be able to open up some office hours for you."

Gail didn't know if he was joking or if he was trying to be flirtatious.

Jason handed her a business card. "My home number is on the back. Call me either at work or home if you have questions about any spiritual matters."

"Here, let me give you my home number as well," Gail said. He pulled out a PDA and wrote in it with his stylus.

They walked to her car, and she thanked him again before driving off.

Once at home, Gail thought about what Jason said concerning sex. On one hand she could see the social implications of random sex, but she didn't think it was such an important thing to God. She thought God was more concerned about issues like hunger and poverty. Besides, she was on the pill so she didn't have to worry about getting pregnant, and she thought Mario was pretty safe. He wasn't bisexual or a drug user.

As for soul ties, Gail knew there was definitely an attraction between her and Mario that neither of them seemed to have much control over. She thought Mario would leave Nina for her. Most women in her position would be glad, but she felt terrified at the thought of Mario leaving his new wife for her. For now she just wanted to have fun and enjoy the time she had with him. She would deal with the long-term aspect of their relationship later.

When Thursday evening rolled around, Gail was ready for Mario. She had the lights low, the candles glowing and dinner ready. When Mario arrived at 7:30, he was not his usual cheerful self. He had dark circles under his eyes and he was in a gloomy mood.

"So how have you been lately?"

"Tired!" Mario said as he plopped down on her couch. "I had a hard week. I'm so glad I can stay here."

"You know you're always welcome," Gail said with a wink. "Hey, I have an idea. Let's eat right quick, and then I'm going to run you a warm bath and give you a full body massage afterwards. How does that sound?"

The look on his face said it all. Gail relished the opportunity to pamper him. She had cooked a delicious beef stir-fry, which Mario rushed through. After they ate, he followed her into the bathroom where she began preparing his bath in her garden tub. As she poured a mixture of oils in the water he began undressing. He noticed her watching and began doing a slow striptease. She was tempted to strip down with him and do some things to him on the bathroom floor, but she decided to stick to her original plan.

"This is a very relaxing combination of oils you concocted," Mario said as he soaked in the warm water.

"Don't get too relaxed. I have plans for you tonight."

"I'm sure you do."

They kept up the playful banter until Mario was ready to get out of the water. Gail left the bathroom when he stood to dry off. She was in the bedroom waiting for him when he walked in from the hallway butt naked.

"I'm ready for you," he said, standing half at attention. She looked at him from head to toe and thanked her lucky stars that this fine, black man was back in her life. She admired his lean, muscular build and smooth, chocolate skin as he sauntered over and stretched across the width of the bed.

She began the massage with increasingly deep rubs down the length of his back muscles. He was quiet for about 15 minutes, and then he began to talk.

"Gail, you know I never told you about what happened with Nina."

"What do you mean?"

"I guess I should say what didn't happen."

"I don't get it."

"Well, I've been married for a month and two weeks and have yet to consummate the marriage."

Gail froze. "What? I don't believe this. The thing she feared most has happened."

"What are you talking about?" Mario turned toward her with a frown on his face.

"Remember I had told you that we talked about her being a virgin before the wedding? She had asked me for advice."

"From what she told me, she got plenty of advice, and I did everything I know to do. We've had a couple of big arguments about it. She's just frigid or something, and I've given up."

"You've given up? You're not going to try anymore?"

"All I know is what I'm going to do right now with you." He didn't look tired anymore as he pulled her on top of him.

When Gail woke up the next morning, Mario was fully dressed sitting beside her on the bed.

"It's time for me to go, love." Mario kissed her cheek.

"So are we still getting together next weekend?"

"You know it. We'll be staying at a suite at the Four Seasons."

"Why such an expensive hotel? We don't even have to stay at a hotel. We can stay here for the weekend."

"I told you I wanted to treat you to something different," Mario said. "So have you decided to go on the trip with me to Corpus?"

"I think I will go. It'll be a nice mini-vacation."

After Mario left, Gail got ready for work. Last night she had been able to put it out of her mind, but now she kept picturing Nina and her innocent questions about sex. Of course, she felt sorry for Nina. She even felt guilty that Nina's loss was her gain. If she weren't having sex with Mario, she would have encouraged him to keep trying with his new bride. He said he had tried everything he knew and things still didn't work out, so Gail could clearly see why he had come running to her. Their chemistry always worked. The dilemma for Gail was how long to continue the charade. If she were going to keep associating with Sara and her friends at The Word, she would have to be very secretive. However, she could just stop going to church and only associate with Sara at work. She would be sure to ask Mario about his plans for their relationship next weekend. There was no need to make any hasty decisions right now anyway.

CHAPTER 11

After an unusually busy Friday at work, Gail was glad to see the day end. Around 3 p.m. she had gotten a call from one of her hanging buddies. They were meeting at the clubTangerines for happy hour. She decided to go since she didn't have to make plans for a visit from Mario.

At Tangerines they sat around drinking daiquiris and margaritas. Gail was glad that all five of her party buddies were present. She enjoyed the spicy conversation and the mix of beauty and brains as they went around the table giving updates on their love lives or lack thereof. They shared advice and laughter over each situation.

Joanna had just started a scandalous affair with a young law school student who was clerking in her office. Tish was dating a boring guy they had all met at Joanna's Fourth of July party. Tish put together catalogs for an educational publisher. Gail thought Tish's job was boring, too. She would probably marry Mr. Boring and have a boring wedding. Gail hoped Tish didn't ask her to be a bridesmaid. Karra was in the process of a messy divorce. Things had gotten complicated recently when her husband spent the night at her house. Now they were talking about a trial reconciliation. Catherine had just ended a two-year relationship with a fine, handsome black man who told her he was bi-sexual. Marsha had a nice, older, white sugar daddy that she didn't talk too much about. He had her set up real nice in a little house in Tarrytown, a quaint neighborhood near downtown Austin. He traveled all the time and she would meet him in Las Vegas or New Orleans at least two times a month. Everyone suspected he was some type of gangster or something like that.

Finally it was Gail's turn to give her update. All eyes were on her as she considered following her first instinct to be discreet about her affair with Mario.

She looked around the table at her hanging buddies. They didn't know any of the people involved so what harm would there be in telling them? She felt so comfortable in their common bond of womanhood and relationship roller coasters, but as she told the story, beginning with the wedding, she felt a bit of shame. Nevertheless, she told them about Mario's difficulty consummating the marriage. The other women were surprised that her situation was more intriguing than Joanna's.

"So girl, is he going to leave his new bride for you or what?" Joanna asked.

"I hope not. I don't think I want to be with him like that. I think we just have a soul tie, some kind of sexual connection."

"Well, it takes more than sex to keep a relationship together anyway. Don and I have great sex! Hell, I wish that was all it takes. We wouldn't be getting a damn divorce today if that was the case," Karra said.

"Child, just enjoy him while you can. Don't get too emotionally wrapped up in him because even though he's seeing you right now, he is still married," Marsha said. She usually offered the most practical advice in the group.

"You say he's a preacher. If his church found out the guy was cheating on his new wife, they may throw him out of the pulpit," Tish said.

"Girl, please. If that was the case, there wouldn't be any preachers any where in the world," Joanna said. "He's human just like any other man. I've had my share of preachers, married and single. They make the best lovers, next to politicians. Now a preaching politician? Yeah, that's some good sex right there." Everyone laughed at Joanna's crass frankness.

"Well, I'm certainly going to enjoy it while it lasts because Mario is a very fine black man and an excellent lover."

"To fine black men and excellent lovers," Joanna said.

"Excellent heterosexual lovers," Catherine said as they clinked glasses around the table and erupted in another round of laughter.

As soon as she got home, Gail checked her answering machine. The alcohol and rich appetizers had made her drowsy, but when she heard Jason's voice on the answering machine she perked up. He left his number and asked her to call him but didn't leave any other information. She figured he was just going to invite her to church again. She had already decided to go, so she saw no need to call him back. She made a mental note to give him a thank you card for the engraved Bible he had given her and wondered what her hanging buddies would think of Jason and his little mysterious ways.

By nine o'clock, Gail was laying on her couch watching television. When the phone rang she figured it was Mario checking in and didn't bother to look at the caller ID.

"Hey you," she said in her sexy voice.

"Hi Gail. This is Jason. I hope I'm not calling too late."

"Hey Jason. No, it's not too late. What's up?" She perked up.

"Well, I know this may sound strange to you. But the Lord laid it on my heart to give you a call and share some things with you."

Gail stifled a giggle and rolled her eyes. She thought this was the worst pick-up line she had ever heard. Was this the way Christian guys came on to women?

"No, I don't think it's strange at all," she said in a voice an octave above normal.

"You sound amused."

"I'm sorry Jason. It was just something funny on T.V. I'm going to turn it off so I can listen to what you have to say." Gail felt bad now. After all, Jason had just given her a nice Bible and here she was laughing at him. She pushed the mute button on the remote control of the television and watched the images as he spoke.

"Well, what I wanted to tell you is this. The thing that you want the most, the thing that you are seeking can only be found in Christ. Once you get in a relationship with God through His Son Jesus Christ, only then will you be able to experience true fulfillment."

Gail was taken aback. His words brought a flood of thoughts into her mind. First of all what did she want the most? The first thing she thought of was that she wanted to get married one day soon. She was tired of always being a bridesmaid and never the bride. What did God have to do with her getting married? She didn't think He was in the match-making business.

As far as fulfillment was concerned, she was quite satisfied with her physical relationship with Mario, but it wasn't necessarily fulfilling. What was true fulfillment anyway?

Jason began speaking again, piercing her thoughts. "Gail, God loves you and wants to be in a relationship with you so you can know His plan for your life."

"Jason you're hitting me with some heavy stuff." She was reluctant to reveal too much to Jason. "I know God loves me. He loves everybody. I know the song, 'Jesus loves the little children,'" Gail gave a hollow laugh, attempting to lighten up the mood of the conversation. She didn't hear Jason laughing on the other end. "So what's that you said about true fulfillment?"

"Well, you can only have true fulfillment when you know why God made you. Everyone has a purpose in life. God put you here for a specific reason. When you know that and fulfill His will for your life, then you have true fulfillment."

"Can't we decide for ourselves what we want to be in life? I mean people change their minds about what they want to do and then they go down a different path. What's wrong with that?" Gail felt her logic kicking in now and things didn't feel so personal.

"When a person is not in a relationship with God, they are really just wandering aimlessly through life, even if it looks like they are headed somewhere. Your life can only have real meaning and fulfillment when you know the One who made you."

"Okay so, we're all a part of God's big, wonderful world. We know He made the world and made us. So what else is there to know? I don't see that there is anything else required of me. I know He loves me, and I go to church and enjoy the services."

"You're headed in the right direction, but there's much more to it than that. You know God loves you, but have you accepted the fact that He loved you so much that He sent His son to die for the sins of the world, for your sins and my sins so that we could be restored into a right relationship with Him?"

"Mmm, I guess that's the part I don't fully understand. What have I done that was so bad? Why did it take all of that. The whole crucifixion thing is so morose, if you know what I mean."

"You're right. It is morose. It's morbid, sad and shameful. It is what Jesus did in your place. See, rightfully, you and I deserved the death that Jesus died."

"And why do we deserve that death? That's what I don't get."

"You know the story of Adam and Eve right?"

"Yeah, they ate the forbidden fruit and were kicked out of the garden."

"Well, God had told Adam that he could eat from every other tree except the tree of the knowledge of good and evil. That tree represented our desire to seek knowledge and understanding without God, basically to pursue our own will without seeking God's purpose for our lives."

Gail chuckled. "You certainly brought that full circle. Right back to the purpose thing. Well, Adam and Eve ate the fruit. I didn't."

"Yes, but we all come from the seed of Adam. Every person is born with the desire to go our own way without seeking the Lord."

"Every person? But some people seem to be just good people all around. They don't do anything bad and everyone likes them."

"Even the nicest person will be separated from God in eternity if they don't accept Christ. The good news is that even though Christ died, He defeated death. He rose again and He lives with the Father. When a believer dies, he or she goes to be with the Father. When an unbeliever dies, that person goes to a place that is eternally separated from God."

"Now there you go, getting morbid again. So good people go to hell?"

"People who are not in a relationship with God do go to hell."

"I think that's messed up, Jason. Doesn't God know the hearts of people? Why would he send good people to hell?"

"God doesn't send a person to hell. We either choose life or death. When you choose to accept Christ in your heart and you believe that God raised Him from the dead, then you will be saved. If you don't accept Him, then you choose death."

Jason was so clear in his explanation that Gail was almost persuaded. There was something holding her back, however. Some desire to control her own destiny, to make her own decisions kept her from fully accepting what Jason was saying. If she could just keep certain aspects of her life under her own control, she would become a Christian. She wondered if this was possible.

"Okay, so I have a question." Gail searched for the right words, trying to be discreet. "What if a person has some things they need to work out. Could they become a Christian and still work those things out?"

"You come to Jesus just as you are. You really can't work things out on your own anyway. First you confess Him as Lord and believe that God raised Him from the dead, and you are saved. Then you repent from your life of sin and turn toward God. As you walk in the light of His word, the things that need to be worked out are dealt with over time. However, some things can change instantly. I've seen drug addicts become totally clean when they get saved."

"Well what if a drug addict gets saved, but still uses drugs?"

"If that person really wants to get off the drugs, they need to apply spiritual disciplines like fasting, praying, meditating on the word of God and fellowshipping with believers. But I know addiction is a powerful thing. Let me ask you this. Does that drug addict want the drug more than they want a relationship with God?"

"I think the drug addict wants both. He just likes the way the drug makes him feel physically, but he also wants to be in good with God."

"See, that's a problem because if a person is addicted to drugs, that is what they will seek. They will only seek to get high, not to do God's will. I know people may think they have heavenly experiences when they are high and spaced out, but it's only a counterfeit. Drug and alcohol abuse allows spirits to access your mind and make you trip out. Then you come down off the drug, but your body is addicted to the high. You don't have time to serve the Lord because you're searching for the next high."

Gail was silent. That was kind of how she felt, but she had only been with Mario two times. Besides she knew she wasn't a sex addict, nor was she addicted to Mario in that way. She just felt a connection with him.

"Are you there?" Jason asked.

"Yeah, I'm still here. I'm just thinking about what you said."

"Well, there's more good news. God has given us the gift of the Holy Spirit who gives us power over things like addiction. I want to share my testimony with you briefly. I know it's late, though, so is it okay?"

"Sure. I don't have anything to do in the morning, but go to the gym."

They ended up talking until 2:30 in the morning. Gail was captivated by his testimony partially because Mario was a part of it. She vaguely remembered Sara's saying something about Mario and Jason being buddies in college, but Jason was filling in the picture for her. He told her how they met through their fraternity and became good friends while Mario was at UT and Jason was at A&M. They would party every weekend, picking a different city each week. They even traveled to other states to attend fraternity functions. It was a fast life full of women, alcohol and drugs.

"Some kind of way, I graduated from college. After that there are about six months of my life that I really don't remember. I guess I wasn't ready for the transition into the real world. I kept going to frat parties, harassing pledges, and I basically stayed drunk all the time. I was supposed to take a really good engineering job right after graduation, but I messed it up. I was celebrating the new gig all weekend and on Monday morning, I was so hung over that I couldn't make it to work. I don't even remember the rest of that week, but I didn't take that job. I had to do something to earn money so I just took some odd jobs like telemarketing to attempt to pay rent somewhere. I usually just crashed at a frat's house.

"Anyway, this went on for almost a year until I was in Dallas one day for a step show and I called up Mario. I hadn't seen him in months. When I contacted him, he was all into the Jesus thing. He was even in seminary. I couldn't get with any of the stuff he was talking about. But he was still my frat, you know, so he let me stay with him that weekend. His folks are rich so he had a very nice condo. I was broke and had missed my ride back to Austin, but Mario didn't seem to mind. Once he realized how messed up I was, he basically turned his condo into a detox center for me.

"I stayed with him in Dallas for about a month getting clean. I craved alcohol and weed, but he just locked me up and made me eat healthy food and protein shakes. He actually cooked every day. We went to the gym and worked out every day too. My body had been wasting away. I never looked in the mirror except to get ready for a party, so I didn't know how much weight I had really lost. When Mario saw me that weekend, I guess he went into rescue mode or something. He told me later that he was shocked at my appearance and surprised that no one had told me how bad I was looking."

Gail was intrigued but not surprised by Mario's actions. She knew all too well how caring he could be. What surprised her was the image of Jason as a drunken party hound.

"Once I got cleaned up, I came back to Austin and easily got a job at Motorola. While I was in Dallas, we went to church at least twice a week, too. I thought that was just too much, but it really helped me straighten up. I got saved one night in Mario's apartment while he was doing a Bible study with some of the other seminary students. It was the coolest thing. I was around young people, male and female, who were reading the Bible and discussing church history instead of trying to see who could screw whom. It blew my mind.

"When I came back to Austin, I was a changed man. Mario had told me about The Word. I joined the first time I went there, and I've been growing in the Lord ever since."

After they got off the phone, Gail was too wound up to sleep. She was trying to trace Mario's life from the time he was a serious young Christian in a Dallas seminary to his current affair with her. Did she cause him to fall from his spiritual position? Was she some kind of temptation he was supposed to resist? What would Jason do if he knew his friend was entangled with her?

CHAPTER 12

Sunday at The Word, Gail had her new Bible and her notebook. Rev. Kline preached from Romans 5, and the sermon was about atonement or reconciliation with God. Gail knew that her understanding of the sermon was due partially to her Friday night marathon conversation with Jason. She took good notes and was excited by the clarity of the word. Each time a question entered her mind, Rev. Kline answered it with his next statement. Gail underlined Romans 5:8 in her new Bible, "But God demonstrates his own love for us in this: While we were still sinners, Christ died for us." That scripture gave her hope. Verses 12-21 helped explain what Jason was saying about Adam's sin of disobedience being relevant to her own life.

After the sermon, Rev. Kline had everyone stand for what Gail thought was the benediction. In the previous services she had attended, Gail thought of this part of the service as just a formality. She was anticipating seeing Sara and Jason after service and thinking about giving Jason her thank you card when something Rev. Kline said arrested her attention.

"Choose the Lord today because tomorrow is not promised to you. No matter what problems you face, you can come to Jesus just as you are. Accept the atonement today. Be reconciled to God today. Don't wait."

As people stepped into the aisle and went to the altar, something in Gail told her to go up as well. However, something else kept her planted flat-footed in the pew. Her hands were sweating and her heart was beating so heavily that she could hear it in her ears. Toward the end of the invitation, Rev. Kline rescued her.

"There are some of you who just will not come to the altar for whatever reason. Well, God can save you right where you are standing. Just repeat this
prayer with those who are at the altar."

Gail repeated the prayer in which she confessed the Lord Jesus Christ and
asked Him to reign in her heart. She didn't doubt that Jesus would do His part,
she just wondered if she would be able to let go of her weaknesses.

After service, Gail was making her way toward Sara to tell her that she had
said the prayer, but she noticed a crowd gathered around Sara. She also heard
people saying something about wedding bells. Gail stood on the outside of a
growing crowd around Sara. She was close enough to see a huge diamond
engagement ring on Sara's finger, mainly because she kept flashing it. Gail got
the gist of the story, which Sara was telling over and over as new women gathered in the crowd. Anthony had cooked dinner at his house and placed the ring
in a glass of water. Once she noticed the ring, Anthony got down on one knee
and told her that just like a man can't live without water, he couldn't live without her. He promised to provide her with a life of love and prosperity if she
would marry him.

When Sara finally noticed Gail standing on the outskirts of the group of
women, she moved toward her.

"Hey did you hear the news?"

"Yes, I heard," Gail said looking distracted.

"I have something very important to ask you Gail. Will you be a bridesmaid
in my wedding?"

"A what?"

"A bridesmaid. Will you be in my wedding?"

"Oh, uh, yeah. Sure I will."

Gail drove home from The Word lamenting. She had promised herself that
she would not be in another wedding until she was the bride. Here it goes
again! At least she had stumbled upon some people who had some money.
Maybe everything would be paid for again, since it was obvious that Anthony
was doing quite well financially.

She got home and made spaghetti and meatballs for dinner. Cooking was
like therapy for her as she pondered her situation. If she really wanted to be a
bride, why was she entangled in a crazy relationship with Mario? She needed to
find an unattached guy like Anthony. Jason was a logical choice, but she didn't

seem to be attracted to Jason like she was attracted to Mario. Jason seemed brotherly to her.

Did she really tell Sara that she would be in her wedding? Surely she could find a way to back out gracefully. On the other hand, Sara would probably be insulted if she refused to be in her wedding. Gail had agreed to be in Nina's wedding without even knowing the girl.

"How did I get mixed up with this group of people anyway?" Gail asked herself as she drained the spaghetti.

When she sat down to eat, she remembered the prayer she had said at The Word. She had been so distracted by Sara's announcement that she had not told her about her new commitment. Sara probably wasn't concerned with that now anyway. Maybe she should call Jason and tell him about the prayer, and ask what she should do next. She remembered that he had told her to read some New Testament books. Maybe she would read a few chapters when she went to bed.

After Gail ate, she called Shawn and they talked for two hours. Shawn's reaction to her latest news about her affair was similar to Joanna and her other friends.

"No wonder the poor guy is chasing after you. If she's not taking care of business, she's just telling him to go out and get some from someone else," Shawn said. "She'll be lucky if she's able to hang on to him after all of this. How serious are you about being with him?"

"I'm not sure about that right now," Gail said nervously. "I think this is just a short term thing. It can't last too long."

"I thought Mario was your soul mate?"

"Maybe he is. But maybe he was a temptation that I was supposed to resist this time." Gail said the words as they popped into her head. She figured her recent decision to try this Jesus thing must have been influencing her thinking.

"What does that mean? Are you going to stop playing with fire?"

"I didn't say that. I don't think I'm ready to give him up just yet. I'm spending next weekend with him. Hopefully, we'll be able to talk seriously about our relationship then."

"Well like I told you before, you can do better. If you really want to get married one day, you'll learn how to date men who are marriage material."

"And just how do I do that? The men I've dated since college have been basically duds."

"You've come across a few guys who could have made the cut."

"Like who Shawn?"

"Well there was that guy Larry."

"He lived with his mother with no plans to move out. He said that if he got married, his mother would still live with him."

"Was she ill or something?" Shawn asked.

"No, they were just close like that. She is perfectly healthy and a nice woman. Her and Larry just had a relationship that I didn't want to compete with."

"What about that dude, what was his name? He had a Mexican name."

"You're talking about Juan and he was a drug dealer."

"No way! You never told me that."

"He's serving time as we speak," Gail said.

"Naw, girl, you've got to be kidding."

"It's the honest truth."

"What about that fitness instructor you were dating when I got married?"

"He's a fitness nut. He was more concerned about having strong abs than having a good relationship. He helped me stay in shape but that was it. Listen, Shawn, I've looked over all my failed relationships enough times to get depressed about it. I'm not saying there aren't any good black men out there, it's just that—"

"You haven't found Mr. Right."

"Exactly, so I'm just going ahead with Mr. Right Now."

After Gail hung up, she decided that she needed to find a local best friend. Her long distance bill was getting way too high.

At work that week, the whole floor was abuzz with Sara's engagement news. Every woman on the floor made her way over to check out the ring. Gail was happy for Sara, but by Wednesday, she was faking it. She was tired of hearing the proposal story. She was tired of hearing about how wonderful Anthony was. He was turning into some kind of idol in the office.

On Wednesday morning, Gail ran into two women in the break room saying that the ring was a five-carat diamond and Anthony was a millionaire. She turned to leave, even though she was clearly being invited into the conversation. On her way out, one of them said that Sara would be leaving her job after the wedding. She certainly didn't think Anthony was a millionaire, but she didn't correct them. It was good public relations for people to be saying something good about a black man for a change. She didn't know about Sara's leaving, though. If Gail hadn't been so reluctant to be involved in another wedding, she could have been privy to all the inside information. Since Monday, Gail had kept her distance from Sara, trying to determine if she would be able to finagle her way out of the wedding party. Besides, Gail had enough going on in her own life and didn't want to get caught up in another season of wedding preparations, especially since she wasn't the bride.

Early that afternoon, she decided to call Jason at work and tell him about her prayer. She was surprised when he answered right away. She expected a secretary or an automated system.

"Jason Tucker speaking," he said in a brisk, business voice.

"Hi, Jason. It's Gail."

"Hey, it's good to hear from you. How are you?" He said more informally.

"Well, I'll get right to it. On Sunday I didn't go up to the altar, but I repeated the prayer for salvation at my seat."

"Gail, this is wonderful news! I'm so happy for you. Your life will never be the same again!" Jason's excitement was contagious, but Gail didn't know what to say. She suddenly had the urge to confess that she was having an affair with his buddy.

Jason didn't seem to notice her silence. He continued, "Now that you are a new creation in Christ, old things are passed away. Everything is new. You know how people say what they would do differently if they had a second chance? Well, you now have another chance, a clean slate. Your life can start over brand new."

"Just like that? Isn't there something else I need to do?"

"Yeah, you should join a local church, preferably The Word. In fact, we have a Bible study tonight."

"I can't make it tonight, but I'll try to be there Sunday." Gail didn't want to tell him she had a hair appointment after work in preparation for her big weekend with Mario. She would probably be able to get away from Mario long enough to attend service on Sunday.

"That's fine. You can join on Sunday. After that, we have a number of Bible classes and Christian living classes that will help you learn about your new life," Jason explained.

"Sounds wonderful. I look forward to learning more. You know, I was really able to relate more to Rev. Kline's sermons after talking to you."

"That's good to hear. Don't hesitate to call me or Sara with any questions you have," Jason said. "I'd love to talk to you longer, but I need to head to a meeting."

"Sure, I'll talk to you later, and I'll see you Sunday."

After work, Gail treated herself to the full treatment at Isis Spa and Salon. Every once in a while, she toyed with a nagging feeling in the back of her mind. Maybe she should try to end this thing with Mario, but by Thursday evening, she was so excited about seeing him again that she could think of nothing else but the warmth of his hugs and the electricity that was ignited when they were together.

Since she would be gone from her condo all weekend, she decided to do some maintenance cleaning that she would have done on Saturday. As she finished up in the bathroom, the phone rang. She went into the living room and glanced at the caller ID. It was Mario's cell phone number.

"Hey, Rio. I can't wait to see you," Gail said. But at the same time, Mario was saying, "Gail. I can't talk long. I have some bad news."

"What?" Gail said, hoping she had heard him wrong. "Bad news?"

"I won't be able to make this weekend, but the trip to Corpus Christi is still on," he said in a rush.

"I've really been looking forward to our weekend."

"I know, baby. But we'll be together again. I promise. But now, I have to get off the phone. I'll see you soon." Click.

Gail was dumbfounded. She stood in the middle of her living room staring at the phone. What was that about? First she just felt disappointment. Then she became worried that something was wrong. She hoped that he would call her back soon and explain a little more. She knew he had family obligations, so maybe something came up. But what could be so important that it spoiled a weekend that he had planned for them? Surely he would call back with an explanation.

CHAPTER 13

By the end of the day Friday, Gail found herself in a blue funk. She went home, changed out of her work clothes and put on a Sade CD. She had checked the caller ID and answering machine. No call from Mario. She thought about going to the gym, but she couldn't muster up the energy. Gail felt herself sliding into sadness, a sort of depression. Maybe she should call Shawn. Thoughts of her last long distance bill stopped her from picking up the phone. She did have Mario's cell phone number. Without thinking, she found his number in her planner and dialed. Disappointment came over her like a shadow when she heard his voice mail message. She hung up without saying anything, knowing that his caller ID would show that she had called. She resigned herself to spending a quiet Friday evening alone. It wasn't so bad. She watched movies all night, ate popcorn and ice cream and fell asleep on the couch.

Saturday, she was still depressed, but she made herself go to the gym because of all the junk food she had eaten Friday night. She kept herself in pretty good shape so she was used to getting stares from men at the gym. However, there was a new guy there who tried to hide it, but he was definitely taking notice of her. It would have been creepy if he had not been so fine himself. He wasn't the overly muscled body-builder type. He was one of those nicely built black men with a neat haircut and a clean-shaven face. She figured he was an engineer or some kind of tech professional new to the neighborhood.

When she went to the water fountain, he took the opportunity to introduce himself.

"Hi, my name is Darien," he said, extending his hand.

"Nice to meet you Darien," Gail said and gave him a million dollar smile.

"So, what's your name?" he asked politely.

"Gail," she answered just as politely.

"Well, it's nice to meet you, Gail. I'm new to Austin."

"Oh? Did you transfer here with your job?" She upgraded his profession to executive management.

"You could say that."

"And where do you work?"

"At Memorial Hospital."

"What do you do there?" She had him pegged wrong unless he was some kind of tech at the hospital.

"I'm an emergency room doctor."

Gail tried not to look impressed. She glanced at his ring finger. No wedding ring and no indentions on his ring finger. An unmarried black doctor. How many of those could there be in America?

"Well, doc, I'd better get back to my work out."

"Sure, no problem. But I hope I see you here again." He looked and sounded disappointed that she was ending the conversation.

"I come here all the time. I'm sure we'll run into each other again," She smiled broadly to let him know that she might be interested. And she probably would have been interested if Mario hadn't been weighing heavily on her mind.

After returning from the gym, Gail checked her caller ID and her answering machine. All she had was a message on her machine from Sara inviting her to lunch at Houston's restaurant after church on Sunday. Gail called back to accept the invitation, but she got Sara's machine. She made her voice sound cheery and left a message saying that she would love to meet for lunch after church.

Sunday morning she headed to The Word, glad to have something to take her mind off Mario. He had been on her mind all weekend.

During the praise service at The Word, Gail thought she was dreaming. On the front row was a man who looked just like Mario from behind. She must have conjured him up by thinking about him so much. Her seat was on one of the side sections of the church, so she wasn't sure it was Mario. She was totally distracted and kept looking in the guy's direction during all the songs. After the praise service, one of the ministers gave a welcome and asked everyone to greet the people around them. That's when she was able to confirm her suspicions. Mario was there on the front row with his wife Nina. Gail thought she was going to be ill as her stomach began to flip-flop. She tried to pay attention to the people greeting her, but she couldn't keep herself from straining her neck to catch glimpses of Mario and Nina through the crowd.

So that was why he had to cancel. He had to bring his wife with him. Why hadn't he just said that instead of being so mysterious? Gail was reasonable enough to understand that the man did have to spend time with his wife sometime.

Gail managed to take a few notes during Rev. Kline's sermon. He preached about the seed, the sower and the enemy, explaining how you can be good ground or bad ground when you hear the word of the Lord preached. She decided that she was not really good ground, even though she was trying to be. She was just too distracted by Mario.

There were so many people at the service that Gail didn't feel like searching for Sara after church and she certainly didn't want to run into Mario and Nina. She went to Houston's Restaurant and waited for Sara and probably Anthony, and hopefully Jason. She got to the crowded restaurant and stood just inside the doors. There were people standing shoulder to shoulder waiting for tables to open up. When the area thinned out a little, she took a seat on an uncomfortable wooden bench.

She checked her watch every two minutes and grew impatient after about twenty minutes of waiting. Restless, she got up to walk outside and Sara finally walked in. Sure enough, Anthony and Jason were with her. As she walked toward Sara and greeted her with a hug, she saw Nina and Mario coming in the door holding hands. She couldn't believe it! She had never dreamed that they would also be coming to lunch. As she hugged Sara, she said into her ear.

"I didn't know Nina and Mario were in town."

"Oh yes, girl, the newlyweds are finally coming out!"

He's been coming out all right, Gail thought. She tried her best to keep cool, turn on some kind of social grace and greet everyone politely, but she dared not look Mario in the eyes.

Anthony had called ahead and their table was ready as soon as they all got to the restaurant. At the table Jason playfully said, "Okay, everybody, boy, girl, boy, girl," and his seating scheme had her sitting between him and Mario. She considered protesting, but thought she would draw too much attention, so she took a bathroom break to regroup.

"Wait up, I'm going, too," Sara said.

"Me, too," Nina said, even as Mario was holding her chair for her to sit down.

As she walked away from the table without waiting for Sara and Nina, Gail could hear Jason asking the other guys, "Why do women always go to the bathroom together?"

She wanted to walk straight past the bathroom and out the door to her car. She went on into the bathroom and immediately into the handicap stall, which offered more privacy. She sat down and thought about her dilemma. Her choices were either to stay or go home. She leaned toward staying. So if she stayed how would she get through this lunch?

Just then she heard the outer doors open and Sara and Nina enter. Maybe they had stayed back to explain to Jason why women go to the bathroom together.

"So girl, how is married life?"

"Well, to tell you the truth, it was rocky for a few weeks, but after I saw my doctor for a few adjustments, it was on and on 'til the break of dawn, girl."

"What?" Sara squealed. Gail heard them giggling and giving high fives like they were still in high school.

This was a new development that Mario had failed to tell her about. She decided then and there that she would stay at the restaurant and find out as much as she could about Mr. and Mrs. Lewis' married life. She flushed the toilet and came out of the stall. She smiled at them and went to the sink to wash her hands. Nina began refreshing her already impeccable make-up in the mirror.

"So did you hear what she said, Gail?" Sara asked.

Gail smiled knowingly at both women in the mirror. "Yes, I did. But Nina, I want some details."

"Details? What do you mean?" Nina paused with her lipstick in mid-air.

Ah, maybe she was putting up a front and still had not been able to consummate the marriage. Nina surprised Gail with a wink and said, "Well, like I said, we had a hard time at first, but Mario accompanied me to the doctor who showed me how to relax my, umm, muscles, you know. All the while, Mario held my hand and encouraged me. It was like some really clinical sex therapy."

"Uh, that sounds weird," Sara said.

"I admit it was kind of strange, but my doctor is a black woman. She's really sharp. I guess I was able to relate to her and do what she said because she knew what was going on down there. With just me and Mario, I didn't know what the heck I was doing, and all he could do was try his best to, you know."

Gail was so glad that the lighting in Houston's was so subdued. Hopefully it was hiding the stunned expression on her face. She managed to ask, "So how many weeks was it before you went to the doctor?"

"We went on Monday. My poor husband had to wait six weeks!" Nina turned to face Gail directly. "But, like you said, he was so understanding and gentle. I really appreciate your advice."

A mischievous grin spread across Nina's face as she looked knowingly at Sara and Gail. Anticipating what was coming, Gail turned toward the mirror and pretended something was in her eye.

"I have to tell you the truth. I am really enjoying our sex life now. I mean, I knew that Mario was virile, but my God! We've been going at it like rabbits since Monday night." Nina and Sara collapsed into their girlish whoops and giggles and Gail thought she was going to be ill.

So this is why Mario had to cancel their weekend, Gail thought. It occurred to her that she shouldn't be upset that the man was actually having sex with his wife. Somehow Gail had been under an illusion that Mario belonged to her as long as Nina was unable to perform her marital duties. As she walked back to the table behind Sara and Nina, she wondered if Mario was going to end the affair soon. She wanted to go home and wallow in her melancholy mood, but she was also curious to see the happy newlyweds together. She wanted to see how Mario would act in this peculiar situation.

Back at the table the men were in rare form, loud talking each other with great pleasure. As the ladies approached, they all stood and held out chairs. When everyone was seated again, Anthony said, "So ladies, this is the question that is on the table." He paused dramatically, making sure he had everyone's attention. "Is the woman that Jason is currently dating here with us today?"

Gail couldn't believe her ears. She knew by Anthony's tone that he was just kidding around, but could things get anymore complicated for her today?

"That's very funny, Anthony. But what we all really want to know is why did it take you so long to get your girlfriend to agree to marry you?" Jason shot back. Everyone laughed but Gail. Glancing at Sara, Gail decided that it must be some kind of inside joke.

"So Mario," Anthony was vying for a comeback.

"Uh oh," Nina groaned. But Mario looked like he was ready for the challenge.

"I hope you and your new bride had sense enough not to get pregnant on your honeymoon." Anthony said. There was laughter all around the table. Nina just rolled her eyes.

"No, brother. We haven't gotten pregnant yet. And, I hope that you have sense enough not to get pregnant before your wedding day."

Everyone laughed and looked at Anthony for his response.

"Well, unfortunately that is an impossibility. I mean fortunately! Fortunately," Anthony said, looking at Sara apologetically. He looked at his buddies for help, but they just rolled with laughter. Anthony was always so businesslike and professional. It was quite amusing to see him so ruffled. Sara had a hurt look on her face, but Gail could tell by the glint in her eye that she was just giving Anthony a hard time.

"If you can't run with the big dogs, stay on the porch, man," Jason taunted.

Nina and Sara looked amused as the men continued to throw comments back and forth. Apparently Nina and Sara were used to this playfulness. Gail found it odd that they never said a word as the men referred to their sex lives. She thought they would at least make a comment. Maybe Mario noticed the confused look on her face.

"Ladies, on behalf of my wayward brothers, let me offer my sincere apologies," Mario began, but was cut off.

"Man, what are you apologizing for?" Anthony said.

Mario went on as if he didn't hear Anthony.

"Please accept my most humble apologies for their rude behavior and lewd comments."

"Are you finished?" Jason asked sarcastically.

"Don't hold it against them, ladies, I know they get rowdy sometimes." Mario looked sincerely at Gail, Nina and Sara, but his gaze ended back on Gail. Nina and Sara just rolled their eyes and shook their heads, but Mario was still looking at her. She avoided direct eye contact, but mumbled that she knew they were just kidding. The conversation moved to other topics and she could tell Mario kept glancing at her, but she pretending to be involved in the conversation on Jason's side of the table.

By the time the main course was served, Gail had become quite comfortable with the group. After laughing at the antics of Anthony, Mario and Jason, she didn't feel nearly as nervous as she did when they all first walked into the restaurant.

She felt apprehensive about the possibility of her brief affair coming to an end, and she felt hurt or angry or both that Mario had not taken the time to explain things earlier. However, she reminded herself that Nina was his wife and was certainly entitled to have sex with her own husband.

Although Gail was initially distracted by Mario's closeness, she got caught up in the general festive nature of the group and laughed with everyone through most of the lunch. She didn't pay much attention to Mario, but she did notice that he and Nina kept feeding each other. She realized it was a blessing that Mario was right next to her, making it easier for her to avoid looking directly at him.

When it was time to order dessert, Jason asked her if she would like to split a cobbler with him. She agreed and caught Sara eyeing them with a raised brow. Everyone ordered dessert but Mario. He took a bite of Nina's brownie, and then to Gail's distress, he turned his attention to her. Nina and Anthony were in a deep discussion about the stock market while Jason and Sara were talking about some gospel music artists that Gail had never heard of.

Mario turned to her.

"So how long have you and Jay been dating?"

She tried to give him a look that said, "No you didn't ask me that!" But instead she said, "I don't know what you're talking about." Unfortunately she looked straight at him, something she knew she needed to avoid. He had a playful look in his eyes and took his time running the tip of his tongue across his bottom lip. She managed to pull her eyes away from his face before she melted completely.

"Well, you can tell me all about it later this week." With that he turned back toward his wife and joined the conversation about stocks. Gail pretended to listen to Jason and Sara debate about some group called Commissioned and some guy named Fred. Apparently, Fred had left the group some while back and Sara felt the group should dissolve. Jason was explaining that gospel music fans still supported the group, and it was all just about the bottom line anyway.

Gail was secretly thinking about "later this week." Mario didn't sound like he was going to end their relationship, but she didn't want to get her hopes up too high. After last Thursday and after what she had gone through when he cancelled their weekend, she knew that she was not ready for things to end so soon.

After a little more banter and dessert, the guys argued over the check and Mario won out by claiming he needed to build up his business expenses for a tax write-off.

"But we're not vendors for your dry cleaners," Jason said.

"Yeah, but you're clients. You still use our stores don't you?" Jason and Anthony looked at each other with raised eyebrows, sending Mario into a tirade.

"That's just like black folk. We don't know how to support our own. That's why we don't even depend on ya'll anymore." Mario went on talking about various ethnic groups and their support of each other, while flashing an impressive looking American Express card to pay the bill.

As they were leaving the restaurant, Jason offered to walk Gail to her car.

They made small talk about the weather until they reached her car.

"So have you been reading your word and praying, my sister?" Jason asked playfully.

"Well...umm, I haven't really read much," Gail said, embarrassed. "But I've enjoyed the sermons. I don't think I was very good ground today, though."

"Is something wrong? Do you want to talk about it?" he asked. "Hey, I mean you can talk to Sara, if you don't want to talk to me if something's bothering you," Jason said.

"I probably just need to take your advice—read the Bible and pray. What was it that Rev. Kline said makes us thorny ground?"

"The cares of life and the deceitfulness of riches. They choke the word and you become unfruitful," Jason said looking more and more concerned.

Noticing the worried look on his face, Gail said, "Oh, don't worry about it. I'll be okay. I just haven't been disciplined, professor. You said I should treat this thing like a class, and I've been goofing off."

"Look, we have a 'Welcome to The Word Rally' next Saturday. It's basically a new members orientation. You meet Pastor Kline and other people in ministry. It'll really help you get grounded."

"That sounds like exactly what I need. What time?"

"It starts at noon. We have a nice lunch and a presentation. It's a really good way to get focused on your new life."

"Thanks Jason, I really do think that's what I need," Gail repeated.

"So are you coming back to church tonight?"

"I hadn't planned on it."

"Come on, Gail. Do you have anything else to do?"

"Well, I guess not."

"Look, you still have enough time to relax before church starts at seven. Do you want me to pick you up?"

"No, I can drive myself."

"So I'll see you there?"

"I guess, Jason."

"Good. It's a laid back service, so you can dress casual."

Gail got in her car doubting that she would go to the service that night, but she did plan to attend the orientation. At the moment she couldn't get her mind off Mario. Since Nina's big bathroom announcement, she felt that things had changed between her and Mario, but then he gave her his little message about talking to her later on. He even seemed jealous of Jason. Gail thought that was ironic.

When she got home she glanced at her answering machine and caller ID. No calls. She changed clothes and settled down to relax. The shock of seeing Mario and Nina had taken its mental toll. Gail stretched out on the couch with the remote and dozed off.

CHAPTER 14

She was sitting upright and saying "hello" into the phone before she was even fully awake. She had grabbed the cordless phone from the coffee table in her sleep and only began to become aware of what she was doing when she heard Mario's husky voice.

"Hey, I didn't expect to see you today at lunch."

"What time is it?" Gail asked. She felt a little guilty about not going to the service.

"It's only nine o'clock. Did I wake you up?"

"I guess I missed it," she said, reclining on the couch.

"Gail what are you talking about? Are you sleep? Wake up, girl," Mario said playfully. "Why did you go to bed so early?"

"I fell asleep on the couch. I was supposed to go back to church with Jason," Gail said before thinking. Mentioning Jason to Mario would bring up a conversation she didn't want to have.

"So tell me what's going on between you and Jay."

"What do you mean?"

"Are you guys dating or something?" Mario asked with a hint of jealousy in his voice.

"Mario, my life is complicated enough without me trying to date someone else while I'm in this thing with you." Gail's voice was more annoyed than she intended, but she was hoping that her tone would signal an end to the topic of Jason.

"This thing? Well, I guess that's a good name for it," he said. "I look forward to exploring this thing with you further in Corpus," Mario said in a business-like manner.

"Umm, oh? You still want to go to Corpus Christi with me?"

"Why wouldn't I?" he asked. "You know I've been looking forward to this trip with you."

"It seems like you might want to go with your wife. She told me that everything is going well with you guys now."

"What exactly did she tell you? I don't think it's a good idea for you and Nina to be chatting like old friends. What's up with that anyway?"

"Don't think it's the most comfortable thing for me. I'm just playing the cards as they were dealt."

"So what did Nina say about us?"

"Let's just say that I wouldn't be surprised if you had to cancel like you did the last time."

"I won't have to cancel. I've already purchased your ticket, and it will be delivered to you this week," he said.

"But since things are working better with you and Nina, wouldn't you rather spend more time with her?"

"Gail, I want to be with you," Mario reassured her smoothly. "I don't know what Nina told you, but as far as I'm concerned, nothing has changed. I want to see you. I can't stop thinking about you. I've got to have you."

"Okay, okay. I get the point. I guess I'm flattered."

"Good. And don't worry about Nina. She'll be occupied with events in San Antonio."

Gail wondered where Nina was at the moment. She checked her caller ID and confirmed that he was calling from his mobile phone.

"So where are you right now?"

"I'm at home. We drove back right after lunch."

"You're calling me from your house?"

"Actually, I'm sitting by the pool and I'm on my cell phone. Why are you asking?"

"I was just wondering where Nina—"

"Is that your phone beeping?" Mario cut her off before she could finish her inquiry.

"Yes, but I'm not going to click over."

"Why? Is it Jay trying to see why you didn't go to church?"

"I don't know," Gail said nonchalantly. She glanced at the caller ID on the end table and recognized Jason's home number.

"Look at your caller ID."

"No."

"Why not?"

"Because I'm trying to have an uninterrupted conversation with you," Gail said. "So what are we going to do in Corpus Christi?"

"Maybe a little shopping, a bit of sight-seeing, a little beach-walking, but mainly a lot of somethin' somethin'," Mario said provocatively.

"Is that all you want from me?" Gail meant it playfully.

"I wanted more, much more. But I'm trying to deal with things the way they are now."

His candor caught her off guard and she was unable to tell how serious he was without seeing his face. She was reminded of the conversation they had when she met him at the hotel expecting him to seduce her.

"Well, I guess we'll also have time to talk about this thing while we're in Corpus."

"We will," Mario said. "I guess I'd better let you go. As usual, I have a long week ahead of me."

"Why do you work so hard all the time?"

"I'm just paying my dues. Things will change soon enough," Mario said. "Before you get off the phone, will you do something for me?"

"What? Do you want to know what I'm wearing or something?"

"We don't have time for all of that right now. Just say my name, you know, the way you do when you scream it."

"I'm not going to scream your name."

"No, just say it."

"What, you mean, Rio? Like that?"

"Not like that. Say it in your sexy voice."

"Rio," Gail drawled softly, gladly obliging as she pictured him reclined on a chair next to his pool in the warmth of the summer night.

"No one has ever said my name the way you do."

The Saturday after attending the new members orientation, Gail decided that she shouldn't go to Corpus Christi to meet Mario after all. She met all the church leaders, filled out forms for membership and had her picture taken. They gave a spiritual assessment that brought out more questions than answers for Gail. The thing that made her not want to go on the trip with Mario was Pastor Kline's comments about purpose and vision. He had said that none of the people in the room were there by accident. According to Pastor Kline, Gail's decision to become a member of The Word was part of God's plan for her life. He said God wanted to reveal His purpose to her. She had sat in the meeting, amazed at the things the pastor was saying. She felt like she was the only person in the room and that finally, some of her life questions were being answered. It began to make sense that the Creator had a reason for her being born. She thought about how misplaced she felt when she was growing up, but if God had a purpose for her life, maybe there was a reason she had experienced the pain and failure of trying to fit in and get the attention of her father and even her stepfather.

"One thing you can be sure about. The devil is not at all happy about this decision, so he's going to fight you every step of the way. As soon as you start seeking the Lord and getting focused on Kingdom living, you will be attacked by the enemy because he doesn't want you to live your life according to God's plan," Pastor Kline had said. He explained how the devil fights to keep people misfocused so that they fail to seek the Kingdom first.

When she was in the meeting, Gail knew exactly what was causing her to be misfocused. Still she needed to bounce these new ideas off someone. She thought about calling Sara, but she couldn't tell her about Mario. She dialed Shawn's number reluctantly, knowing that her phone bill wouldn't be going down any time soon.

"Girl, I'm so glad I caught you," Gail said when Shawn picked up. "What are you doing today?"

"I was actually on my way out, but I can talk for a little bit. What's up?"

Gail gave a synopsis of Pastor Kline's talk at the meeting that morning and explained how she felt that Mario was a distraction keeping her from focusing on God's plan for her life.

"Well, Mario may be a distraction, but all that other stuff sounds a little extreme to me."

Gail's call waiting beeped. "Hold on a minute while I see who this is."

She clicked over.

"Girl, I've been thinking about you all week."

"Mario! Umm, I'm on another call."

"Well, hang up so we can talk."

"Just a second." Gail clicked back.

"Shawn?"

"It's still me. Who's Shawn?"

"Hold on." Gail clicked again. "Shawn?"

"Yes, it's me."

"Girl, Mario is on the other line."

"What are you going to do?"

"I guess I'll talk to him. He sent me a ticket to Corpus. I'm supposed to meet him there next Friday evening."

"Well, here's my advice and then I'll let you go. I think you need to play the whole thing out so that you get him out of your system. Go on the trip and do whatever, but eventually, I think it's going to end, unless he wants to leave his wife for you."

"I don't want him to leave his wife."

"Whatever, Gail. I'm going shopping now. I'll talk to you later."

Gail clicked back over the Mario.

"So is Shawn a guy or a girl?" Mario asked as soon as she got on the line.

"She's my best friend. Why does it matter, Mario?"

"I just want to know if there's any competition for your attention."

"Well, I guess I should tell you about the doctor I met at the gym."

"What? Who is he? At the gym? Girl, don't talk to guys at the gym. It's just a big meat market anyway."

"Hold up, Mario. I was just kidding. Besides, you're the one who's married with obligations."

"I didn't even call to talk about that. I just wanted to make sure you got your ticket."

"I did, but I've been having second thoughts about this trip. Maybe we should wait." Gail tried to conjure up the same resolve she'd had at the new members orientation.

"Oh, please don't say that. I need a break from work and from everything else. Please go with me. I really need to spend some time with you."

Gail was surprised at the pleading tone in his voice.

"What would you do if I just didn't show up?"

"I'd catch a plane to Austin and beg you to go with me. Why are you having second thoughts about the trip?"

She considered telling him about Pastor Kline's talk about purpose and vision, but she didn't want to insult him by calling him a distraction. She tried an indirect approach.

"You know I joined The Word and all. I've been getting more involved and maybe we should cool it for now."

"Gail, if you had said that with some conviction, I may have believed you."

"Well, this church stuff is all new to me. You know more about it than I do. But I do know that the Bible says adultery is wrong."

"It was also wrong for me to marry someone that I don't love."

Gail was shocked and unable to respond. She held the phone, eyes wide, mouth hanging open, heart beating wildly.

"I shouldn't have said that. But I think it's the truth," Mario said quietly.

Gail felt sorry for him, but she still didn't know what to say. If he didn't love Nina, was he going to stay married to her? She was too afraid to ask him that and other questions running through her mind. She wasn't prepared to handle the answers. Maybe next week she would ask him what he was going to do about his loveless marriage, but for now, she would tread lightly.

"Look, just meet me in Corpus next weekend, and maybe you can help me sort all this out. I just want to see you and be with you again."

"Okay. I guess."

CHAPTER 15

That Sunday at church, Sara greeted Gail in the foyer.

"Hey girl! I heard the good news." Sara gave Gail a big hug.

"What news?" Gail asked, returning Sara's hug.

"About you getting saved and joining church. I had to hear it from Jason. Why didn't you tell me yourself?" Sara asked.

"Jason was the one calling me every day to make sure I was coming to church. He even gave me a Bible," Gail said.

"I didn't know all this. Well, I'm so excited for you. This is a big decision."

"I guess so. But I have some things I need to work out."

"Just trust God to work things out for you. Don't trust in your own understanding. Get enrolled in one of the classes in Christian living and you'll see what I mean."

Sara linked arms with Gail and headed toward the sanctuary. "For now, let's enjoy the Lord. It's time to get our praise on."

As usual the service at The Word was exciting and lively. Praise service was in high gear as they entered and found seats near the front. Rev. Kline was on the stage wearing a flowing black robe. During the song he began explaining why it's important to praise. The band kept a rapid beat behind him as he spoke.

"You see God inhabits the praises of His people. When we give Him glory, we give notice to the spirit world that we are aligned with the Most High God, the Only God. Praise is a form of warfare for the believer. Jesus has been given a name that is above every name. So at the name of Jesus everything must bow." He let out a loud "Hallelujah" and started dancing across the stage.

Then he cried out, "Come on men. Come on warriors. Let's lead out in praise."

Men moved from their seats all over the sanctuary and started dancing in the aisles and running around the church. Pastor Kline's dancing became more and more rapid until he was just a blur moving around the stage. Everyone was dancing, clapping, stomping. Gail tried to keep up with the frenetic beat and moved over to give Sara room to dance next to her. She didn't even attempt to dance herself, but she did feel a connection. Maybe it was some ancient link from Africa that connected her to these people. She didn't know, but she did feel the joy and the elation of praising God. The beat began to slow down to half time until the praise leader began singing the familiar, acquiescent, "Yes," song. Rev. Kline had left the stage and the service moved on to the greetings and announcements followed by tithes and offerings. The choir sang a fast song with a funky beat called "This is War" led by a male and female who sounded like professionals to Gail. She asked Sara if they had ever recorded.

"The choir is releasing their second CD later this year. They're good aren't they?"

Rev. Kline came back to the stage after the song and went immediately into his sermon.

"We've already launched our attack on the enemy. So let's discuss some strategies for the warfare you will face this week. Let's be on the offense for once. We're not going to be running scared this week. Every morning when you wake up, I want you to have demons trembling."

Rev. Kline's sermon title was "Winning the War" and he read from Deuteronomy 20:1-4. "When you go to war against your enemies and see horses and chariots and an army greater than yours, do not be afraid of them, because the Lord your God, who brought you up out of Egypt, will be with you. When you are about to go into battle, the priest shall come forward and address the army. He shall say: "Hear, O Israel, today you are going into battle against your enemies. Do not be fainthearted or afraid; do not be terrified or give way to panic before them. For the Lord your God is the one who goes with you to fight for you against your enemies to give you victory."

The sermon was a charge for battle and the crowd was so hyped that many people stood during the entire sermon. He preached about being aggressive and fearless in war because nothing and nobody could defeat God. By the end of the sermon, Gail wanted to participate in the battle, but she felt like an inadequate soldier. She wasn't even sure who the enemy was right now.

CHAPTER 16

On the plane heading to Corpus Christi Friday evening, Gail contemplated how she could tell Mario that their relationship needed to end. She had thought about simply not showing up, but when she had received her tickets in the mail, Mario had included a note: "Can't wait to hold you in my arms again. Your touch is the most refreshing thing in my life right now. –M."

Part of her felt like a completely different person since she joined The Word, but another part of her longed to be with Mario. Although no man had ever satisfied her so completely, Gail knew this was about more than just sex. She had tried to deny it, but as she sat looking out of the window of the plane, she admitted to herself that she wanted Mario. She should have been the bride instead of Nina. If Gail were married to Mario, he wouldn't be sneaking off on a rendezvous with an ex-lover.

Yes, she wanted him, but she still didn't want him to end his marriage for her. That would just be too embarrassing. She liked her new church and her new friends, and she couldn't handle disgracing herself in their environment. The only way she could deal with being with Mario in the open would be if they ran away together. Considering his ties to his family business and his own church in San Antonio, she didn't think he would want to run away.

What was she thinking anyway? The logical thing to do would be to end it before she got too emotionally involved. She would try to come up with something by evening. She could break it to him gently at dinner.

When she got off the plane, Mario was standing at the gate waiting for her looking handsome as usual in a casual blue cotton shirt, dark blue linen pants and brown leather sandals. He took her carry-on bag and swept her into a warm embrace. The little resolve she had to end the relationship was melting quickly. How could she resist this?

After they picked up her checked bag, Mario guided her to a rented red convertible and they headed to the hotel with the top down. Gail enjoyed the feel of the warm sea air whipping through her hair on the breezy August evening. He drove the car up to the valet station at a beautiful hotel by the beach. Mario had already checked in, and he led Gail to an extravagant suite on the top floor.

"I have a surprise for you," he said, smiling gleefully as he pulled out his key card.

"I'm sure you do."

Gail found the opulent suite breathtaking. She admired the view of the gulf beach through floor to ceiling windows. It was a clear night with brightly shining stars. She was mesmerized.

With little pretense, Mario pulled Gail from the window and took her into the bedroom. Trays of tropical fruit and champagne were next to the bed. There were massage oils on the nightstand. After a long embrace, Mario began lighting candles throughout the room. She took her overnight bag into the bathroom and showered quickly. She put on a red silk teddy with a short, matching robe that she had bought with him in mind.

When she stepped back into the bedroom, Mario was opening the champagne. He gave her an appraising look and let out a low whistle as she walked toward him.

"You look absolutely delicious," he said and popped the cork. He poured champagne into their glasses. "I'm really glad you came."

Gail just smiled and sipped some champagne. An unfamiliar feeling of unease came over her. It must have shown on her face.

"Are you all right? You don't like the champagne? It's one of the best they have." Mario looked alarmed.

"Oh, I'm fine. The champagne is fine. Really. I guess I'm just feeling shy all of a sudden."

The scenery was perfect for a night of pleasure, but Gail was surprised that she didn't feel in the mood.

"I don't want you to feel uncomfortable, baby." Mario said taking her hand and sitting with her on the bed. "Let's just sit here and relax."

He placed a piece of pineapple in front of Gail's mouth. Holding it there he said, "Sometimes we just need to take things slowly." He placed the fruit in her mouth along with the tip of his finger. She sucked both until he pulled his finger out. He fed her more pieces of fruit and spoke in a soothing voice.

"It feels so good being with you. I want you to have a good time. This feels so right to me. When I'm with you all my worries melt away. There's so much pressure in my life, but you're like an oasis for me. It means so much to me that you came on this trip. I want to give you so much. Right now, all I can give you is this weekend, and I want you to enjoy every bit of the time we have together."

It didn't take long for her to get back in the mood as she listened to his smooth voice and ate the bits of fruit.

He started rubbing her feet with peppermint foot lotion and moved up her body, changing to different oils for each body section. On her legs, he used a cucumber gel. When he moved to her arms, he used a lush citrus-scented lotion and took his time giving her a tension releasing hand massage. He slowly took off the robe and teddy and continued the massage. Gail's body felt like liquid under the deft moves of Mario's hands, lips and tongue. After a few rounds of slow, languid sex, Gail drifted into a very light sleep with Mario's arm draped across her torso.

Suddenly, she was wide-awake. She stared up at the ceiling as a wave of guilt began to flow through her. She lifted Mario's arm from her body and slipped out of the bed. She found her suitcase, slipped on some jeans and a t-shirt and went into the living room.

Gail fell on her knees and the tears began to flow.

"Lord, I know this is wrong, but I don't know how to stop. Help me get out of this," she prayed. She stayed on the floor crying quietly. After a while she heard the bedroom door swing open. She wasn't prepared to explain why she was laid out on the floor, and she didn't bother turning around. After a few seconds, she heard the door close quietly.

Maybe he figured I was praying and wanted me to have some privacy, she thought. "Well, I've got my answer and there's no time like the present," she said quietly.

Gail went into the bedroom with determination, but she was not prepared for what she saw. By the moonlight shining through the window, she saw Mario on his knees at the side of the bed, apparently praying. She didn't know if he was mocking her, but at the moment she didn't care.

She went to the closet and located an extra pillow and blanket without addressing him. As she was leaving the room, Mario rose from his knees and followed her into the living room.

"What are you doing?" he asked. "Come back to bed, baby."

"No, I'm going to sleep out here." She turned on a lamp and spread the blanket on the plush couch.

"Why are you dressed? What's going on, Gail?"

Gail sat down and took her time considering Mario. All he had on was his briefs and she acknowledged that he still looked good from head to toe. However, instead of the usual feeling of lust, she just felt sorry for him.

"So tell me, Gail, why are you sleeping out here?" Mario sat in a chair directly across from her.

"Do I really have to explain it, Mario?"

"Just tell me what's going on with you right now."

"You sound like a concerned counselor," Gail quipped.

"I'm a concerned friend, someone who cares a great deal about you."

"Right now, I'm feeling guilty because what we are doing is just wrong. I never should have come here with you."

"Well, I'm sorry you feel that way, but there's no sense in wasting a beautiful weekend in this lovely city," he said. "But you don't have to sleep on the couch. I can get you another room so that you can be comfortable."

"No, I'm fine right here."

"Actually, I insist. I can call right now and arrange it."

"But it's 3 a.m."

"Oh, they'll just bring a key right up and move your things for you."

"So you're kicking me out?"

"No. I'm trying to make you feel more comfortable so you can have an enjoyable time."

"I don't think that's possible at this point." Gail was annoyed at Mario's businesslike manner. "Do you even feel bad about all this? It's adultery isn't it?"

Mario stared at Gail and heaved a deep, long sigh.

"Well, do you?" Gail insisted on an answer.

When he finally spoke, his voice was so soft, she had to lean forward to hear him.

"The only thing I feel badly about is that I let you get away the first time, and it looks like it's going to happen again."

"I can't be your mistress, Mario."

"I'm not asking you to be my mistress, Gail. I want to be with you."

"No, Mario. We just need to end this before it gets out of hand."

"I want to be with you all the time." Mario was leaning forward and looking so sincere.

He really wants me, Gail thought. What should I do? An immediate answer came to her. Don't be deceived.

"What do you mean by that?" Gail asked. Mario moved from the chair and sat close to her on the couch.

"I mean that I love you, Gail. I want you in my life. I know that things are rather complicated right now, but if you just give me some time, I'll get out of this situation," he said.

Gail was speechless and confused. She knew the Holy Spirit was telling her not to be deceived, but Mario was so convincing.

"Look, Gail. All I'm asking for is time. Just take the weekend and think about it." Mario took her hand and looked into her eyes. "I really love you, Gail. Just give me time to make things right."

"I don't know, Mario. You just got married. You can't just leave. Give Nina a chance. If I weren't in the picture, you wouldn't even be thinking about leaving your marriage."

"That's not necessarily true."

"Well, why did you marry Nina if you really didn't want to?"

"I've been trying to answer that question myself. You don't know how close I came to walking away from that altar and running away with you."

"How do you know I would have run away with you?" Gail smiled.

Mario looked surprised, but a smile was teasing his lips. "Oh, you would have. I saw the way you were looking at me that day," he said playfully and pulled her to his chest.

She pushed away. "Me? How about the way you kept gazing at me? I'm surprised people didn't notice."

"I wouldn't have cared if they did."

Gail wondered if Mario was as sincere as he seemed. If he hadn't said he loved her, she could have gone on with her plan to go back to Austin first thing Saturday morning. Now, she felt like she would be breaking his heart if she tried to leave before the weekend was over.

Mario pulled her close again. "So what do you want to do right now? Come back to bed with me or I can get you your own room."

Gail stifled a yawn. "I think I'll just stay right here." She stretched out on the couch, forcing Mario to stand.

He stood over her with his hands on his hips.

"Suit yourself. But if you come to your senses, I mean change your mind, you know where I'll be."

CHAPTER 17

Gail woke up to the smell of bacon frying. She looked over the back of the couch and saw Mario in the kitchen cooking and humming to himself. He glanced at her and flashed a dazzling smile. He was wearing a bright orange shirt that complemented his smooth, dark skin.

"Rise and shine," he said. She went to the bathroom and took her time showering and getting dressed. She was buying time. Her plan of action had been so clear last night after she had prayed. But after Mario said he loved her, she became totally confused. At least she had managed to stay on the couch. But now he was in the kitchen cooking and looking so handsome and enticing. Surely she could enjoy a day with him without getting into too much trouble.

That night, Gail found herself laying next to Mario and staring at the ceiling again. She felt guilty, but she was too ashamed to pray this time. After breakfast, Mario had whisked her off on a site-seeing tour, which seemed innocent enough. Lunch was at a beautiful seaside restaurant. They had a lovely walk on the beach and did more site seeing and some shopping. By evening, Gail was glad she had decided to stay in Corpus Christi. They had dinner at a small, expensive restaurant by candle light with a spectacular view of the sunset. She had not been aware of the subtle seduction. But thinking back on the day, she wondered how calculating Mario had been. Or maybe he was just being his natural self. He had bought her some pricey coral jewelry, but she knew he was generous. The site seeing and restaurants were not out of the ordinary, either. As much as she wanted to blame Mario, she admitted she could only blame herself for having sex with him again. She had practically thrown herself at him.

All day he had not tried to kiss her or touch her suggestively. When they returned to the suite after dinner, Mario went into the bathroom and started getting ready for bed, saying he was tired after such a full day. He walked through the suite in silk pajamas and barely looked at Gail as he got some juice from the refrigerator. She stared at him as he drank the juice in one long gulp.

He headed back to the bedroom and she blocked his path. He stopped in front of her, but she didn't know what to say.

"So are you sleeping on the couch again tonight?" he asked.

"What do you think?"

In response he merely kissed her on the forehead and went into the bedroom. She followed him and got in the bed. She initiated everything, but he responded with vigor to every move.

She had been so sure about ending things after she had prayed. Then afterwards when she saw him praying, she didn't know what to think. Was he praying because he saw her praying? He was supposed to be a minister, but he didn't seem nearly as serious about things as Jason was. More puzzling to Gail was that Mario had apparently been responsible for getting Jason into the church. Maybe she was just Mario's weakness. He certainly was hers. She knew it would take much more prayer for her to get over him.

The next morning Gail woke up to Mario sitting on the bed fully dressed in a dark suit.

"Wake up, sweetheart," he said, rubbing her naked back.

"What time is it?" Gail asked.

"It's eight, and your flight leaves at ten. I ordered breakfast already."

"Why are you so dressed up? You're going to travel in a suit?"

"Oh, no, I'm not leaving until tomorrow. I have to preach this morning."

"Preach?" Gail sat up in the bed. "Mario, I just don't understand you."

"What do you mean?"

"You know what I mean. You got me down here with you on one of your preaching trips?"

"Well, not really."

"Maybe I should go with you to see just what the hell you preach about." Gail stomped into the bathroom.

"Now, there's no reason for you to be so testy." Mario followed her.

"Testy? I'm down right angry because of your hypocrisy!"

"You weren't angry about my hypocrisy last night. In fact, you were the one who got things started. I thought you were going to be sleeping on the couch again." Gail noticed a playful gleam in his eyes.

"Oh, you knew exactly what you were doing. Not touching me all day. Making me want you even more."

"What? Now, what exactly are you accusing me of?"

"You think this is funny! Do you take anything seriously?"

"I take you seriously." Mario's gaze wandered over her naked body.

"No you don't." Gail reached for a towel to cover herself. "You don't even know me, Mario."

"I know that you enjoy being with me. I know you want me. You know Nina could never make me feel the way you do. That's one of the reasons you continue to be with me. I'm not proud of what we're doing, but I'm not going to apologize for my feelings for you. You think I'm being a hypocrite, but I have prayed about this predicament and right now, I can only lean on God's grace, okay." Mario turned and walked out.

"I'll be waiting for you downstairs to drive you to the airport," he said over his shoulder.

"No. You go ahead. I'll take the airport shuttle. And don't try to stop me. I insist."

CHAPTER 18

Once Gail got back to Austin, she thought about calling Shawn. She picked up the phone and slammed it back down. She couldn't talk to Shawn about Mario and his hypocrisy. Shawn would probably just say something about all church folk being hypocrites. Besides, if Mario was a hypocrite, what did that make Gail?

She could not deny that Mario made her feel good. He knew exactly which buttons to push. When she was with him, she felt like his queen. He wasn't shy about sharing his feelings. He was everything she wanted in a man. He was attentive, handsome, successful and wealthy. Had she really missed out on an opportunity to be his wife?

Gail also could not deny that she had clearly heard the Holy Spirit speak to her when she had prayed on the living room floor of the hotel in Corpus Christi. She wanted to be delivered from this situation with Mario once and for all. If she were going to be set free she needed some practical advice about what she should do. Sara would probably be glad to give her some pointers about how to avoid sex with an old boyfriend. Gail thought about how adamant Sara was about celibacy. Yes, Sara would definitely be able to help her. Gail would go to the Sunday evening service and get Sara to talk to her after church.

Pulling into the church parking lot, Gail felt tired and drained. As Mario had promised, there had certainly been a lot of "activity" in the last couple of days. Not only was she physically tired from having sex, she was also mentally and emotionally drained. She flashed back to the summer when she first met Mario and remembered how intense he was about their relationship, which to her was just a summer fling. He would spend time after they would have sex talking about how she made him feel from the moment he saw her that day. He did the same thing now. Just last night, after she had acted like a sex-crazed nymphomaniac, Mario had held her and whispered sweet things in her ear. She sat in the car with the engine running, thinking about the things he said and trembling.

But now she was determined to rid herself of Mario Lewis once and for all. She hurried into the sanctuary and found the congregation in corporate prayer. One person was praying on a microphone, but people were crying out all over the church. Some were even on the floor praying. Some were kneeling at the altar. Some were walking around speaking in tongues.

The church was not full to capacity like it was on Sunday mornings. It was about seventy-five percent full and she struggled to find Sara in the crowd. She spotted Jason first and took note of his fresh haircut and nicely tailored suit. As the prayer leader transitioned to praise service, an usher led Gail to a seat in the fourth row of one of the side sections, but she still had not found Sara. She wasn't worried, though, because she knew Sara was at church. Sara would have to be in the hospital or out of town before she would miss a church service.

The first song of the praise service was a slow song that Gail was familiar with. She sang along casually,

"I love you. I love you. I love you, Lord today.

Because you care for me in such a special way

I praise you. I lift you up. I magnify your name.

That's why my heart is filled with praise."

After two stanzas the saxophonist played a solo, and Gail got lost in the melody of the song. Then the praise leader said,

"Let's make this a personal thing. Do you really love the Lord? Do you really know how much He cares for you? God loves you in a way that no one else can love you. He made you. He created you in His image. He is the reason that you are even breathing right now. You are His child. Love Him in your own special way. Cry out to Him, saints. Praise Him. Lift Him up. Magnify His name."

Then he began singing again,

"My heart, my mind, my soul belongs to you.

You paid the price for me way back on Calvary

And yes, I praise you. I lift you up. I magnify your name.

That's why my heart is filled with praise."

Gail's cheeks were wet with tears as she experienced an overwhelming sensation of love. She knew it was the presence of God. Her knees were shaking and her heart was lurching in her chest. How could God love her so much after the terrible things she did with a married man? Who was she that the Lord would allow her to feel so loved in a sanctuary full of people who seemed to have this Christian thing all together? She couldn't answer those questions, but she shook off the shame and basked in the presence of the Lord. This was the first time that she had become totally immersed in praise service. She didn't notice what anyone else was doing. She was focused on singing praises to God. She sang to the Lord like she was the only one in the sanctuary.

The praise service was longer in the evening than in the morning service, and Gail was glad about that. She didn't exactly dance in the aisle, but she got a few steps in during the fast songs. She was just glad to be able to express her praise and her love to God. If He loved her so much, surely He would help her get out of a bad relationship.

When Rev. Kline stood to deliver his message, Gail was ready with her notebook and the Bible that Jason had given her. The pastor's style was much more laid back than in the morning service. He even wore more casual clothes. She was used to seeing him in formal looking suits and even robes, but tonight he had on a gray shirt and slacks. He read from John 4:23-24.

"But the hour is coming, and now is, when the true worshipers will worship the Father in spirit and truth; for the Father is seeking such to worship Him. God is Spirit, and those who worship Him must worship in spirit and truth."

As the pastor began giving the history of the text, Gail's face burned with shame. She felt like she was the woman at the well. Her eyes filled with tears as she read verse 18 over and over, "and the one whom you now have is not your husband." She stared at the page until the words were a blur. She could hear Rev. Kline speaking, but she couldn't focus on what he was saying until she heard him repeat something three or four times.

"I'll say it again, beloved, we are all like that woman at the well. We constantly seek for things that cannot satisfy us, whether it's relationships, jobs, money or whatever else. If I could just get this car, I'll be satisfied then. You get the car and after about two weeks you want something else. Sister, you say, well if I could just get that man, I know I'll be satisfied. You get married to him, and then you come running to me asking for counseling sessions." Most of the congregation laughed, but Gail was experiencing inner turmoil that was quite different from the love of God she had felt during praise service.

"But don't get upset with me. I'm going to tell you how to get some satisfaction so you can stop singing the old song," Rev. Kline broke out singing, "I cain't get no," and then he held the microphone toward the audience who sang back, "Sa-tis-fac-tion."

This time Gail cracked a smile and chuckled a little.

"So let me tell you the big secret. The only way you can find satisfaction in this life is to live a life of worship unto the Lord. He is actually searching. He is roaming through the earth seeking sincere worshipers. I want the Lord to be able to look into these four walls and see some sincerity. Even more, I want the Lord to see you outside of these four walls and see you living a life of worship. Do you want to be a sincere worshiper?"

As usual the congregation responded with shouts of "yes," "teach," "that's good, pastor." He continued his teaching and gave four basic components of a life of worship. Gail took notes and memorized the four aspects of a life of worship, which were prayer, fasting, devotion/meditation and studying the Bible. He called these four things level one, the foundation of a worship life and said that he would deal with building on that foundation next Sunday night. Gail was most impressed with his teaching on meditation. In speaking about devotion, Rev. Kline explained that a Christian should meditate on the scriptures. He said that Christians associate meditation with New Age and Yoga, but the Lord commanded His people to meditate on the word in the Old Testament. Gail felt like meditation was exactly what she needed. Constantly thinking about the wrong things is what got her to Corpus Christi with Mario. When she wasn't with him, she thought about him and the things they did together. Now she would practice meditating on the word and thinking about God's will for her life.

After service, Gail was making her way through the crowd to Jason to ask if he had seen Sara when she ran right into Sara in the middle aisle of the church.

"Hey, I was just looking for you," Gail said.

Sara hugged her. "I missed you this morning. Were you here?"

"No, but I got here as soon as I could tonight. The praise was awesome!"

"Yeah, I really like the evening service because we spend more time in praise."

"Sara, I need a really big favor from you tonight."

"What is it? Are you all right?"

"Can we go for coffee or something? I mean if you don't have plans with Anthony."

"Oh, no. Anthony and I don't have plans."

"Well, if it's not too late for you, can we go somewhere like Magnolia Café and talk?"

"Sure, Gail. That'll be fine. I'll meet you there in 20 minutes unless you want to ride together."

"No, I'll meet you there. The one on Congress."

On the way to the 24-hour restaurant, Gail rehearsed what she would say. She wanted to be careful not to identify Mario. After mulling over what to say, she decided to call him Mike and leave out the fact that he was married.

Arriving at the restaurant at the same time, Gail and Sara made small talk while they waited for a table. After they were settled in a booth, they talked about the church service until they ordered their food. When the waitress left, Sara finally asked,

"Okay, sister-friend, what did you really want to talk about?"

Gail took a deep breath. "Well, I guess I need help getting untangled from an old relationship."

"I see," Sara said. Gail thought she sounded like a psychologist.

"So Dr. Martin, do you have a prescription for this illness?"

"I don't, but Dr. Paul gives a prescription in Romans."

"What? You lost me on that one."

"Well, Paul writes about struggling with the flesh in Romans 7 and 8. You can read that sometime, but I don't want to just throw scripture at you. Tell me about this old relationship."

"It's been going on and off for a few years, and I thought it was just sex, at first. But I think he may want to take things further than I want to go."

"He wants to marry you?"

"I'm not sure about that, but he definitely wants to go to the next level. Because of the things I've learned at The Word, I just don't think this relationship is good for me."

"Why not?"

"Mainly, I guess it's because we have sex and we're not married." Gail paused, thinking Sara would say "I told you so." When Sara remained quiet and showed no change in her inquisitive expression, Gail continued, "He also causes me to be misfocused. All I think about is him. He distracts me from church. He's the reason I wasn't there this morning," Gail said, worrying that she was already revealing too much.

"Sounds like he has a pretty tight hold on you," Sara said. "So you feel differently about sex outside of marriage now?"

She wasn't exactly saying, I told you so, but Gail caught the hint of sarcasm in Sara's voice.

"I don't know if that's what I'm saying. I still think it would be okay for you and Anthony to have sex. Look at that big old rock on your finger. It looks like you need a sling to help keep your wrist up." They laughed and paused the conversation as the waitress placed their food on the table. They ate in silence, savoring the first bites of giant blueberry pancakes, potatoes and eggs.

"Sara, I know you don't struggle with this, but I really need some practical advice about getting out of this relationship."

Sara sounded like she was choking on her food.

"Girl, you think I don't struggle?" She gulped some water and started laughing. "I'm engaged to this handsome, wonderful, successful man who placed this 'big old rock' on my finger, and you think I don't struggle?"

This was new information for Gail. She did agree that Anthony was handsome, although he was a little too "pretty" for Gail's taste. She much preferred the more rugged good looks Mario possessed. Anthony was built like a track runner. Mario was built more like a football player. Mario's strong chest muscles were obvious even when he wasn't flexing, but he was not too bulky. He was just right, and she loved to lay her head on his chest. Shaking her head quickly, she pulled her thoughts from Mario's body.

"Well, Sara, you certainly gave me the impression that you were not tempted by sex like other women I know."

"I didn't mean to give that impression. I'll be real with you. If it were up to us and our flesh, we would be having sex. However, we really want to have a special night on our honeymoon. We want our covenant to be sealed on that night. We get carried away every once in a while, but one of us always stops before things go to far."

"What does that mean? How far do you go?"

"Just kissing and stuff."

"What kind of kissing and stuff? French kissing?"

"A little French kissing."

"What kind of stuff?"

"A little touching, but no disrobing or anything. Hey, I thought you wanted me to give you some advice about getting out of a relationship."

"This is helping me. It makes me know you're real. I mean, you can relate to me more if you at least know what it's like to desire somebody so much that you melt if they touch you."

"Yeah, I know about melting, but I'm waiting for the right time for the full meltdown." They shared a knowing laugh together.

"I admire that, Sara. I don't know how you do it, but I guess you're doing what's right for you."

"So, let me give you my opinion on how to get delivered from an old relationship. First, you have to see the relationship for what it is. And I think you have. It seems that you've determined that you need to get out of the relationship because you are having sex with no plans on marrying this guy. What's his name?"

"Umm, his name is Mark." Gail immediately realized her mistake. His name was supposed to be "Mike", but it was too late to fix it. She had come so close to saying Mario that she leaned heavily on the "k." She just hoped Sara didn't see through her lie.

"So, since you've decided that your relationship with Mark needs to end, now you have to cut your ties to him. You have to go cold turkey. No phone calls. No email. No letters. Just end it."

"That sounds too simple."

"Well, it is that simple, but you have to fill your life with other things to help you grow spiritually. It's a process. God leads us up a path, and we allow the light of His word to shine on our lives. As the light shines, He reveals to us the things we need to change about our lives. In your case, God has shown you that this relationship is one of those things. But He wants to give you something in return for this relationship with Mark. God wants to give you a more intimate relationship with Himself."

Gail didn't know if a more intimate relationship with God would be enough to pull her out of the hold Mario had on her right now. Sara must have noticed the look of doubt on her face.

"You have to weigh the two things," Sara continued. "What is more important to you?" She put her hands up to represent two sides of a scale. "Here is God, the Creator, the Everlasting Father calling you to Him. And over here you have some half-committed man just wanting to get in your panties."

Gail laughed. "Well, when you put it like that, it's obvious. But when I'm in the same room with Mike, it's hard for me to think about how much I desire a relationship with God."

"That's why you have to avoid being in the same room with Mike or Mark or whatever his real name is," Sara said.

Gail's face flushed as the blood rushed to her cheeks. She was embarrassed and confused. Telling Sara half the truth was harder than she thought it would be.

"That's okay, Gail. I don't have to know his real name, as long as you're being real with me about what you're going through."

"Let's just say, I'm being as real as I can be right now."

"That's fair. Now, let's take the Pastor Kline approach to this thing. You know he always gives us practical steps to help us apply the word. You can start with the things he said tonight about living a life of worship, but specifically, let me tell you some things you should do to avoid Mike-Mark."

"You are too funny," Gail said in response to Sara's combining the pseudonym. "Number one, you said I need to cut my ties to him."

"Exactly. That means no calls, either way. Just screen all your calls at home and at work. Hey, wait a minute!" Sara's eyes widened and she put her hand over her mouth. "Girl, is this the same guy who sent those beautiful flowers to the office?"

"Maybe so."

"So he's not a keeper, huh? That's too bad. Does he go to church at all? Maybe there's hope for him," Sara joked.

"Believe me. There is no hope. I need to end it for real."

"You're right, I guess. But the brother is certainly persistent. He doesn't send you cheap arrangements. He must really be stuck on you."

"He might be. But I've determined that I need to get out of the relationship, remember?"

"Okay, I got distracted. Back to the list. You may want to have a closure conversation with him if possible. If he's really into the relationship, it's only fair to explain why you're cutting him off. This part is up to you. If you think he can convince you to stay in the relationship, it may be self-defeating to attempt to have this conversation right now."

"Well, I did plan on at least telling him that I was breaking up with him."

"This could get tricky, though. See, if you guys are physically involved to the point that you usually end up having sex when you're together, he may be able to win you over while you're trying to have the break-up conversation."

"So what do you suggest?"

"Like I said, create some distance first. Give yourself some time to grow in your intimacy with the Lord and your sensitivity to the Holy Spirit before you allow yourself to be alone with Mike, I mean Mark."

"Let's just call him Mike," Gail said.

"Okay, Mike. But on second thought, when you have the conversation, I would suggest it be in a public place and that you have a limited amount of time with him so there is no opportunity for sex."

"That's a good idea." Gail knew just the place. She would ask Mario to meet her at the same Omni restaurant where he began his seduction of her. But she would give herself a few weeks to grow first. Otherwise, she would certainly be up in a room with him. "So I create the distance, immerse myself in my relationship with the Lord, have the closure conversation and then what?" Gail asked.

"And then you continue walking with the Lord. He'll show you what's next. God wants you to have an abundant life. He wants what's best for you. He'll deliver you out of this relationship and set you up for something far greater."

"That sounds pretty exciting."

"A relationship with God is the most exciting relationship you can have."

"Thanks, Sara. This has really helped me."

"I want you to know that I'm here for you, and I'm praying for you. If you need anything, anything at all, just call me."

When Gail got home, she saw the blinking light on her answering machine. She didn't even check the caller ID. She went straight to the bathroom and took a shower. She got ready for bed and was about to kneel in prayer when she decided to go ahead and listen to the messages. The first one was from Joanna, her hanging buddy, inviting her to happy hour at some club on Sixth Street the following Wednesday. The next three were from Mario.

"Hey, love. I know you were a little upset with me, and maybe I was a little stupid. But I just…" Mario paused and took a deep breath, making Gail think about the warmth of his breath on her neck. "I can't stop thinking about you. I'm a nervous wreck. I don't even have an appetite. I haven't eaten a thing since I left you this morning. And I've even asked myself why I left you there by yourself. I guess I was a little upset myself. But I can't stay mad at you for any reason. Look, I just want to see you. Give me a call when you get in tonight, sweetheart."

Gail pushed delete and the next message started.

"Hey, Gail, I just called back because you haven't called, and I want to make sure you're all right, that you made it home safe. Just give me a call so I can hear your voice and know that everything is fine."

Delete. There was one more.

"Okay, I've concluded that you're not going to call me." He heaved a long, sexy sigh into the phone. Gail checked the caller ID and saw that this last call came in right before she got home. "I guess you're still upset. Look I know you have this big concern about my marriage, but let me tell you, this thing was not based on love. This was practically an arranged marriage. Our families have known each other for years and they have always wanted Nina and me to be together for political and economic reasons." Gail had some vague memory about Nina's father and San Antonio city politics. "In any case, I've told you before, and I'll tell you again. I love you and I want to be with you. We can work this out. Give me a call, love. I'm aching to hear your voice. Sweet dreams."

Gail took a little longer to press delete. Instead she pressed repeat and listened to the message again. Maybe he *was* pressured into marrying Nina. That made sense. On the other hand, he didn't have to bow to the pressure. If he didn't want to be with the girl, he shouldn't have married her. In any case, it wasn't her job to figure out Mario's life. She was about to press the delete button when the phone rang and she jumped as her heart leaped into her throat. Then she felt indignant. Surely he wasn't calling her at one o'clock in the morning. She glanced at the caller ID. It was Mario calling from his cell phone.

She didn't bother answering the phone. She turned the ringer and the answering machine off and went into her bedroom. The phone in the bedroom continued to ring and she was tempted to answer it just to stop the ringing. Then she was tempted to answer it just to hear Mario's voice.

"Oh, I've got to pray!" The ringing continued as Gail knelt beside her bed. She fervently pleaded with the Lord to take away her desire for Mario. Then she prayed that the Lord would increase her desire to read the word and grow in her Christian walk. That's when she felt peace and then the phone stopped ringing. She continued praying and resting in the peace that enveloped her.

For the first time in weeks, Gail's last thoughts before she went to sleep were not about Mario, but about God. Remembering her experience in the presence of God in the praise service earlier that evening, she sang herself to sleep. "I love you. I love you. I love you Lord, today."

CHAPTER 19

The next morning at work, Gail was waiting for her computer to boot up when a huge bouquet of red roses was delivered to her cubicle. It was another extravagant arrangement in a crystal vase, and as usual, a crowd of women came out of nowhere and assembled at her cubicle. The comments ranged from "Someone really loves you," to "Does he have a brother?" After pumping her for information about who sent the flowers, the women gradually left when they realized that she wasn't going to share any of her business with them. There was only one woman left at her cubicle.

"So I guess these are from Mike," Sara said, gently brushing a petal on one of the perfect flowers.

"It's a nice try, but it will take more than a dozen roses to change my mind about the decision I've made. Sara, I experienced God like I never have before last night. It was so real."

"I know what you mean. God is good. No man can compare when it comes to the security and love from God, but…" Sara paused. "This guy seems to really be sincere and he's trying hard. He is definitely going to follow up these flowers with something like a visit or at least a call."

"Oh, I know he'll try to call me, but I've taken your advice and I'm screening all my calls. I know I'm not ready to talk to him, yet."

"From what I've seen so far, he can be pretty persistent."

"You're right about that, so I'm going to keep my distance."

"Does he live or work near you?"

"No, but he gets around. Like you said, I wouldn't be surprised if he tried to visit my condo, but I would refuse to see him."

"Well, if there's anything I can do to help, let me know."

After Sara left, Gail read the note.

"I understand if you need a little space right now, but please don't keep me out here yearning for you too long. Love, –M."

How sweet. He was really trying hard. That meant she would just have to pray that much harder.

Over the next few weeks, Gail engulfed herself in activities at The Word. Although memories of Mario kept popping up in her mind, they had at least faded into the background. It helped that he didn't call or try to contact her after sending the flowers. She was glad he didn't have her email addresses.

Once in a while some pretty vivid memories of Mario invaded her thoughts, but she was more fascinated with all the new things she was learning about God. She developed a fervent prayer life by waking up early every morning and praying before she started each day. Initially her prayers were about the relationship with Mario. She repeatedly asked God to forgive her and to give her the strength to stay away from him. Eventually, she began to pray about her own growth and understanding of spiritual things. Gail used Pastor Kline's sermons and Bible study books she found in Christian bookstores to help her study the Bible. Her evening routine was to do a Bible study every night and to read one chapter of the Old Testament and one chapter of the New Testament.

She also attended church on Sunday mornings and evenings and on Wednesday evenings. As Gail learned more about the Bible, she began to understand what it really means to be a Christian. She realized that her thinking about her life had to change after Pastor Kline preached from Romans 12:1 one Sunday. A light bulb went off in Gail's mind as he explained the process of offering "your bodies as living sacrifices." She discovered that she must separate her body, her mind, indeed, her entire life so that she could be used by God to accomplish His will. It was all so clear to her that Sunday. She had a purpose, and that purpose was in Christ. Her purpose was not about getting married, although that was a good thing. Her purpose involved telling others about the gospel, just as Jason and Sara had told her.

After three weeks of personal devotions and attending every church service, Gail was surprised when she practically began to yearn for Mario again. She knew it was a combination of things that caused her to think of "what if" scenarios with Mario. The numerous happy couples at The Word made her wonder if she could have been among them if she had played her cards differently. Maybe she should have returned his calls and emails while she was still in college. Maybe she should have pressed him about leaving Nina. Maybe not.

She was also constantly bombarded with wedding plan news from Sara at work, and although Gail tried to deny it, feelings of jealously were rising within her. The last thing she wanted to do was alienate Sara, so she took her issues to God one evening and asked the Lord to teach her how to be happy as a single person. She had purchased a Bible study that was specifically for single women, but she had avoided reading it until that evening. After praying, she began the first lesson, and immediately started getting answers to the questions that plagued her mind. The first lesson dealt with the desire to be married and placed the desire in perspective. It confirmed that her desire was not a bad thing, yet she had to keep it under control so it didn't turn into an obsession.

She wasn't surprised when the subject of Pastor Kline's Bible study on Wednesday was from Philippians 4:11. He taught about being content and gave practical points that helped Gail tremendously. She thanked God for answering her prayers. The Lord was actually teaching her how to be happy as a single person.

After service Sara informed Gail that Pastor Kline and his wife were hosting an informal reception at the church.

"They do these receptions about once a month to fellowship with the members."

"I remember hearing about them at the new members seminar."

"Well, Pastor Kline specifically asked me to make sure you came to this one."

"What?" Gail's eyes widened. "I didn't even know he knew who I was."

"Of course he knows who you are. You're at the church every time the doors are open. Besides, that's his job. He's supposed to know who you are. He's watching over your soul, trying to make sure you learn the word and grow in the Lord."

"He's done a great job. I'm a different person than I was last month."

"You certainly are. It seems like just yesterday you were saying you couldn't understand why a person would need to go to church more than once a month."

"That's exactly how I felt. But now I know. The services and Bible studies are so helpful to me. God has made a miraculous change in my life. I feel like I'm growing more in the word every day."

Gail followed Sara to another part of the church into a large room set up with a buffet of hot hors d'oeuvres and fruit and cheese trays. People were socializing throughout the room, and Gail was reminded of the parties she had been to at Joanna's house. The conversations would probably be much different here. After Gail and Sara got their plates, Sara guided them to a table where Pastor Kline and his wife, Serene were sitting with a few other people. Gail sat next to Serene and Sara sat across the table.

This was Gail's first time seeing the Pastor and his wife up close. She felt nervous, like she was meeting someone famous, but Pastor Kline's easy-going personality made her feel at ease. She soon discovered his comedic side. Although he was more soft-spoken than when he was preaching, he was telling sidesplitting stories about growing up with his siblings in Mississippi. As he spoke, he slipped into a Southern accent that Gail had never noticed.

Gail was sure that Serene had heard the stories a thousand times but she was laughing just as hard as everyone else. Gail had admired her from afar at church, but up close, Serene was even prettier to Gail. She had a stunning smile and flawless skin that accented her unusually light hazel eyes. And Gail was close enough to see that Serene did not wear contacts. Gail also noticed that the long hair flowing halfway down Serene's back was not a weave.

Eventually, Serene turned to Gail and asked her how she had come to The Word.

"I work with Sara, and she invited me over and over until I started coming."

"So you finally came just to get her to stop asking?" Pastor Kline asked with a grin.

Gail was somewhat embarrassed as everyone around the table focused on her. "I guess you could say that. I didn't understand why she went to church so much, but I know now."

"I think you come to more services than I do now!" Sara said. Pastor Kline and the people around the table laughed, easing Gail's discomfort. People began different conversations with each other and Serene asked Gail where she was from. Gail fell into an easy conversation with Serene. She found out that Serene had a degree in accounting, but she also had an M.B.A. and was the director of a foundation that funded organizations that helped children.

Gail wanted to ask Serene about her marriage, but she didn't know what would be an appropriate question. She asked about Serene's children, hoping to work her way to the questions she really wanted to ask.

"So you have four children?"

"Yes. We have three boys and a girl. The oldest boys are twins."

Serene's figure in no way revealed that she had been pregnant three times. Gail felt comfortable enough to comment. "You have certainly kept in shape. Do you work out or what?"

"I power walk five days a week. I use the time to pray, but it does help me stay in shape. Every once in a while, I lift weights and run a little."

Gail was still trying to find a way to ask about her marriage. She decided to just ask right out.

"So how did you meet Pastor Kline?"

"Oh, we grew up together in Mississippi. He says I always had a crush on him, but it was the other way around."

"Were you childhood sweethearts?"

"Not at all. He was my brother's best friend and treated me like his little sister when we were growing up. I was actually working in Manhattan when he started trying to court me."

Gail smiled at the old-fashioned word "court."

"What were you doing in New York?" Gail asked.

"I was working at a Fortune 100 company in mergers and acquisitions."

"Are you serious?"

"Yes. I was on my way to the top. When Nate asked me to marry him, I had to make a choice between a promotion at work or a promotion in the spirit."

"How did you make the choice?" Gail asked, fascinated.

"It may have been the size of the diamond he put on my finger," Serene said waving her left hand in front of her face. They both laughed like they were old friends. "Seriously, though, he prepared me for about two years before he actually asked me to marry him. He had this great vision to quit the law firm and start a church in Texas."

"Where was he working?"

"At my dad's law firm in Mississippi. He and my brother both became lawyers and worked in my father's firm."

"So you dated for two years?"

"I wouldn't call it dating. He wrote me letters and came by to visit whenever he was in town, but there wasn't anything official. I saw other people occasionally, but I was so wrapped up in my job, I didn't have time for relationships."

"So were you surprised when he asked you to marry him?"

"I was actually shocked, but I should have known something was up. He had called on a Thursday and asked me to have dinner with him at a very nice Italian restaurant the next evening. I didn't even know he was in town, and I actually had a date that Friday night, but for some reason, I cancelled the other date and got kind of excited about seeing Nate again. He showed up at my door looking so handsome in a dark suit, with a fresh haircut, face all clean-shaven. I should have known he was up to something."

"He asked you at the restaurant?"

"Yes, he did the traditional thing and got down on one knee. People were watching us and actually applauded when I said 'yes.'"

Gail glanced at the dazzling ring. Nathaniel Kline must have been doing well in his law practice. "This is the ring he gave you that night?"

"The very same one."

"So was it a struggle leaving your job? You were about to be promoted?"

"I struggled with it a little, but he had spent two years telling me about starting a ministry here and helping people. I didn't know what he was doing, but he was actually preparing me for the proposal. He wasn't just asking me to marry him. He was asking me to work in ministry with him as well."

"How did you move from being like siblings to being romantically involved?"

"Looking back on it, Nate took a very systematic approach to our relationship. He was wooing me, but not in the traditional romantic way. He just shared his vision with me and asked for my input on different things. I was working in New York, he was working in Biloxi, and we were actually discussing some of the very programs that we've implemented here. I don't know how he did it, but he got me caught up in the vision, and by the time he proposed, I was ready to move forward."

"But didn't you still think of him as a brother?"

"I think when he was down on one knee holding my hand and placing the ring on my finger, my whole perception of him changed in that moment." They shared another laugh.

"That's a wonderful story. How long have you been married?"

"It will be eleven years in October."

Gail was still wondering how the relationship developed without the romance. Pastor Kline was a handsome man and Serene was a beautiful woman, and it was hard for Gail to believe that they didn't get involved with each other romantically or intimately. Maybe it was because they were like siblings. She wanted to ask more questions, but one of the church staff members came to the table and started taking pictures. Gail posed with Serene and the pastor, and then other people crowded the table trying to get a picture with the pastor. Gail moved away from the table and went around to mingle.

After speaking to a few people she knew and making small talk, Gail wandered up to Sara and two women that Gail had first met when she went bowling with the single's group. Sara had Diane and Jeannette engaged in an animated conversation when Gail walked up.

"Oh, Gail, I meant to tell you earlier, we're invited to a party at Nina's and Mario's next month," Sara said.

"What?" Gail's face screwed up in a frown.

"Yeah, Nina told me to make sure you come. She really appreciates what you did for her."

"That was really nice of you to fill in like that," said Diane.

How could she get out of this one? "I think I have to do something with my family that weekend. I won't be able to go."

"Can't you get out of it? You can spend time with your family any weekend. Nina is definitely looking forward to your being there."

"I don't know. I'll have to think about it," Gail said. "I'm about to head out now."

"Wait for me. I'm leaving, too."

They gathered their purses and Bibles. On their way out the door, they passed by a table full of plants, with a sign that said "New Growth."

Sara picked up a plant and handed it to Gail. "Have you gotten one of these yet?"

"No, but I'll take one. How much does it cost?"

"It's free. We give them to new Christians to represent their new lives in Christ. It doesn't seem like you're new anymore, but you still get a plant."

"Well, thanks. This is nice. Where are the watering instructions? I don't have any real plants because they always die from neglect." The plant had luscious green leaves that she hoped would stay alive in her apartment.

"This particular plant doesn't need much sunlight, but you'll want to keep it pretty moist. Just make sure the soil always feels wet. It'll flourish if you keep it watered."

As they were walking to their cars in the parking lot, Gail commented, "Serene told me about how she was working in the corporate world when Pastor Kline asked her to marry him."

"Aren't they a great couple? And they've been so successful together."

"Did they start the church as soon as they got married?"

"No, I think they waited for about three years, but they had been planning it for a long time. Their timing was perfect. The city was growing with new people moving in from all around the country. All of the black churches here were the traditional denominational churches. This town was ripe for something new," Sara said.

"I don't know why I never visited before. I remember hearing about this church, but I guess I was one of the people who was used to traditional churches. I'm glad I'm here now."

"I am, too. Gail, I really hope you will make it to the party at Nina's. It's a barbeque and swim party. Every time I talk to her, she asks about you."

"She does?" Gail wondered if Nina was suspicious about her relationship with Mario.

"Yes. She wants us to all hang out again soon. You know, her and Mario, me and Anthony, you and Jason."

"Oh yeah? So now you're trying to pair me up with Jason, but I haven't been in contact with him much lately."

"According to Anthony, Jason and his brother are trying to get some kind of contract for their business. It's a pretty big deal, and it's taking a lot of work."

"I hope things work out for them. I like hanging out with Jason, but right now the only relationship I'm concerned about is my relationship with God."

"I know that's right. No other relationship can work anyway if your relationship with the Lord is messed up."

"I have come to understand that in a very real way. Jason did tell me that he was praying for me last Sunday. You know, I think he's more concerned with my spiritual life than anything else. That's what makes him, and you, such good friends."

"Oh, now, don't get all weepy on me."

"Is Jason going to the party?"

"I'm sure he'll be there. Mario and him are pretty tight."

"Well, like I said, I'll think about it."

They talked for a few more minutes and then got in their cars and headed home.

Driving home, Gail wondered if she was strong enough to be around Mario now. More than likely she would be paired with Jason at the party and could avoid Mario all together. Whether she went or not, she needed to bring closure to her affair with Mario.

That night when she prayed, she asked God to remove every inkling of feeling she had for Mario. She wanted to be able to hear his name without her heart rate increasing. She wanted to feel like it was completely over between them. She wanted complete closure. She walked into the bathroom and looked at her birth control pills on the counter. That's what she needed to do. She had to stop taking those pills. She threw them in the trash, and determined that she would not get the prescription filled again. That was her symbol for closure. If she weren't taking the pill, she would not be able to have sex. In the back of her mind, she thought about other methods of birth control, but she had a strict rule about having sex without protection. She had seen too many women get pregnant because they were careless about using protection, and Gail was not going to let that happen to her. So if she were not taking the pills, she would not have sex. It was as simple as that. She felt like a weight had lifted and she laid down to a peaceful sleep.

CHAPTER 20

Gail continued in her routine of work, church, personal devotion and Bible study. Faithfully, she took care of the plant she had gotten from the church, considering it a symbol of her growth in Christ.

One Thursday night, Gail was engulfed in her nightly Bible study when the phone rang.

"Hello," she said, answering the phone without looking at the caller ID. Whoever it was, she wanted to get the conversation over quickly so she could get back to her study. She was fascinated with the F.F. Bruce commentary on Romans 1 and the historical and New Testament use of the word "righteous."

"Oh Gail, I'm so glad I caught you at home." At first she didn't even recognize the smooth, sexy voice. But her heart jumped into her throat and other parts of her body began to respond to Mario even before her mind fully identified him. Words were slow to form.

"Uh, well. What do you want?"

"I really don't want to talk to you on the phone. Would you have a cup of coffee with me? I need to talk to you about something in person."

His tone was so familiar and friendly, she found herself saying "yes" before she could put up her defenses.

"Good. I'll be there in 15 minutes." He hung up. Gail's mind was spinning as she began to stack her books and put them away. She went into automatic pilot, making sure her condo was tidy. Everything was in order and she was fresh and clean, having showered and gotten ready for bed before she began her Bible study. She was changing into some Guess jeans and a t-shirt when the doorbell rang. That was less than 15 minutes. He must have been sitting outside in his car. Opening the door, Gail suppressed a gasp. Mario stood in the door looking and smelling good. She noticed the neatly trimmed mustache and the perfectly faded haircut. He was dressed in tan linen slacks and a cream colored casual shirt. The physical attraction seemed to be intensified, and Gail thought about Romans 12:1. She prayed that she had the discipline to be a living sacrifice to God and not become a sacrifice to her flesh before the evening was over. How did she get into this situation? This was her moment of truth. She would simply bring full closure to the relationship by letting Mario know that things were over. He had her in a sensual embrace before she could say anything.

"Ummm," he murmured into her hair. "It's so good to see you. It has been way too long."

A couple of moments went by before Gail pushed him away.

"I'll drive," she said grabbing her keys.

"That's fine with me. I've been driving up and down I-35 between here and San Antonio for two weeks, and I'm tired."

"No, I mean, let's take separate cars."

"Don't be silly. That's just a waste of gas. I'm not some dangerous stranger."

"Whatever," Gail said, exasperated.

"Let's go to the Starbucks on Duval. I like the atmosphere there. It's more artsy than commercial."

She shrugged her shoulders and quickly headed to her car. All the Starbucks were the same, no matter where they were located. She concentrated on remembering certain scriptures she might reference and barely responded to Mario's small talk on the way to the coffee shop.

From the sensual hug to the intimate ways Mario touched her while they ordered, Gail could sense that Mario's plan was to talk his way back into her bed. But she would initiate her closure conversation before he could fully launch his attack.

After Gail ordered an iced latte and Mario ordered a regular coffee, he steered them to a secluded table. Gail began talking as soon as they sat down.

"Look Mario, before you say anything, I have something to tell you." She looked fully into his face to gauge his reaction to every word. "This relationship is over. After I got involved with you, I came to know the Lord in a very real way, and now I know that I can't continue in an adulterous affair with you. It's wrong and it's not good for me, for you or for your new marriage."

Mario seemed to listen to her intently, but his expression revealed no emotional reaction to her words.

"You know what, Gail. I totally agree with you."

"What?" Gail was shocked.

"Yes, you are absolutely right. That's why I am prepared to end things with Nina."

"No! That's not what you should do. You should work things out with her. You just got married. You and I need to go our separate ways, Mario. It's not going to work."

"I don't know what I'll have to do to win you, but my marriage is over, no matter what."

"What do you mean? Has she left? What happened?"

"Let's just say that I'm going to end the charade before things get any deeper." Mario grabbed both her hands in his and leaned toward Gail across the tiny table. "I told you before. My marriage is just a sham. I did what everyone expected me to do, but you know what, Gail? I want to follow my heart, and my heart belongs to you."

Even though Mario sounded like a corny soap opera Don Juan, Gail was captivated by his intensity. She looked at his face and into his eyes trying to detect deception, but he really seemed serious. When she saw him standing at her doorstep, she had wondered why she should even try to resist him. What was the point in keeping herself from this man? Nevertheless, she had made a vow to end the relationship.

"Well, even if things don't work out with you and Nina, I need to concentrate on growing spiritually, and I don't have time for a relationship right now."

"Okay, that's fine." Mario sat back and rubbed his hand across the top of his head, drawing Gail's eyes up to his soft waves. "But all I ask is that we remain friends."

"Oh, I don't know about that."

"What's the harm in that? I'm trying to grow in the Lord, too. I'm striving every day just like you are."

"We wouldn't be able to have much contact. My life is pretty full right now with work and church."

"All I would want is to call you every now and then and to have dinner with you once in a while."

"I don't know, Mario."

"You can't deprive me of all contact. You're like Bathsheba to me. If I can't even talk to you, I don't know what I'll do. All this time, I left you alone, but it was so hard for me. You're all I thought about the whole time. I was always wondering what you were doing and where you were, but I kept myself from calling because I knew you needed some time after the trip."

"Didn't David have Bathsheba's husband killed?"

"What?"

"And didn't the prophet rebuke David for what he did?"

"Oh, so you're a Bible scholar now?" Mario asked with a smirk. "All I meant is that I love you dearly. But I'm glad you don't have a husband or serious boyfriend that I have to deal with because then I don't know what would happen," he said, raising his eyebrows playfully.

"But you have a wife to deal with." Gail had to avoid looking too deeply into Mario's eyes so she wouldn't be drawn in. "Nina is a wonderful woman, and she deserves for you to at least try to work things out with her."

"Look, I already told you about that situation. Why are you so worried about Nina? You don't even really know her."

"Don't get mad at me. You're the one who married her. If you didn't want to do it, you could have walked away."

"You're right, and I made a terrible mistake. I should have walked away. But now, I know exactly what I want."

"It's too late, Mario. I've committed to living right. I really love the Lord. I can't be with you right now."

"I know. I know. Okay." He dropped his face into his hands and sighed heavily. He raised his head slowly and gave her a longing look. "I don't know what I'm going to do without you. Can you at least promise me that I can see you every once in a while?"

"I can't make you any promises."

Gail felt victorious as they left Starbucks. She was almost home safe. Back at her apartment, Mario insisted on walking her to her door because it was so late. He stood too close to her as she struggled to get her key into the lock. He placed his hand over hers just before she turned the knob to go inside.

"Wait," he breathed softly onto the back of her neck. "I have one last request." He turned her around gently. "Just one kiss before I go."

"No." She pushed her arm into his chest, but he didn't step back. "Mario, I can't kiss you."

"Why not? Just a simple kiss on the cheek."

"No. You want more than just a simple kiss."

"Oh, I do? How do you know?"

"Because you sound all lustful."

"Lustful? What does that sound like?"

"And you're standing too close to me."

"Too close for what? Do you want to kiss me as badly as I want to kiss you?"

"There will be no kiss tonight."

"Come on, Gail. Really. Just a good-bye kiss, okay?" He leaned his head toward her face cautiously. "Just a peck like this." He kissed her lightly on the cheek. "See, that's all I wanted."

Gail stood, rolling her eyes.

"Okay, I have to tell the truth. That's not all I wanted. How about this?" He kissed her mouth lightly and leaned back again. "And this." He kissed her mouth again and pressed a little harder with his soft lips.

"Is that all?" Gail had to stop him before she lost all control.

"No. If I could get just a little more response from you, I'll be satisfied. Give me one real kiss and I'll go."

What harm could there be in one kiss? Gail allowed Mario to kiss her again, and this time he softly plied her lips open. Within seconds they were in a full French kiss. Once she crossed the line, a familiar ache crept up from a familiar place. Mario played her like a violin until he got the door open and they were standing in her living room pulling off each other's clothes. They were completely naked by the time they made it to the bedroom. Gail put all thoughts of spiritual growth aside as she fully enjoyed the delights of Mario's skilled lovemaking.

CHAPTER 21

Driving to San Antonio, Gail thought of all the reasons she had ended up entangled with Mario again. She had thought that immersing herself in spiritual activities would keep her from falling, but when she saw Mario standing at her door, she was unable to resist the pull of the attraction between the two of them.

That night, after their passion had been satisfied, Gail poured her heart out to Mario. She had pulled herself out of his arms and sat up in the bed.

"Mario, I need to tell you something. I was really trying to end this relationship with you. I know that it's wrong and I've been praying that God would give me the strength to resist you."

Mario's eyes went from sleepy to alert as he listened to Gail.

"I know, Gail," he sighed and sat up. "I've tried to resist you as well. But believe me, I've been honest with you all along. I really do love you. I'm not just trying to be a dog. I think marriage should be taken seriously just like you do."

"Well, why did you show up at my door? I was really making progress in my walk with the Lord, and now I feel like I've taken a giant step backwards."

"You shouldn't feel like that. God knows the sincerity of our hearts."

"If we were so sincere about God, we wouldn't be here committing adultery."

"That's not necessarily true," Mario said. "Remember when we were talking about David and Bathsheba earlier? David had some terrible flaws, but God still used him. David had to pay for what he did to Bathsheba's husband, but he still loved her dearly and went on to have a son with her, and that son, Solomon, turned out to be one of Israel's greatest kings. I'm not trying to be

David, though. I'm ready to make a clean break with Nina so that I can minimize the damage I've done."

"But I've already told you I don't want you to leave Nina for me. I'm not sure our relationship would work."

"I know you feel that way, but it won't stop me from trying."

As much as she wanted to resist, Gail allowed Mario to gently pulled her into his arms and make slow, passionate love to her again.

Now here she was on the way to his house. She had totally forgotten about the end of summer party when Sara reminded her at work that Friday morning after Mario had spent the night at her house.

"Girl, Nina called last night to make sure you come to the party," Sara said. "She would have called you herself, but she didn't have your number."

Gail wondered for a moment if Nina might suspect something between her and Mario. She hoped Nina wasn't setting her up. Somehow she didn't think Nina would do something like that. And, to hear Sara tell it, Nina was enjoying marital bliss. But, of course, ignorance is bliss, Gail thought.

"I guess I'll go. What time does it start and how do I get there?"

"I sent you the email. It has all the details in it. I hope you didn't delete it. If you did I'll resend it to you," Sara said. "You seem so disinterested, but I must say I'm glad about the change in you."

"What change?"

"Haven't you noticed? The only thing you get excited about is church and Bible study. I think that's a wonderful change. You never talk about going to parties or clubs with your other friends anymore."

"You're right. I haven't been to a party or a club with them in ages. What kind of party is this at Nina's?"

"It's a swim party and barbeque."

"A swim party? That sounds kind of out there for Christian folks. Are people going to have on bathing suits, bikini's and stuff?"

"If you had read the invitation you would know. It asks that women wear tasteful bathing suits which translates to either a one-piece or if you wear a bikini you should wear shorts over it."

"How is a person supposed to know all that?"

"I guess a person would have to ask if she were planning to go to the party."

"I guess so."

Gail had decided to go to the party more out of curiosity than anything. She wanted to see Mario's house. She also wanted to see Mario. After Thursday night, she had given up on trying to resist him. She had gone back to thinking that if she just let the affair run its full course, she could get him out of her system. For now she couldn't find the strength to resist the incredible pull he had on her. Gail was beginning to believe Mario really did care about her, but she was not ready to trust him to follow through with getting a divorce and being with her.

She followed the directions from the printed out email and made her way into a neighborhood of large homes with huge trees lining the streets. The invitation said to look for palm trees, but she was surprised by the palm tree lined drive that led to Mario's house. She followed a car into a semi-circular drive and was greeted by a valet. She couldn't tell if the woman who greeted her and other guests at the door was hired just for the party or was a part of the household help, but she was certainly impressed. They were led straight from a grand foyer into a courtyard that seemed to be in the middle of the house, so she was unable to see much of the interior. The first person she saw that she knew was Jason.

"Wow, you look fabulous!" Jason's eyes went from her hair down to her sandals. "You look really great."

Gail had made a 7 a.m. appointment with Lanelle at Isis Salon on Saturday morning. Her thick hair fell in soft waves to her shoulders. She'd gone shopping Friday night to buy the perfect outfit. She had on a turquoise one-piece bathing suit with a turquoise ankle length sarong skirt and a matching sheer boat neck top with flowing sleeves. She had found matching high-heeled sandals that showed off her fresh pedicure. When she walked, her legs were revealed to mid-thigh. She knew she looked too sexy, but she had followed the dress code.

"You look great yourself," Gail said.

"I don't mean to stare. I guess I haven't seen you in a while." Jason gave her a quick hug and led her down some steps into an even larger courtyard. From there Gail took in an impressive view of a multi-level yard that was obviously built for entertainment. There was a hot tub on one level, two levels of seating areas, one level with a large stretch of grass where people were putting golf balls, and a huge pool on the lowest level. Lush shrubbery and large colorful flowers gave the grounds a tropical atmosphere. Gail thought back to a phone conversation she'd had with Mario when he'd said that he was sitting in his backyard by the pool. He'd made it sound so ordinary, but there was nothing common about the Spanish-style home and luxurious grounds.

"You've met a lot of the people here. Most of them were at the wedding," Jason said, interrupting her thoughts. Gail walked around greeting people with Jason. While Jason was leading her to a buffet table full of brisket, ribs, sausage and all the typical side dishes, Gail spotted Nina and Mario holding court on the grassy level that contained the putting green.

"I guess I should greet the hosts before I get a plate," Gail said.

"You go ahead. I spoke to them already," Jason said, eying the ribs. "I'll hold your plate for you. This food was catered by the best barbeque restaurant in San Antonio."

"I don't want to go down there by myself."

"Why not? You were in their wedding, and I know you're not shy."

"Come on. Please?" She placed her hand on his arm and gave him a gentle tug.

"Oh, all right." He reluctantly turned away from the buffet table.

Gail made note of the precise moment when Mario saw her. He was unable to hide his admiration, and she felt his gaze as she walked toward Nina and gave her a hug.

"I'm so glad you made it." Nina greeted her with a warm hug.

"It's good to be here. Thank you for inviting me."

"Hello, Gail. It's a pleasure to see you again," Mario said with proper social formality.

She offered her hand, but Mario pulled her close and gave her a quick, but meaningful hug.

"Enjoy yourself," he said. "Have you gotten something to eat, yet?"

"That's exactly what we were about to do," Jason said.

"We'll talk to you later," Nina said, giving Gail a wink, as Jason pulled her away.

Gail and Jason went through the buffet line and found a table in the upper courtyard where they enjoyed the delicious food.

"I can't believe this house," Gail said as casually as she could.

"Yeah, Mario's family is loaded," Jason said. "You should see his parents' house."

"His dad got rich from dry cleaners?"

"They own a chain of dry cleaners, but they actually got rich from real estate."

Mario had never mentioned real estate to Gail. He made it sound like he had to work so hard to keep the dry cleaning stores in shape.

"So why does Mario work so hard all the time?"

"That's totally by choice. Mario doesn't have to work. His family has diversified their wealth to the point where they make money no matter what's going on in the economy. In fact, they probably make more money when the economy is bad."

"How do they manage that?"

"When the economy is bad, people sell land and houses cheap. That's when people like Mr. Lewis come in and clean up, no pun intended."

Gail chuckled and ate the rest of her potato salad.

Jason leaned back in his chair, swirling his iced tea in a glass. Gail felt him staring at her, but she pretended not to notice.

"So, are you going to enjoy a swim?" Jason asked.

"We can't swim until thirty minutes after we eat," she said playfully.

"I might just enjoy that hot tub. It's huge."

"I want to see this beautiful house. Do they let people just wander around or do they give tours?" She asked.

"I don't know. I guess I could find out for you," Jason said.

Just then, Mario stepped into the courtyard and kept his eyes on Gail even as he spoke to people who continually greeted him as he walked. He didn't head in their direction. Instead he motioned for Gail to follow him through a door on the opposite side of the courtyard. He was obviously trying to avoid Jason.

"I think I ate too much potato salad. I'm going in to find the ladies room and then I need to relax before I do anything else."

"Are you sure? I could give you a tour if you'd like."

"No, you go on to the hot tub, and I'll see you a little later." Gail rose from the table and headed into the house before Jason could say anything else.

She didn't know what Mario had in mind. As soon as she walked through the door, he grabbed her hand and led her upstairs and into a secluded hall that led to a small bathroom. She was yearning for him to the point that every time he touched her, she felt shock waves go through her body from the point of contact straight to where she wanted him to touch her the most.

"All this could be yours," he said jokingly as he locked the door.

"Would you really leave Nina to be with me?" Gail couldn't help wondering if she had really missed the opportunity to be Mrs. Mario Lewis.

"Yes. And I'll go do it right now if you don't believe me." Mario began to open the door.

"No. This is not the time for that drama." Gail gave him a half smile. She was hoping they would never have to face Nina with their relationship, but if Mario was as serious as he seemed, Gail knew it was inevitable.

"So," Mario drew her to him. "When will I see you again?"

"That's up to you." She let her body get caught up in his embrace. "You seem to be calling the shots now."

"Well, if I'm calling the shots I'm going to just slip this off and see what's under here." Mario loosened the knot on her skirt. He deftly pulled her top over her head and had her down to her bathing suit in seconds. "You look absolutely delicious, and you smell like something I've been craving."

He stripped her bathing suit off, and it didn't take long for them to become fully engaged in a standing position. Gail unbuttoned his shirt and pressed into his strong chest as he set their rhythm. She ran her hand up and down his back, relishing the feel of his muscles.

She was fully enjoying the unexpected tryst when she caught a glance of the two of them in the mirror. It was as if she had left her body. In the mirror she saw two depraved people fulfilling a disgustingly lustful primal urge. Scripture flooded her mind.

"Now the body is not for sexual immorality but for the Lord, and the Lord for the body," Gail quoted.

"What?" Mario asked, but didn't miss a beat.

Gail was confused. She didn't know she had spoken out loud.

"I said stop," she said adamantly and tried to push him away. He had one of her legs in the crook of his elbow and the other propped on the toilet seat and he was pressing her into the bathroom wall. She couldn't get her feet on the ground or leverage her weight to push him out of her. He kept his rhythm.

"Mario, I mean it. Don't! Stop!"

"I won't, baby."

"No. I mean stop right now."

"Gail, I can't. I'm too far gone. It'll be just one more minute."

"No!" Gail tried to twist her body back and then forward again in an attempt to disengage, but Mario seemed to misinterpret the move and pumped harder and faster.

"Did you not understand me? I said no, Mario!"

All he did was groan in pleasure and continued. She pulled her head back and looked into his face. She knew that look all too well. He was enraptured, on his way to a powerful orgasm. He began to twitch and shake like he was having a fit. She waited for him to finish so she could just get dressed and leave, but then she was surprised by the warmth that started at a tiny spot and spread through her thighs and up into her belly. The orgasm overtook her body, and Gail had no idea she could feel such pure pleasure and such intense revulsion at the same time. She tried to quell her own shivers as another wave spread through her groin. Mario looked into her eyes with complete satisfaction.

"And what was that you were saying?" he asked, loosening his grip on her.

She pushed him away as tears flowed down her face.

"I wanted you to stop."

"Gail, please. I know you enjoyed that."

"That's not the point. I said stop, Mario."

"Okay, then. I apologize, but you know I can't hardly resist you." He moved closer to her and tried to kiss her.

This time the feeling that spread through Gail's body came from her stomach. She really had enjoyed too much of the potato salad. Before she knew it, vomit was spewing onto Mario's chest.

"What the hell is this?" Mario screamed and jumped back.

Gail was able to get the toilet lid open and the next wave landed there.

"What is wrong with you?"

"Just leave me alone," Gail said as she flushed the toilet.

"Damn, girl! Do you need to take a pregnancy test?"

"Mario, if you don't get out of here, I swear, I won't be responsible for what happens."

"Okay, but we need to talk about this later." He pulled some towels from under the sink and wiped the vomit from his chest and shirt. "I'm going to change. Your clothes are here on the counter. I don't think you threw up on them. Everything seems to have landed on me," he said angrily. His voice softened, "Are you sure you're all right?"

"Mario, just leave." Gail hovered over the toilet dry heaving. Her stomach was empty now.

"I'm going. Uh, I guess I'll see you outside or something."

Once she was alone, Gail immediately started to pray. "Lord what is wrong with me? How could I think that anything good could come out of this crazy relationship? Please show me how to walk away. Teach me how to walk in your word so that I can resist this urge to fulfill the desires of my flesh. I can't do it without you, Lord. I don't want this to get any worse. Please help me."

Gail cried until she realized she would be missed at the party and someone may come looking for her. She had told Jason she wasn't feeling well, so maybe he would think that's why she left the party.

CHAPTER 22

Gail sped away from Mario's house and wandered through the streets until she found the highway back to Austin. She didn't know why she had fallen so easily into Mario's arms on Thursday. If she could have just resisted him, she wouldn't be feeling so disgusted now. Was she really the depraved woman she saw in the mirror in the bathroom? Before Thursday, she had been growing in the Lord and feeling strong in the Spirit. Surely there was some method she could employ that would keep her from ending up having sex with Mario every time she saw him. She had really wanted him to stop, but she couldn't exactly call what he did "rape." She had consented for the most part.

Once she was out of the city limits and the road was clear, Gail set her cruise control and listened to the smooth sounds of Take 6 as she calmed her nerves and talked herself out of being angry with Mario.

As soon as she made it into the comfort of her condominium, she turned off the ringers on her phones and switched the answering machine off. The caller ID showed that Mario had already called four times. She did not dare listen to the messages he left.

In her short time at The Word she had learned that after falling into temptation, she should repent, ask the Lord for forgiveness, and walk in restoration. Repenting meant she had to turn away from her relationship with Mario and change her mind about it as well. Her biggest obstacle was that she practically craved him and wasn't sure she shouldn't have him. On the other hand, she felt like being with him right now was violating her relationship with God. She was guilty because he was married. Otherwise, maybe she wouldn't feel so bad.

Gail took a long, hot shower, and picked up her Bible before crawling into bed. She read from Romans, and turned the television in her bedroom to TBN and watched Christian television all evening.

The next day at the Sunday morning service, Gail had a hard time getting into the praise service. The songs were familiar, but she felt awkward. She tried to ask the Lord to forgive her for falling again, but she couldn't focus her mind on anything. By the time Pastor Kline began his sermon, her mind was even further from the service. She had gone back to Thursday night and began replaying all the wrong decisions she had made. She should have just told Mario that she could not see him. Why had she let him come to her house in the first place?

Gail managed to take a few notes from Pastor Kline's sermon. After all, she needed the sermon notes to do her personal Bible studies. He talked about how to deal with strongholds. The title was "Your Mind is the Battle Field." He sang parts of gospel songs that said, "I'm on the battle field, and I'm fighting for the Lord." He went through several different songs that all said the same thing and then asked the question, "Where exactly is the battle field?"

"Is the battle field really on your job? Is it in your home? Is the battle field out there somewhere?" he asked. "Or is it right here?" He pointed to his head. "I submit to you today that the battle field is your mind."

"You may come in here every week and sing and dance and even run around the church, but if you don't work to master the thoughts that go through your head you will allow the devil to mess up your mind. If you think wrong thoughts, you will end up feeling and doing wrong things."

Gail made a half-hearted attempt to take notes and then decided to just get the tape. Her mind was wandering so much that she was only hearing bits and pieces of what he was saying.

Pastor Kline read from II Corinthians 10:4-5 "For the weapons of our warfare are not carnal, but mighty through God to the pulling down of strong holds. Casting down imaginations, and every high thing that exalts itself against the knowledge of God, and bringing into captivity every thought to the obedience of Christ."

Gail hadn't given Mario any serious thought previous to Thursday night. She had not pictured herself with him in weeks, but somehow it all came back to her in a whirlwind when he showed up at her front door.

"An unexamined, uncensored thought will become an imagination. An imagination will become a stronghold. A stronghold is something that has control over you. It's something that you struggle with because you want to gain mastery over it," Pastor Kline said.

"But don't be alarmed by the struggle. Just learn how to fight. The enemy knows you well enough to push the right buttons in your life. There are some thoughts that come to your mind that barely get a blip on your radar screen. For most people, weird thoughts of bestiality or cannibalism don't do a thing for them. But if the right thought about the right person doing the right thing to you comes through your mind, you could be physically sitting here listening to me, but mentally not here."

Gail said an "amen" to that because she knew she was not good soil at that moment. After the service ended, she went straight to the bookstore to buy the tape and headed home. She was still feeling depressed when she got home, so she called Shawn in California hoping that hearing her voice would cheer her up. She got Shawn's answering machine and left a message.

Not wanting to sit around idle, Gail ate a quick salad and headed to the gym. She settled into her routine of 30 minutes on the treadmill and then moved to the free weights. She had noticed Darien, the doctor, when she was on the treadmill. He slowly made his way toward her as he worked his way through his weight exercises. She was working her biceps when he finally walked up to her.

"Hi, Gail. I've missed seeing you here in a while. Did you change your schedule?"

"I've been more involved in my church, so I haven't been coming to the gym as much."

"What church do you go to? I've been wanting to find a good church to attend."

"I go to Living Word Christian Fellowship. People call it The Word."

"Someone has suggested that church. I'd love to visit there with you."

"That would be nice," Gail said half-heartedly. She knew she was supposed to be inviting people to church enthusiastically, but she was somewhat suspicious of Darien's motives.

"When is the mid-week service?"

"Wednesday night. It starts at seven."

"Are you going Wednesday?"

"Yes, I'll be there, but if you want a good introduction to the church, you may want to go on Sunday. That's a better day for visitors. Wednesday night is a pretty deep Bible study."

"Oh? How deep do you have to be to attend?" Darien asked, raising his brows.

"I didn't mean it like that," Gail was embarrassed.

"You think that because I'm a doctor, I don't know the word?" Darien teased.

"I didn't mean to sound like a spiritual snob."

Darien laughed, and Gail noticed how straight and white his teeth were.

"I guess church folk can be just as snobbish as rich folk," Darien said.

"Well, I'm not a snob in any sense of the word," Gail countered.

"Why don't you prove it to me by having some coffee with this poor man after you finish working out?"

"You? Poor? How is that?"

"Two words: student loans."

"Say no more. But I think I'll have to pass on the invitation."

"Please come with me. I'm new in town, and you're the nicest woman I've met."

"I have plans that I can't change. I'm sorry." She didn't want to tell him that she was going back to church that night because he may try to invite himself along.

"Okay," he said softly. "But I'd still like to go to church with you Wednesday night."

"Why don't you meet me there? I'll wait for you in the foyer."

"I'll do that."

"Do you know where it is?"

"It's on Turner Avenue, right?"

"That's right. I'll see you Wednesday." Gail picked up her weights and started lifting again as Darien walked away. That was interesting, Gail thought. She wondered if he was sincerely interested in church. It was obvious that he was interested in her. She would be sure to meet him Wednesday, and at some point she would find out if he were truly single. He would be a good catch for somebody.

Gail made the mistake of trying to take a quick nap after she got home from the gym. By the time she woke up, it was 8:30, and she didn't feel like walking into church so late. She turned on TBN and lounged around. A quick scan of the caller ID showed that Mario was still calling. She erased all his messages without listening to them. She wasn't angry with him, but she was not ready to talk to him.

Monday was the Labor Day holiday so Gail took advantage of the sales at the mall and found some good buys. She also treated herself to dinner and a movie. She knew other single women who didn't do things like that by themselves, but Gail liked spending time alone. She had a book about how to have intimacy with the Lord, and she read it while she waited for her food to come and again while she waited for the movie to start.

When she got home that evening, there was a gift bag on her doorknob. She knew it was from Mario, and she started to just throw it in the trash. Instead she opened the box and gasped at the double-strand diamond bracelet. It was simple and elegant, and it was obvious that the diamonds were real. There was also a card in the bag. She opened it reluctantly and read Mario's note:

℘

Dear Gail,

I'm so sorry I have to apologize for my actions once again. It's just that you are so irresistible to me. When I saw you walking toward me Saturday, you looked like my Aqua Queen, and I fully understood what a mistake I made on my wedding day. I married the wrong woman, and now I have to make things right. I'll be in touch with you in a couple of weeks. Until then, please accept this bracelet as a token of my love and sincere apology for my lack of restraint on Saturday. You mean the world to me, and I don't want my stupid actions to jeopardize my chances of being with you.

Love, Mario

The tears that flowed down Gail's face surprised her. She felt such a mix of emotions. Maybe Mario was the right person for her, but he just came at the wrong time. She put the bracelet on and admired it on her wrist as the light bounced off the diamonds.

Gail was late for church on Wednesday night because she had worked until six, something she rarely did. Sara had gotten backed up in her work and had asked for Gail's help. It didn't take long for Gail to see that Sara was behind because she was doing more wedding planning than working. When Gail took Sara the spreadsheets that she had checked, Sara was on the phone with the wedding planner. Gail just left the stack on Sara's desk and headed home for a quick dinner before church.

Praise service had begun when she arrived, and she regretted staying at work. Darien was not in the foyer and she would have a hard time finding him in the crowd. She didn't even know if he was there, so she went into the sanctuary.

"You're Gail, right?" the usher asked her as soon as she entered.

"Yes," Gail knitted her brows at the man. He was familiar to her, but she didn't know his name. She glanced at his nametag. "And you're Bobby."

He chuckled and said, "You have a visitor here. Come this way."

He led her to a seat next to Darien, who was fully involved in the service. His hands were raised in praise and his eyes were closed. She didn't want to interrupt him with a greeting so she just stood quietly next to him, and tried to get into the service herself. He must have gotten there early because he had secured seats on the third row. Pastor Kline's Bible studies were immensely popular, and Gail would have been sitting in the back of the sanctuary if Darien had not saved her a seat.

After praise service, Darien turned and greeted her with a quick hug as they sat down. She recognized the rich smell of sandalwood in his cologne.

"It's good to see you," he said in her ear.

"I'm sorry I wasn't here earlier. I had to work late."

"Oh, that's okay, I can certainly understand that," Darien said with a smile. "I'm so glad I came. This is the kind of church I'm used to. I can't wait to hear the word. I know it's going to be good."

"You're right."

Pastor Kline taught such a stirring message on the destiny of the believer that the whole crowd was standing by the end of the teaching. Gail was pleasantly surprised by Darien's reaction to the word, but she was moved herself. After listening to Pastor Kline, she felt like she could do anything; especially get over a petty thing like her illicit relationship with Mario. She understood that the relationship was just a way for the enemy to get her off the course that God had planned for her. She could not let a man, even one as handsome and enticing as Mario, stop her from fulfilling her destiny in Christ.

After church, Darien was bubbling over with how much he enjoyed the word. They went to the bookstore so Darien could purchase some tapes.

"When I was in D.C. in med school, I attended Abundant Life. It was big like this church and the word was awesome."

"That's great. I really didn't go to church before I started coming here," Gail said.

Just then, Jason walked up to them.

"Gail! How have you been?" He hugged her and held on a few beats too long. She noticed Darien's slightly annoyed look.

Pulling herself gently from Jason's grasp, Gail introduced Darien. "Jason, this is Darien. Tonight was his first time here."

"Nice to meet you. I'm Jason Tucker." They gripped hands and Gail could tell it was a strong grip.

"Darien Washington. I had a great time in the service. I was just telling Gail that I used to attend Abundant Life in D.C."

"I've heard of that church. It's a powerful ministry. So you just moved here from D.C?"

"I've been here a few months. I met Gail at the gym and she invited me to church," Darien said.

"I hope you come back, man. If you're looking for a church, I can give you more information about our ministry." Jason turned to Gail. "Mario told me you left the party sick Saturday. Why didn't you find me? I would have driven you home."

"Oh, I was fine. I just had to get home and lay down. I ate too much of that rich food, but I'm doing okay now."

"Gail, I'm going to pay for these now," Darien cut in.

"All right. I'll wait for you here."

"So, Gail, are you really okay?" Jason asked after Darien was out of earshot.

"Of course I am. I'm fine."

"I wanted to make sure I didn't do or say anything to upset you."

"Why, because you were flirting with me from the moment you saw me?"

Jason blushed and looked at his shoes.

"I'm just teasing. You weren't flirting that badly."

"You may accuse me of flirting again, but I have to admit that I was quite taken with how beautiful you looked. I mean you always look good, but that outfit was so nice on you," Jason said and it was Gail's turn to blush. "So, I'm glad you're feeling better."

"Yeah, everything is okay. I'll see you Sunday." Gail turned toward Darien and the cash register. "By the way, thanks for the compliments," she said to Jason over her shoulder.

After paying for his tapes, Darien walked Gail to her car. He continued talking about The Word.

"Thanks for telling me about the church."

"You would have come eventually. Someone had already told you about it."

"But you are the one who inspired me to actually come."

"And how did I do that?" Gail couldn't resist asking.

"I knew that I'd see you here if I came since you refused to go out with me."

"Dr. Washington, are you coming to church just to chase some girl?"

"By no means am I doing that. I'm serious about my relationship with the Lord, but I am a single man hoping to be married one day. I just need to meet the right woman."

"I'm sure you will." Gail fished in her purse for her keys. "Well, I guess I'd better get going."

"I'll see you on Sunday morning."

Gail smiled to herself all the way home. She was getting the message loud and clear that there were plenty of eligible men available and she didn't need to be fooling around with a married one.

CHAPTER 23

By the end of September, Gail had settled back into her routine of work, church, daily Bible study and prayer. Darien had surprised her by his consistent church attendance. She thought a doctor would be too busy to attend church as much as he did.

"Gail, one thing you will learn about me is that God is priority in my life. I want all the things that other people want in life, but I know they won't mean a thing without the Lord," he said when she asked him how an emergency room doctor found time for church two to three times a week.

She enjoyed talking to Darien after church, but he surprised her again by not flirting with her or asking her out. Although she never saw him talking to anyone else, she began to wonder if he had his eye on another woman at the church.

At work, Sara was still happily planning her wedding, and Gail was actually beginning to get excited with her. Even though Gail wasn't looking forward to being a bridesmaid again, Sara's joy was contagious. Sara's wedding was almost a year away, but she was concerned with every detail, jumping from subject to subject so quickly that Gail could barely keep up.

"And girl, you know I tried to pick the right date so I wouldn't be on my period during our honeymoon."

"Now, that would be messed up. I've never thought about that. How can you calculate it a whole year from now?"

"I'll have to get on the pill at just the right time." Sara chattered on about when she would start her prescription, but Gail's mind was trying to do her own calculations. She abruptly ended the conversation and made her way to her cubicle. She pulled out her calendar and saw that her period was only a week late. It would take her body some time to regulate itself after getting off the pill, and it would also take some time after being off the pill before her body would be fertile again. This was further motivation for her to stay away from Mario. She simply would not have sex if she were not on the pill.

Mario had left a long message on her answering machine about how he was ready to present Nina with divorce papers, and Gail needed to make a decision about their relationship. She thought he was just bluffing, and she didn't return his calls. However, she still wore the beautiful bracelet he'd sent.

Every day Gail anticipated her period. After another week, she started praying to God, asking for her period to come. She became consumed with her private worry. She didn't dare give voice to her fear. Another week passed, and she knew something was wrong.

It was the Monday of the third week, and Gail was on her way back to her cubicle after checking for red in the bathroom. She passed Sara's desk.

"Hey, girl, what's up?" Sara said with her usual cheeriness.

"Nothing much. What's up with you?"

"I talked to Nina last night. She's been giving me lessons about how to be a good wife. She bought this great book titled *365 Nights of Great Sex* or something like that. The pages are sealed so that only the woman can open her pages and only the man can open his pages. Each page is some sexual surprise for your spouse. The girl has done some wild stuff!"

Gail knew she was being rude, but she practically walked away while Sara was in mid-sentence. So Nina was becoming the model wife? If she was such a good wife, why was Mario still calling her leaving his sexy voice on her answering machine? She wasn't sure what she was going to say, but she was going to return his calls that night.

Mario answered his cell phone on the first ring.

"Hello, sweetheart."

"Hi, Mario."

"Are you ready to begin a new life with me?"

"Why would you want to begin a new life with me when your wife is doing such a good job keeping you satisfied."

"She could never satisfy me like you do."

"She seems to be trying very hard."

"You think so?"

"Sara says she's buying books and experimenting and things."

"Do I detect a hint of jealousy?"

"This is not what I called you about."

"Did you call to thank me for the bracelet?"

"It's very nice, but that's not why I called, either."

"What do you need, I'll do anything for you."

"I've missed my period."

"You what? Well, that's just, I mean, I can't believe it."

Gail listened closely to his voice, looking for a hint of doubt, denial or anything that would cause her to lose the tentative grip she had on her emotions. She didn't know what to expect from Mario. She was surprised by his next comment.

"This is absolutely wonderful, Gail!"

"Wonderful?"

"Yes. It is. Have you been to the doctor yet?"

"No."

"I'll be there first thing in the morning. We'll spend the day together. Can you call in sick?"

"I guess I could, but you don't have to come down here."

"Oh, I insist. Hey, tomorrow is my birthday, so we can celebrate! And, look, you need to make a doctor's appointment as soon as possible. And drink plenty of orange juice with calcium and eat a lot of leafy green vegetables."

"What are all the instructions for? This may be nothing."

"Or it may be something wonderful."

CHAPTER 24

Gail didn't really believe she was pregnant, but she was curiously pleased that Mario was coming to see her. She felt guilty about the satisfaction she got from being able to pull Mario away from Nina if only for a short time. Hearing that Nina was working hard to be a good wife triggered something in Gail that she couldn't explain. She would bask in Mario's attention for a little while and then let him know that it was a false alarm after her period started.

Mario called early Tuesday morning and said he would pick her up in time for lunch. She headed to the mall as soon as it opened and found a store that sold fancy writing pens. She picked one and had it personalized for Mario. On her way out of the mall, she pondered what Mario had in mind for the day and how they would end it. Remembering her pledge to not have sex, Gail thought about the most effective means of over-the-counter birth control. She thought about stopping at Walgreen's, but time was running short and she hurried home to get ready for Mario to pick her up.

Mario chose Pappadeux's restaurant for his birthday lunch. He asked for an intimate table in the back of the restaurant. The hostess obliged Mario, and they were seated in a back corner that was partially shielded from the main part of the restaurant by a big wooden column.

After they ordered, Gail explained to him that she had stopped taking her birth control pills and her body was probably just getting used to regulating itself.

"That may be the case, but I want you to make an appointment and get yourself checked out anyway," Mario instructed.

"I'll make an appointment. I promise."

"May I ask why you stopped taking the pills?"

Although Gail didn't think he was accusing her of trying to get pregnant on purpose, she decided to be totally honest with him.

"Frankly, I had planned to completely end my relationship with you, and in my new commitment, I promised the Lord that I would be chaste and live a celibate life while I'm single."

Mario just stared at her with a mischievous grin on his face. She knew what he was thinking, and was sort of glad he didn't say anything. Instead of discussing Mario's ability to make her break a promise she had made to the Lord, she took his gift out of her purse.

"Here's your birthday present."

"Oh, Gail. You didn't have to get me anything! This is sweet." He opened the box and made a big deal out of the gift. "You know me so well. This is a perfect gift for me. Thank you, Gail."

He leaned over and gave her a kiss on the cheek, and then he brushed her lips lightly with his and started sweet-talking her the way he did when they were in bed. Gail simply enjoyed the attention, because in her mind, the end of the relationship was drawing near.

"I'm glad you're wearing the bracelet," he said fingering her wrist and the sparkling diamonds. "It looks beautiful on you."

"It is a very nice gift, but you shouldn't have bought something so expensive."

"I bought it because I love you. If you want me to, I'll tell Nina tomorrow that the marriage is over, and you and I are going to be together."

"There's no need to do that just yet. Let's just get the results of the pregnancy test first, and then we can decide what to do."

"If you say so, baby," he said as he gave her another kiss, this time pressing her lips with his tongue until she yielded to him and opened her mouth to his kisses.

"What is this?" Gail and Mario turned at the same time to see Nina standing at their table with balloons and gift bags in her hand.

"You said you were meeting one of your managers here for lunch! What is this?" Nina's body started shaking as she looked from Mario to Gail and the reality of the situation dawned on her. Gail turned to Mario to find him just as speechless as she was.

To Gail's horror, Sara and Jason walked up behind Nina. They were holding gift bags as well.

"Surprise!" Sara gushed. She didn't realize what was going on. "We need to get a bigger table."

"Umm, Nina, let me talk to you outside," Mario said, standing.

"No. I'm not going outside with you. You need to explain to me what is going on here."

"Uh oh," Jason said.

Nina threw down the presents and the balloons drifted up to the ceiling. She placed her hands on her hips.

"What *is* going on? I thought we were throwing a surprise party," Sara said, still clueless.

"I gave you everything, Mario. I gave you my virginity and this is what you do in return?" Nina glanced at Gail and shook her head. "I can't believe this." She turned back to Mario. "I did everything you wanted. I did my best to make you happy, but apparently, it wasn't enough." Tears began to flow down her cheeks.

"All I wanted was to be a good wife for you," Nina sobbed.

"Oh, Nina, please don't do this," Mario's voice was tender. "Baby, let's go outside and discuss this alone."

Gail looked at Mario in shock, wondering why he was taking this approach. Here was his chance to end it with Nina, and he was suggesting that they talk about things alone. It wasn't that she really wanted his marriage to end, but he had just been telling her how much he wanted to be with her and not Nina.

"No!" Nina yelled, drawing the attention of everyone in the back of the restaurant. "I know I'm not perfect, but I did my best for you! Why are you doing this to me? If you didn't want to be with me, you should have ended it before we got married. You are just a dirty dog, Mario!" Nina's voice escalated with every word.

"Nina," Jason intervened. "We need to get out of here with this."

"I'm not going anywhere. Did everybody know about this except me?" She turned to Jason and Sara.

"Of course not. It's not even clear what exactly is going on," Sara said, turning to Mario as if there were a logical explanation.

"I'll tell you what's going on. When I walked in here to give my husband a surprise party for his birthday, he was sitting here kissing this woman, who claimed to be my friend. This is some mess. That's what it is!" Nina yelled. The manager of the restaurant was now standing next to Jason, asking if everything was all right.

"Nina, look, we need to discuss this somewhere else," Mario said with his teeth clenched.

"Mario, I'm not discussing anything with you. You have ruined my life. I can't believe you're doing this to me."

"It's not about you, Nina! Gail and I had a relationship back when we were in college."

"So you arranged to have her in our wedding so you could have a sleazy fling with her at your bachelor party or something? Sounds like some sappy movie. This is ridiculous, Mario, and you are a low-down, dirty dog. My daddy is going to kill you." Nina wiped the tears from her cheeks and looked down at Gail. Pointing her finger in Gail's face, Nina unleashed another wave of her wrath.

"You know what, Gail? Women like you allow men to act like dogs. You let them treat you any kind of way. All the while, they actually want to be with women like me who demand respect and honor from them," Nina's venom made tears well up in Gail's eyes, but she refused to cry.

Nina continued her speech. "I've done my best with this one." She jerked her head toward Mario. "I honestly thought God had brought about a change in his life, but apparently not. So you can have him. Good luck with him." Nina turned and pushed her way through Jason, Sara and the restaurant manager and stomped through the restaurant toward the door.

"Sara, please don't let her leave here alone! Go with her," Mario commanded. When Sara didn't move, he ordered her again. "Hurry, go, right now!" Sara turned and ran after Nina.

Gail sat in her seat, stunned and uncertain about what to do. She watched Mario give the manager a large bill and gather up the presents that Nina had dropped.

"Come on, Gail. We'll drop you at your apartment," Mario said.

Gail walked through the restaurant behind Mario with Jason trailing her. As everyone openly stared at them and whispered as they passed, Gail felt like she was in a parade of shame. She was numb as Mario escorted her into the back seat of his car. Jason sat up front with Mario, but they were completely silent as they drove her home.

As soon as Mario stopped in front of her condo, Gail got out of the car and headed into the house without looking back. She listened for Mario to get out of the car and turned as he called to her. He had rolled his window down, but he didn't get out of the car.

"Gail, I'll call you, okay?"

Granting him a fleeting glance over her shoulder, she kept walking and lifted her hand in a half wave as she entered her building.

Gail collapsed on the couch and cried. She felt totally humiliated and abandoned. Mario had sent Sara after Nina, but he didn't have anything to say to her. She wondered what Jason and Sara thought of her. What was she supposed to do now? Was she really pregnant with Mario's baby? If she were pregnant, she would make sure he paid child support. She didn't think he really wanted to be with her. What Nina said really hit home. It was true. She didn't require much from Mario so he did act like a dog. Instead of setting herself up for disappointment, Gail decided to follow through with her plan to end things with Mario. If she had ended things sooner, she could have avoided all the embarrassment she suffered at the restaurant.

CHAPTER 25

The next day at work, Gail managed to avoid Sara on her way in. She busied herself all morning. Around 10 a.m. a huge bouquet arrived from Mario. Gail didn't bother reading the card. At noon, Sara came to her cubicle and stood looking at the flowers.

"I guess I know who these are from now."

"This is a terrible situation," was all Gail could manage. She braced herself for the worst, but Sara took a reserved but friendly tone.

"We should talk about this. Let's set aside an evening when we're both free. Is that okay with you?"

"I guess," Gail said tentatively.

"You may not feel like you owe me an explanation, but I guess I would like to hear your side."

Gail had a fleeting thought that Sara may be trying to spy on her for Nina.

"I don't know about that. I mean, you've known Nina longer, and I know you're pretty close."

"Well, I'll just say this much. I'm not surprised that Mario cheated on Nina. She's a sweet girl in her own way, but she and her family put a lot of pressure on Mario to marry her. I've known Mario for a long time, too, and this is no surprise. Frankly, I'm more concerned about how you're doing right now. If you want to get together tonight, I'm available," Sara offered.

"What about Bible study?"

"I hadn't planned to go tonight because I'm packing for my trip to Louisiana. I'm leaving in the morning. We could wait until I get back next week if you would like."

"No, I want to talk tonight. Come over and I'll make dinner."

Sara came to Gail's condo at seven. Since Sara was on a diet, Gail made chef's salads. After they ate, Gail continued talking about safe topics while she put the dishes in the dishwasher. After avoiding the main topic through dinner, Gail and Sara sat in the living room, and Gail told the entire story, starting with meeting Mario at UT and ending with the potential pregnancy.

"I can understand your trying to stop taking the pills, but you had sex with Mario almost immediately after that. I don't understand that part."

"I didn't plan that. Besides, you have to be off the pill for months before you're able to get pregnant."

"That's not always the case. Women do get pregnant while they're taking the pill. Come on, Gail, as much as you talked about being educated about sex as a women's health issue, you should know better." Sara said.

"I've had friends who have had trouble getting pregnant after getting off the pill." Gail shrugged.

"Gail, do you think you were, perhaps subconsciously, trying to get pregnant?"

"That's ridiculous. I may not even be pregnant anyway. And, I wasn't trying to get pregnant. I was trying to stop having sex, and I thought that if I got off the pills it would be more motivation for me to be celibate."

"It takes the power of the Holy Spirit to live holy, Gail. You can't trick yourself into it."

"I know that. I'm just telling you what my thinking was at the time. This thing with Mario has really been a struggle for me, but I'm ending it now."

"Were those flowers a good-bye present or something?"

"I don't know what those flowers are about, but he'll know where I stand soon enough."

"Gail, apparently you've tried to end things with Mario before, and nothing has worked so far."

Gail sighed. She was tired of Sara being right about everything.

"Well, since you've known him for so long, what do you suggest I do?"

"If you want to end things with him, you have to really cut him off—absolutely no contact. The only way he'll get the message is if you are consistent with him."

"I've thought about why I ended up in this situation and I'm dealing with my issues, but why did he come on to me so strong when I saw him at that reception before his wedding? Once I realized Nina's fiancé was someone I'd had a fling with, I tried to get over it and go on, but he just kept after me until we ended up in a full blown affair."

"You have to understand something about Mario. He grew up an only child, and his parents spoiled him rotten. He was a golden child. He could do no wrong in his parents' eyes. It's not totally his fault that he's so selfish and manipulative. He's used to everybody liking him so when someone doesn't, he either tries to win them over or move them out of his life space. He thinks he can get away with anything because, for the most part, he has all his life."

"But he's so attentive and nice," Gail said.

Sara rolled her eyes. "That's all a part of his game. Being nice wins people over. He may even be loving and tender, but he's also a cheater and he is manipulative."

"Jason told me that Mario nursed him back to health from alcoholism after they finished undergrad."

"Jason and Mario were partners in crime. Of course, he's going to help his fraternity brother."

"At the time, Jason said Mario was in seminary and having Bible studies at his house. He encouraged Jason to get his life in order with God."

"I don't know what Jason told you, but it sounds like he idealized the real Mario. Look, I'm not saying Mario doesn't have some redeemable qualities. I'm just trying to warn you about the kind of person you're dealing with. He is a manipulator."

"Is Nina a manipulator?"

"What do you mean?"

"She got him to marry her. Didn't she and her parents put a lot of pressure on him? You said so yourself."

"They put a lot of pressure on him, but Mario made his own decisions. There was plenty in it for him. My question for you is, are you going to be able to walk away from him?"

"I've already walked away from him," Gail said. "But I have a question for you. Why do you dislike Mario so much?"

"It's not that I dislike him. I just want you to get some insight into the kind of person he is."

"I understand." Gail was cautious about her next question. "I know this may not be appropriate, and you don't have to answer, but how is Nina doing?"

"As well as can be expected," Sara said. Gail didn't sense an open door to ask any more about it. Sara rose and prepared to leave.

"I start my vacation tomorrow. I'll be gone for about a week, but if you need to reach me, call me on my cell phone."

Sara gave her a hug and left.

Gail tried to figure out how Sara could even talk to her if she were really Nina's friend. Maybe they weren't as close as Gail thought they were. Mario had to practically yell at Sara before she went after Nina at the restaurant.

CHAPTER 26

Gail anticipated the Sunday morning service, knowing she would find direction in the word. She had been under a dark cloud since the scene at the restaurant. Hoping the gloom would be lifted by the praise service, Gail arrived early enough to get a good seat in the front. She was pleasantly surprised when Darien sat next to her right after praise service started.

She let the tears flow as she sang and worshiped God through every song. She confessed and repented again concerning her relationship with Mario and asked God to restore her. The sermon was a practical teaching about prayer. Pastor Kline explained how prayer should be a time when the believer lines up with what God is saying rather than a time when you only make requests. He said the things you request must be based on God's word. Gail took good notes and looked forward to her personal study time on Luke 11. Maybe this was the key to being able to totally break free from Mario. She needed to use the word in her prayers about the situation.

Immediately after the benediction, Darien said he had to leave. He apologized for not walking her to her car, but she said it was okay because she wanted to go to the bookstore before she left.

Gail bought a journal on prayer and fasting that Pastor Kline had recommended. She was on her way out of the church when she saw some women gathered and staring at her. She recognized them from the single's ministry fellowship and walked up to them, flashing a smile, which quickly froze on her face.

"There's the home wrecker," someone in the group said. Their eyes were like daggers boring into her as she stood in shock. Surely they didn't know what had happened at the restaurant.

"What's done in the dark will come out in the light," someone else said.

A woman stepped closer to her and said, "You know, you really hurt Nina. How could you do something like that after being in their wedding?"

Gail was too indignant to defend herself. She turned to walk out the door and blocked out their comments, which they continued to hurl at her.

"Gail, wait!"

She recognized Jason's voice but refused to turn around. After what just happened she didn't think she would ever come back to The Word. She kept walking to her car, and Jason kept calling. As she placed the key in the lock, he caught up to her.

"Gail, I saw what happened. Please don't let that stop you from coming back to church."

"I have to go." She opened the door, and got in, leaving Jason standing in the parking lot as she drove off.

When she got home, she decided to listen to the messages that Mario had left. He sounded tired, but he was asking about her health and whether she had made her doctor's appointment yet. The phone rang. She didn't recognize the number that showed on the caller ID, but it looked like a cell phone number.

"Hi, Gail, this is Jason."

"Jason, I really don't want to talk right now."

"Wait, Gail. I just want to apologize for what those girls did."

"You can't apologize for what someone else did, Jason. You weren't the one who told them what happened, were you?"

"I think Nina had something to do with it. But you have to understand that this is just a ploy of the devil to keep you from coming to church."

"It may be better for me to find another church anyway," Gail said.

"Why would you do that? You need to just hang in there and keep coming no matter what people say."

"Jason, I am not going to The Word and have people staring and talking about me every time I walk through the door."

"Look, Gail, I talked to those girls and they won't be bothering you anymore."

"Jason, I think I know women a little better than you do. It doesn't matter if they talk or not, they will still make me feel unwelcome in that place. It's not like they're accusing me of something I didn't do. Maybe this is what I deserve."

"Don't say that, Gail. People make mistakes. You'll get over this."

"I know I'll get over it, but that doesn't mean I'll still go to The Word."

"Don't make your mind up about it right now. You're just upset."

"I guess you're right," Gail said just to keep him from trying to convince her. "I'm surprised that you and Sara want to have anything to do with me considering that you're both friends with Mario and Nina."

"You're our friend, too, Gail. We wouldn't abandon you in a time like this. You need friends right now."

Gail wondered how Nina felt about them trying to be her friends. She knew it wouldn't be appropriate to ask Jason any questions about Mario and Nina so she just thanked him for calling and got off the phone.

Although Jason and Sara's attempts to reach out to her encouraged Gail, she definitely was not going back to The Word. She couldn't face the embarrassment of everyone knowing about her affair with Mario and what happened at the restaurant.

Restless and frustrated, Gail went to the gym and had an extra hard workout.

CHAPTER 27

Monday morning at work Jason showed up at Gail's cubicle around lunchtime.

"Hi, Gail," he said quickly. "Before you get mad at me, I just came by to give you this tape. It's from Sunday night, and I just thought you may want to hear it."

He said good-bye and walked away before Gail could even respond. Of course he knew where she worked, but she didn't have a clue how he found her cubicle. Sara was still on vacation. Either he knew other people who worked there or he went through great lengths to locate her in the huge building.

She looked at the title of the tape. It said "The Root of the Matter." Her curiosity was peaked, so she listened to the tape as soon as she got home that night. She was moved by the message as if she had been sitting in the actual service. Pastor Kline explained that many issues people deal with as adults are based on things they went through as children. Gail's first reaction was to assess the concept as basic psychology until Pastor Kline explained the spiritual aspects of the negative seeds planted in people's lives when they are children.

"These seeds often grow into tangled vines of insecurity and low-self worth that hinder a person's emotional growth. I am purposeful about planting healthy roots in my children individually, especially my daughter," the pastor said. "There is a love that only I can give her. If she doesn't get that love, she will seek it in other men."

Gail listened to the tape a second time. She stayed up late Monday night thinking about the root of her problem.

Although she wasn't close to her mother now, she remembered getting basic nurture and comfort from her mother when she was a child. What Gail felt she missed the most was a healthy relationship with her father. The poor quality of her relationship with her father was highlighted by Pastor Kline's description of his relationship with his daughter.

Pastor Kline gave instructions on how to deal with the root of the matter even if it meant getting in contact with people you hadn't spoken to in a long time. In some cases, getting to the root meant forgiving, in some cases, asking for forgiveness. He gave many examples of the benefits of dealing with issues at the root, and Gail was convinced she needed to get in touch with her father. When she thought about all the times he sent money instead of visiting her himself, she started to get angrier by the minute. She needed to tell him just how neglected he made her feel, and he needed to apologize for not being there for her. Gail was tired of men disregarding her and taking her for granted, and it had all started with her father.

Tuesday morning when she got to work, she called her father's office but he was not available. She left a message, and was surprised when she got a call back from him within the hour. She wasn't prepared with how quickly she would be able to deal with the root of the matter.

"Gail! I'm so glad you called," Phillip Adams said. "Lillian and I will be in town tomorrow. We could have dinner if you're available. I have something very important to talk to you about."

"I'll be available," Gail said, a little stunned. "I wanted to talk to you about something as well."

"Can it wait until tomorrow, or do you want to talk right now?" He sounded accommodating and uncharacteristically patient. Depleted of the venom of the night before, she decided to wait.

"We can talk tomorrow. That'll be fine." She gave him directions to her condominium.

"I look forward to seeing you tomorrow then," he said.

Gail had expected her father to be unavailable and inattentive as usual, but all of a sudden he was on his way to Austin. Phillip visited Austin frequently, and he never called her for dinner or anything else. Almost a year ago, Gail had accidentally run into him and his wife Lillian at Landry's Seafood restaurant. They were on their way out and she was with a couple of her hanging buddies, Joanna and Marsha. She made quick introductions, but her dad seemed to be in a hurry to leave. Her friends teased her about how handsome her father was and even asked about his availability. She had told them that he would only break their hearts.

Tuesday, Gail left work early so she would have enough time to clean her apartment before they arrived. Since Lillian was a bit fussy about housekeeping, Gail wanted to make sure everything was in order on their first visit to her condo.

They arrived at 6:30 and when Gail opened the door, she immediately noticed that something was different about them. Flashing a bright smile, her father was as handsome as ever.

"Gail!" He said, embracing her in a bear hug. "It's so good to see you."

"It's good to see you, too, Dad." Gail returned his hug, relishing the security she felt in his arms, if only for a brief moment.

Lillian also reached out and gave her an awkward hug. They sat in the living room and made small talk. All the while, Gail noticed little changes that made them seem so different than the last time she saw them. Her father had always seemed distracted to her, like his mind was always somewhere else. But now, he was totally there with her and Lillian. He was laughing and joking in his usual way, and by the time they left for the restaurant, Gail was sure that something had changed in her father's life, but she didn't know what it was.

Gail suggested a ritzy Mexican restaurant, Z-Tejas, and found that it was one of her dad's favorite Austin restaurants. Ever the gentleman, her father opened both car doors on the passenger side and ushered the women into his midnight blue 6-Series Mercedes.

He had operated a lucrative import business for as long as Gail could remember, but she always wondered if he was a drug dealer or did some other illegal things. Maybe it was because she had seen him with other women on several occasions over the years. If he cheated on his wives, maybe he also cheated in business.

He had always been very generous with his money, especially when her birthday and holidays rolled around, but Gail was never able to establish a relationship with him because he never spent time with her or paid much attention to her. Now, as she listened to the easy banter between her father and Lillian, she sensed a definite change in him.

He didn't leave her wondering for long. As soon as they were seated at Z-Tejas he launched into a story that kept her riveted to her seat.

"I want to begin by saying that I'm a changed man, and I've been evaluating my life. I made some terrible mistakes when I was married to your mother, and even after I remarried, I wasn't a faithful husband."

Gail didn't bother to hide her shock as she looked from him to Lillian who was simply gazing at her father with loving admiration. With raised eyebrows, she thought to herself, Okay, this is weird, but she made no comment.

He continued on, "I want you to know that you have two brothers besides your sisters Lisa and Leslie. I don't plan on going anywhere soon, but when I die, I don't want you to be shocked about Jeremy and Michael if they show up at my funeral. I would like all of you to get together with me one day soon, if at all possible. I can't express to you how sorry I am for not being the kind of father you needed. You've done very well for yourself, but I know it's not because I was a great dad to you."

Gail still couldn't believe what she was hearing. She had two brothers? She had only heard about one. This confirmed the rumors. He was definitely a changed man. He sounded nothing like the aloof man who paid little attention to her, no matter how well she did in school or how obedient she was when she stayed at his house in the summers. She was a much better behaved child than her stepsisters, but it seemed to Gail that they always got all the attention.

She had a question burning in her mind, and she was finally able to speak after the initial shock.

"What has brought about this change?"

"That's the best part of my story. It all started when Lillian brought home these videos of different preachers. All the messages were about manhood and God's call for men to be leaders. At first, I thought I was looking good because I've always been a good provider for my family and all my children. But when they talked about faithfulness, fatherhood and real manhood, I always found a reason to leave the room." He smiled at Lillian, and she winked at him.

He continued, "We also attended a marriage encounter weekend where I learned so much about myself. You see, my father and mother never divorced, but my dad is a smooth-talking lady's man. My mother was also unfaithful to the marriage and her lover was around so much, I considered him my uncle. He lives right down the street from them!"

"Are you talking about Uncle Bud?" Gail remembered him from the times she had been at her grandparents home. She knew there were a lot of secrets in that household because there was a lot of whispering and people talking behind closed doors. She had thought that some of it had to do with how her father carried on with so many women. She had no idea that the same kind of drama was going on in the generation above him.

"That's right. Uncle Bud. And he still lives down the street from my parents."

Gail couldn't imagine that her grandparents still carried on like they did when they were younger. Her father was the oldest of six siblings. She wondered if any of them were by Uncle Bud, but she was certainly not going to ask.

"At the marriage encounter, we had to do a family relationship history, like a family tree. That's when things became clear to me. My tree was so convoluted it was unbelievable. I had never looked at my family history like that before. I'd followed the same pattern in my life, and I don't want my children to inherit that legacy. My life changed that weekend. The people who did the workshop were so real and transparent. God used them to bring about a mighty change in this old man," he said smiling at Lillian.

"The Lord spoke to me clearly that weekend. He let me know that I could not prove my manhood by how many women I could get or how much money I earned. Over the last few months, I've learned how much God loves me and what manhood and fatherhood are really about."

Lillian remained silent as she dabbed her eyes with her napkin. Feeling a huge lump in her throat, Gail fought back her own tears.

Her father reached across the table and took both of her hands in his. "Gail, I want you to know that I love you, and I am going to do my best to establish a real relationship with you."

Gail was overcome as the tears streamed down her face.

"I love you, too, Daddy." Through her tears, she saw her father looking at her with such love and care in his eyes. She wanted to crawl into his lap and curl up. The waiter discreetly clearing the table broke the mood.

"Now," Phillip said, almost businesslike. "You said you had something you wanted to talk to me about as well?"

"Actually, umm, I just wanted to catch up with you and see how things were going," Gail said, feeling a tinge of shame.

When Gail's father asked her if she had a relationship with the Lord, she reluctantly shared a little about getting saved and attending The Word. He and Lillian were so excited about her experience that it made Gail rethink her decision about not going to The Word anymore. They said they would be sure to schedule their next trip so they could visit the church with her.

Gail considered the unexpected visit from her father an answer to the prayer she refused to pray after listening to the tape about the root of the matter. She knew she had purposely misinterpreted the gist of what Pastor Kline was saying. She had gotten angry about the lack of a relationship with her father, and if she had said all the things she had planned, there may not have been a reconciliation.

In spite of Gail's initial attitude, God brought an instant healing to the relationship. Gail felt like her father, Phillip, was digging up all his roots and replanting them with the compassion that can only come from knowing God. If Phillip followed through, at some point she would have to explain how she ended up pregnant before she got married, but surely he, of all people, would understand how that could happen.

When they dropped her off, Gail was actually sad to see the evening come to an end. She was refreshed by the fellowship, and she didn't look forward to the gloominess of her lonely condominium.

She went inside and immediately checked the caller ID. Mario had called again. Maybe this is a sign, Gail thought. If God could bring about such a great change in her father, maybe there was a chance her relationship with Mario really was meant to be. Mario seemed so sincere when he told her that he loved her. If she gave him a chance, maybe she would find out that he really was the man for her. He said himself that he had made a mistake marrying Nina. The chemistry between Gail and Mario was quite undeniable. If she could make it work with Mario, she would prove everyone wrong. She would show Nina that Mario really did want her, and she would show those women at church that she was a good woman who just happened to fall in love with a man who had gotten himself mixed up in an arranged marriage.

Picking up the phone, she quickly called Mario's cell number before she changed her mind.

"Hey, sweetheart. I'm so glad you returned my call. I'm on my way over."

"On your way over here?"

"You didn't listen to my message?"

"No, I just saw your number on the caller ID, and I called you."

"Well, I said I wanted to come over to see how you are doing. I want to spend time with you. We need to talk. I'm not far away."

Now she was nervous. Was this really the right thing to do? Sara had told her that she should cut him off completely. Maybe she *would* cut him off, but she would at least see what he wanted to talk about and how far his professed commitment would go.

CHAPTER 28

Two weeks later, Gail was sure that Mario was definitely committed to pampering her. However, she didn't know if it was because he loved her or because he was concerned about his unborn child. When Gail had finally gone to her gynecologist, the doctor expressed concern about the progression of the pregnancy. Dr. Hartman told Gail in no uncertain terms that she had to cut back on her work schedule and get as much rest as possible. Mario had insisted on being in the room with her, and he assured the doctor that Gail would do exactly what the doctor said.

Mario's attentiveness would have been irritating to her if she had not been worried about the pregnancy. Once the test came back positive in the doctor's office, she began to look forward to having Mario's child. Now that the doctor was expressing concern about the viability of the pregnancy, she was anxious for everything to be all right. Mario practically moved into her apartment and took over her life. He bought groceries, did all the cleaning and cooking, and he drove her to work every morning. She reduced her hours so that she got off at 2 p.m., and Mario was there each day to pick her up. Gail did her best to avoid talking to Sara at work, and thankfully, Sara never brought up Mario, even though Gail was sure Sara knew that Mario was staying at her condo. Mario told Gail that he and Nina were separated and he was filing for a divorce.

At least twice a week, Mario took Gail shopping for expensive maternity clothes, which she didn't even need yet. He wanted to buy things for the baby, but Gail persuaded him to wait until after the third month of the pregnancy. One Saturday evening they were in a mall department store, and Mario led Gail to the children's section to look at the baby clothes. Mario fell so in love with the little outfits by Ralph Lauren and Tommy Hilfiger that Gail couldn't keep him from buying a few.

After Mario paid for the clothes, Gail mentioned that she was in the mood for some ice cream so Mario insisted that they head for the food court. He was trying to get her to eat as much as possible because she had been losing weight. As they neared the food court, Gail recognized two women from the group that had confronted her at The Word the last time she had attended church. The women were walking straight toward Gail and Mario with daggers in their eyes.

"Let's go another way," Gail said, pulling at Mario's arm.

"Why? I thought you wanted some ice cream."

"Do you know those women coming toward us?"

"I know one of them. She goes to your church. Keep your head up. Stay by my side and keep walking," Mario gently commanded. He then proceeded to stare the women down as they made their approach. They were clearly prepared to say something mean, but their original plans were thwarted by the look on Mario's face. All they did was mutter half-hearted greetings in response to Mario's "Good evening, ladies."

Gail was grateful for Mario's boldness, but she couldn't hide her feelings of shame as they sat in the food court to eat their ice cream. Unable to enjoy her pralines and cream, she let it melt in the bowl.

"Gail, I know you're not going to let those girls spoil some good ice cream."

"It's not them," Gail lied. "I guess I've lost my appetite."

"You're probably just tired and hungry for some real food. Let's go home."

Back at the condo, Mario began preparing dinner, and Gail sat at the bar to keep him company as he cooked. She noticed the new growth plant she had gotten from The Word. It was in the corner of one of the kitchen counters, and the leaves were withering. She had been neglecting the plant and didn't even remember how often it was supposed to be watered.

"Do you know anything about plants?" she asked Mario.

"I know this one needs to be pruned." He grabbed the plant and started pulling off the dead leaves.

"What are you doing?"

"I'm pruning it. It also needs to be put in a larger pot."

"Well, maybe you can keep it alive."

Gail loved to watch Mario cook. His culinary talents were a cross between a gourmet chef and a down home southern cook. The brother could throw down on everything from fruit crepes to fried chicken. Tonight's delight was smothered pork chops, mashed potatoes and steamed broccoli. Gail didn't understand why she had lost weight because she certainly couldn't resist Mario's good cooking.

After dinner, Mario led her to the couch and began giving her a foot massage.

"Look Gail, I know what those women did at the mall bothered you."

"You're right it did, but it was nothing that couldn't be fixed by your TLC."

"I'm glad you feel that way because I've been thinking about some things."

"Like what?" Gail had been thinking about some things as well, but she didn't want to press Mario about the future until her pregnancy had progressed more.

"I don't intend to leave you alone with our baby. This condo is wonderful for the two of us, but we'll need more space for the baby. How would you like to live with me in my house in San Antonio?"

Gail didn't know what to say.

"Just think about it. Whenever you're ready, I could move you in and we could begin decorating the baby's room."

"What about Nina?"

"She moved out. I told you we were separated."

"Where did she go?"

"I guess she got her own place."

"I don't know about moving to San Antonio, but I'll think about it."

As Mario's expert hands soothed her feet, Gail said to herself, "This is almost perfect." Although Mario's house was a dream home and Gail could see herself living in it, she wanted to be absolutely sure about Mario's commitment to her before she did something like move out of her condo.

Gail woke up the next morning to the familiar smells of Mario's big Sunday breakfast. Their Sundays consisted of watching football, reading the paper, and sometimes a leisurely walk in the park a couple of blocks from Gail's condo. Anticipating another languid day with Mario, Gail put on some jeans and a sweatshirt. She wasn't showing yet and all her clothes still fit. She would have still denied being pregnant if the tests had not come back positive at the doctor's office.

When she went to the kitchen, Mario was all business.

"Gail, I have to go to San Antonio this morning. I'll be back tomorrow night."

"What? When did you know about this? Why are you just now telling me?"

"Sweetheart, I've been vacationing here with you for a month now. You know I have a business to tend to," Mario said.

Suspicion crept through Gail's mind. She wanted to stop the words, but they were past her lips before she could control her tongue.

"Are you going to see Nina?"

Mario chuckled as he put Gail's plate on the dining room table. He had made her an omelet full of vegetables and cheese with pan sausage and biscuits from scratch. She was almost distracted by the mouth-watering food.

"In the future, could you give me more notice? I didn't know I would be spending today alone," Gail pouted.

"I think I can manage that," Mario said. He squeezed her in a hug and whispered apologies into her ear. Gail welcomed his coddling. After a few minutes, he placed her in a chair at the table. "Now eat your breakfast before it gets cold."

Mario's trip to San Antonio was actually a blessing for Gail. Once he left, she felt a strange sense of relief. She was breathing easier, and she immediately knew why. One of Mario's idiosyncrasies became more obvious after he left.

Gail was generally a very tidy person, but Mario was obsessive, not only about cleanliness, but also about things being orderly and lined up straight. If he had not been staying with her, she never would have known Mario's need for order. She thought it was wonderful that he did all the cooking and cleaning, so she didn't complain about his obsessions. He had lined up everything on her bookshelves including her little figurines and pictures of her family. She went through her condo, moving things around until she felt more comfortable. When she got to the kitchen and saw how all the spices were lined up and how the food in the refrigerator and on the shelves were in perfect order, she decided not to move anything around. She didn't want to take a chance on him getting pissed off in the kitchen and refusing to cook for her. A thought occurred to her and she opened the shelf where the spices were and looked at them again. Sure enough, they were in alphabetical order. That was kind of spooky. Nevertheless, Gail decided to put Mario's obsession out of her mind. Many people thought she was a neat freak, so she didn't want to be judgmental about Mario's habits.

By the afternoon, she was settled on the couch to watch football games. Since Mario had moved in, they had begun letting the answering machine pick up all calls, so later in the day when she heard the click of the machine, she remembered that it was time to check her messages again.

The first week Mario was there, she got a call almost every day from Darien. Jason called three times leaving brief messages. She knew he was just trying to encourage her to go back to The Word. Joanna called inviting her to happy hour one week. Gail looked forward to showing Mario off at one of Joanna's holiday parties. She usually had one before Thanksgiving, one before Christmas and, of course, a New Year's Eve party. The only calls that Gail promptly returned were those from her father. He would call to give her updates on the holiday plans. He had been thinking about taking everyone on a skiing trip for Thanksgiving, but had settled on having a traditional holiday at his house in the Dallas area. The call that had just come through was from Sara. Gail certainly wasn't going to return that call.

CHAPTER 29

❀

After a rigorous Monday at work, Gail was tired and glad her days ended at 2 p.m. Maybe this was what it was like to feel pregnant. As she waited for the elevator, she was so tired and sleepy that she couldn't wait to get home to rest.

"Hey, Gail, hold the elevator for me," Sara said as the elevator door opened. "I'm leaving early today, too."

"Oh, hi, Sara," Gail said half-heartedly.

"How have you been doing?" Sara asked with a hint of her usual cheerfulness.

"I'm kind of tired today."

"I'm sorry to hear that. Could we talk briefly before you leave?"

"Well, I think I should get home," Gail said.

"Really, it will only take a minute. We haven't talked in weeks."

Gail wished Mario were waiting outside to pick her up. She couldn't honestly give Sara a good excuse for not giving her a few minutes of her time.

They went to the cafeteria on the first floor and sat down.

"So. How are things going?" Sara asked, smiling broadly.

"Actually, things are fine," Gail said. "The doctor wanted me to work fewer hours and get a lot of rest, but I feel great most of the time. What did you want to talk to me about?"

"I'll get right to the point. Jason told me what happened at church with those girls, and I just want you to know that I personally spoke to them. You should feel free to come back to church without worrying about what they may say or do."

"I've pretty much made up my mind about that, Sara. I won't be going to The Word anymore."

"Well, where will you be going?"

"I haven't decided, yet."

"I can recommend some places if you want me to. It's important that you attend church somewhere so you can continue to grow in the Lord."

"You know Mario is staying with me now," Gail said, eyebrows raised.

Sara heaved a huge sigh. "To tell you the truth, Gail, I didn't know that. However, I am not at all surprised. He's still being true to form."

"What do you mean by that?"

"Just what I said. He's just being himself."

"Well, he's been very kind and considerate to me. He's been taking real good care of me since the doctor told me to reduce my hours and get a lot of rest."

Sara looked away, shaking her head and sighing.

"What, Sara? Do you know something I don't?"

"Gail, I told you what you need to know about Mario, and you have still chosen to deal with him." Sara began gathering her things to leave. "Look I don't want this to end on a bad note. Just remember that you can always call me if you need anything. Please try to come back to The Word. If you don't want to go there, make sure you find a church where they preach the word without compromise."

Driving home, Gail grew more and more suspicious of Mario's trip to San Antonio. Sara was definitely trying to tell her something, but Gail had a hard time reading between the lines. Mario had proven to her that he cared for her, but Sara was saying that she shouldn't trust him. Gail didn't know what to believe. What if he did see Nina during his trip to San Antonio? They were still married. He had a right to see his wife if he wanted to. He had made it clear to Gail that he wanted to be with her and not Nina. She decided to believe Mario's actions rather than Sara's words.

When Mario returned from San Antonio later that night, he had plenty of action for Gail. He lavished her with gifts of perfume and bath oils as well as with his gentle lovemaking. Satiated, Gail fell into a restful sleep in Mario's arms.

Hours later, Gail was startled by the ringing of the doorbell. A glance at her alarm clock showed 2:12 a.m. Gail attempted to move Mario's arm from across her waist.

"Who could that be at this hour?" Mario asked groggily, pulling her closer.

"I don't know. Maybe they'll go away," Gail said, settling down, hoping to go back to sleep. The doorbell continued to ring incessantly. Suddenly, Gail was fully awake, and she knew exactly who was at the door.

"Mario, I think you'd better get the door."

"What? Why? They obviously have the wrong door."

"Then I'll get it," Gail said, jumping out of bed.

"No, wait. I'll go. You stay here. It might be someone dangerous." Mario threw on his robe and went to the door. Pulling on her own robe, Gail followed close behind him.

He looked through the peephole.

"Gail, go back to the bedroom," he commanded.

"I will not. Open the damn door or I will."

"I don't think this is a good idea, Gail."

The ringing of the bell was replaced with banging.

"Mario, this is becoming a public nuisance, and if you don't open the door, one of my neighbors will call the police."

Immediately, Mario turned the locks and opened the door.

"What the hell are you doing?" he hissed through clinched teeth and pulled Nina into the condo.

"I don't know what I'm doing, Mario. I followed you here and sat in the car for hours. I know I said I would give you time and space, but the very thought of not having you in my life makes me crazy," Nina said. Turning her attention to Gail, Nina continued, "Gail, please let him go. If it's true that you're pregnant, we'll pay child support. We'll take care of the baby, but please let Mario come back to me."

Gail was almost shocked speechless. "Don't put this on me. I'm not holding Mario hostage in here. He came here on his own."

"It takes two, Gail. If you hadn't been all up in my man's face at my wedding, he wouldn't be in this mess," Nina yelled. "And then coming around us like you're dating Jason when all along, you're trying to get Mario in your bed."

"You don't know what you're talking about!" Gail hollered. "You need to get your facts straight before you come up in somebody's house making accusations. I don't appreciate you coming in my house at 2 a.m. acting like a damn lunatic! You need to leave, right now!"

"I'm not leaving until Mario packs his things and comes with me! What are you going to do about that?"

"Nina, Gail, stop this right now," Mario said forcefully.

A dull ache rose in Gail's stomach and she felt like she needed to lie down. "It's time for this drama to end. Nina, if you don't leave, I'm calling the police."

"You can call the police if you want to. I'm the one with the diamond ring and the marriage license. I wish women like you could get arrested for stealing people's husbands."

A sharper pain hit Gail's lower abdomen and she almost doubled over. "If your husband really wanted to be with you, he wouldn't have been kissing me and seducing me the Thursday before your wedding," Gail said with venom. The pain in her stomach was increasing and her vision became blurred. Gail could see Mario struggling to keep Nina from physically attacking her even as she crumpled to the floor, fighting to stay conscious. She couldn't see or speak. All she knew was the pain, and she vaguely felt something wet and warm oozing between her legs. She was losing her battle with consciousness.

"Aw, hell. Look what you've done!" Mario yelled.

"I didn't do this. There's blood! Oh, God, Mario, she's having a miscarriage! Call 911!"

Gail felt herself being lifted from the floor.

"No, open the door, we'll take her. The hospital is not far from here! Get the damn door!"

CHAPTER 30

"Gail? Gail, can you hear me? Do you know where you are?" Gail didn't want to open her eyes. She still felt that terrible pain in her abdomen, and if she opened her eyes she thought it would get worse.

"Give me something for the pain," she whispered toward the familiar voice.

"Gail, do you know who I am?"

"I do, but it hurts, Doc."

"I'll give you something for the pain, but I need you to open your eyes and talk to me."

Gail opened her eyes and was surprised by the tears that were released and streamed down her face as she looked into the face of Dr. Darien Washington. She felt a mixture of shame and relief. How was she going to explain this to the good doctor? When she noticed the I.V. in her arm, she became alarmed and began sobbing.

"Don't cry, Gail. You're going to be all right. Your friends are very concerned about you," Darien said.

"What friends?"

"The ones who rushed you here. They were both quite hysterical, but I calmed them down. I let them know that I'm a member of your church, and I would personally take care of you," Darien said. Gail calmed down and used the tissue Darien gave to her.

"Where are they now?"

"I sent them to the chapel to pray for you," Darien said. "They found your father's phone number in your purse and called him."

"They did what?" she said, trying to rise up.

"It's okay. I talked to him and assured him that you're going to be fine," Darien said gently.

"Why would they call my father? I don't understand."

"You lost a lot of blood, and they were alarmed, Gail. They were just trying to help."

"What happened to me? Why did I lose so much blood?"

"We're running some tests right now, and a specialist will be in to talk to you later this morning."

"What kind of specialist?"

"We'll talk about that later," Darien said. He turned to speak at length to a nurse who had quietly stepped into the room and began working with the I.V. bottle that led to Gail's arm.

When he turned back to Gail, she was already drifting off to sleep. "Right now, we're giving you some more medicine for the pain. It's going to make you sleepy, so I'll be in later to talk to you."

Gail was suddenly overcome with apprehension, but she was too drowsy to protest and welcomed the comfort of unconsciousness.

"Please don't leave me," she tried to whisper before slipping away again.

Gail understood the message of the dream as soon as it began. Everything she saw was beautiful, but none of it was real. She discovered this because if she really looked at a thing, it disappeared or turned into something ugly. A beautiful bouquet of flowers turned into a pile of writhing snakes. A huge oak tree disappeared when she looked up at its massive height. A pretty, inviting meadow turned into a lake full of blood when she walked toward it. Okay, okay, I get the point. This dream needs to end right now, she thought. But the dream went on. More and more beautiful things came into her peripheral vision, causing her to turn her head from side to side so she could see everything. Finally, she discovered that if she looked straight ahead, she could move faster. And still faster she moved until she was flying. She liked flying. It felt completely wonderful. She turned her body, hoping to make a loop in the air, but then she was falling, falling and falling. Oh God, help me, she thought.

Trying to open her eyes and rid herself of the dream before she hit bottom, Gail awoke with a start. She welcomed the face of Darien, even though he looked quite worried.

"What's the matter Darien? Is something wrong with me?" Gail automatically reached for his hand.

"You've had a miscarriage, Gail," Darien said quietly. "I was hoping the gynecologist could be here to explain it all to you, but he was called to an emergency."

"Why did this happen?" She didn't bother stopping the tears that began rolling down her cheeks.

"Usually a miscarriage means that something's not developing correctly. This may have been a blighted ovum, which means the embryo wasn't developing at all. We were concerned with the blood loss, but it looks like you'll be fine."

The technical information did little to ease the emotional pain or answer her question. Where was Mario, now?

"You'll have a D&C to clear out your uterus later today," Darien continued. "Miscarriages are quite common with first pregnancies." Gail was glad Darien assumed correctly that this was her first pregnancy.

"My doctor must have known something was wrong. She practically put me on bed rest," Gail said.

"This was probably inevitable. It just wasn't a viable pregnancy," Darien said.

"So am I allowed to have visitors?" Gail pictured Mario pacing the hallway, but she couldn't imagine where Nina would be.

"I guess you could have visitors for a short time," Darien said.

"So, where are the people who brought me here?"

"You mean Mario and Nina? They left." Darien turned away from Gail and opened her chart. He was unable to hide an unmistakable look of disgust. Maybe he knew Mario was the father of her miscarried child.

"You know, Gail, I forgot to tell you that sometimes a blighted ovum is caused by weakness in the sperm," Darien said without taking his eyes from Gail's chart.

Gail surprised them both by bursting out laughing. But the tears flowed as well. She continued to laugh and cry, until she was overwhelmed with sadness. While she laughed, Darien stood staring at her, but when she broke down in sobs that wracked her body, he held her firmly in his arms. His soothing words calmed her.

"You just have to wait for the real thing, Gail. God knows what He's doing in your life. This was just a counterfeit. Wait on the Lord and have patience and courage. He has great things in store for you. Everything is going to be all right."

He held her close and tight, but there was nothing seductive in his comforting touch. Nevertheless, Gail thought, why was I messing around with a crazy guy like Mario when this wonderful man was in my life-space all along?

Darien had arranged for Gail to be in a private room and for her to have a D&C immediately to avoid any chance of infection in her uterus. It was only when she overheard the nurses talking that she realized he was pulling strings at the hospital. He was by her side during the awful procedure, and continued to comfort her during her crying spells throughout the day. If he had not been there for her, she would have felt totally abandoned in that sterile place. He only left her side a few times during the day. When she was released late that evening, Gail didn't know how she was going to get home.

"I took the liberty to buy you some clothes to go home in," Darien said, pulling a light blue Nike sweat suit and t-shirt out of a bag. There was a smaller bag that contained underwear and socks. He also placed a box of gym shoes on the bed. Gail hadn't even thought about clothes.

"I'll be back in a few minutes to drive you home."

"Darien, I'm really grateful for all you've done today. Thank you so much."

"It's the least I could do."

CHAPTER 31

Gail took a leave of absence from work. Her physical recovery was quick and painless, but she just didn't feel like going into the office. Darien called to check up on her everyday, and he tried his best to get her to go back to The Word. She was leaving for Dallas to spend Thanksgiving with her father the next week, so she used that as an excuse, claiming that she was getting ready for the trip. Her father called every day to check on her. Having spoken with Darien when she was in the hospital, her father knew much more than Gail wanted him to know. Although she was grateful he didn't ask questions about the pregnancy or the father of the baby, she was also surprised he didn't probe more.

Since she wouldn't go to church, Darien dropped by and gave her some tapes from recent sermons. Emotionally, she was not ready to face Sara and Jason or anyone else at The Word. She felt like such a fool for believing Mario. When she returned from the hospital on Tuesday, all his things were gone, and he had not called her since he left. He didn't even leave a note when he left. She knew it was over, but he could have at least called to see how she was doing.

Nina or Mario must have told Sara and Jason what happened because they both called her Wednesday and she let the answering machine pick up both calls. Jason just said he hoped everything was all right, but Sara said she was coming over with some chicken soup. When Sara arrived, she handed the warm pot of soup to Gail at the door.

"Come on in, Sara," Gail said.

"No, I'm supposed to meet Anthony in a few minutes, and I'm sure you need to get your rest."

"Actually, I'm well-rested, Sara." Gail left the door open and went into the kitchen to put the soup on the stove. She looked over her shoulder and saw Sara reluctantly follow her into the kitchen.

"You don't have to keep yourself from saying, 'I told you so.' I've learned my lesson well."

"Oh, Gail. I wouldn't say that to you."

"So how is everyone?"

"Jason is fine. The church is doing great."

"What about Nina and Mario?"

"I can't believe you asked me that."

"Well, I haven't heard from him, and I did go through something very traumatic."

"I thought you said you were doing fine."

"Physically, I feel fine."

"Well, if you want to heal emotionally, you should just forget about Mario."

"Okay, let's change the subject," Gail said. "What are you doing for Thanksgiving?"

"We'll be at Anthony's parents' house in South Austin. What about you?"

"I'm going to my dad's in Dallas."

"That's great," Sara said walking back toward the door. "I'm sorry I have to go now. I hope to see you back at church soon. I'll give you a call after Thanksgiving."

As usual, Gail felt like Sara knew more than she was willing to say. It was definitely over between her and Mario, but she was still curious about him.

When Darien called her on Thursday, she was determined to question him about the night she was brought into the emergency room.

"Darien, I guess you know that I was seeing Mario."

"I assume that's over now."

"What exactly happened when they brought me in?"

"Well, they were both pretty hysterical. You were conscious for some of the time. You don't remember anything?"

"The only thing I remember is talking to you in the hospital. Before that, the last thing I remember was falling out at home."

"I thought you would have remembered more."

"I don't. So will you tell me what happened?"

"I'll tell you, but first I want you to know you are better off without Mario in your life."

"I've come to that realization."

"Well, like I said, they were hysterical. Nina had called your father on her cell phone and he was quite upset. She had the presence of mind to grab your purse at your place, and she went through it looking for someone to contact in an emergency. She found your dad's number. I spoke to him the first time when they rushed you in. Once you were stabilized and after I talked to you, I went to tell Nina and Mario that you were going to be fine. They were already in a heated argument when I approached them. Mario asked to see you, and Nina told him that this was punishment from God for his cheating on her. I didn't feel comfortable letting Mario see you under the circumstances, but he was quite insistent. Nina kept up her tirade, and their argument escalated until I put them both out."

"You said you sent them to the chapel to pray for me."

"I did when you first got here. That's where I found them arguing. I'm glad you realize that Mario is not the man for you. You can do much better."

"Right now, I just need to get myself together. I listened to the tapes you brought to me. I noticed you threw in a lot of tapes about relationships."

"You caught that? I wasn't being sarcastic, though. I figured you might find comfort in Pastor Kline's teachings."

"Well, I feel like I have so much baggage now. I'm not fit to be in a relationship with anyone."

"And you shouldn't feel any pressure to be in a relationship. All you need to concern yourself with is your relationship with the Lord. Focus on God and allow Him to heal you. It's a process that won't happen overnight."

"You're right as always, Darien."

Gail told him she would be spending Thanksgiving at her father's house, and he said he would be spending Thanksgiving, Christmas and New Years working.

"That doesn't sound like a lot of fun," Gail said, frowning.

"I don't mind. It's all right for now, but when I get married and have children, I won't work these kind of hours," Darien said. "I can bring some holiday cheer to the unfortunate people who end up in the hospital at this time."

"There's one other thing, Darien. How much information did you give my father?"

"Actually, Nina was the one who told him you were having a miscarriage even before we had made a proper diagnosis. I spoke to him a couple more times because he kept calling. I had to convince him not to come down here. I'm sure he'll be relieved to see how well you're doing."

"Yeah, but I would have preferred if he didn't know about this whole fiasco. I haven't even told my mother."

"You'd better hope Nina hasn't called your mother, too," he said with a chuckle.

"Very funny," Gail said. "I really appreciate everything you've done for me.

"Don't mention it. You just follow doctor's orders and get plenty of rest."

Although Gail agreed with everything Darien said about relationships, her heart flip-flopped when Mario called her late Saturday night.

"Oh, Baby. You don't know how much I wanted to be there to hold you and comfort you. Are you all right?"

"I'm fine, Mario. I thought you would have called sooner than this."

"Things have just been crazy. I can't even talk long now. But I'll make it up to you. We'll talk after Thanksgiving."

"No, Mario. We really don't have to talk anymore at all," Gail said even though she wanted him to call her again.

"Don't be silly, Gail. You know I love you, and I want to be there for you no matter what. I'll call you after next week. I promise."

CHAPTER 32

Thanksgiving at her father's house was interesting for Gail. When she got to their house, Phillip and Lillian greeted her with extra long hugs and hovered over her, making her feel uncomfortable.

"Gail, are you sure you're okay?" her father asked.

"Dad, really, I'm fine."

"Is there anything I can do for you?"

Turn back time is what Gail wanted to say, but she just shrugged her shoulders.

"Well, Gail, just know we are here for you, and if you want to talk about anything, we are available any time," Lillian said.

None of Phillip's other children showed up, even though they were all invited. Gail could tell that Phillip was disappointed. Lisa was spending the holiday at her in-laws in Detroit. Leslie was trying to make a good impression on her fiancé's family in Houston, and Jeremy and Michael were apparently not so receptive to their father's new interest in their lives.

"Everyone says they'll come for Christmas, though," Phillip said brightly. "I'm just glad you're here, Gail. I can't say my other children share the same beliefs we do just yet, but God is still in control."

They had a bountiful spread of food. Phillip's parents, Anna Marie and Clarence, and to Gail's surprise, Uncle Bud rounded out their Thanksgiving table.

Because her father had told her about the history of her grandparents and "Uncle" Bud, Gail paid close attention to how they interacted. Strangely enough, she could see how the three of them coexisted in an interesting triad. Clarence, Gail's grandfather was gregarious and fun loving. He didn't take himself or anyone else very seriously. It seemed that everything was always all right with Clarence.

Bud was Clarence's altar ego. He was quiet, introspective and loved literature and jazz music. Bud was always reading a book, and although he didn't talk much in a group, he would talk endlessly to Gail about every author from Henry James to Octavia Butler and any jazz musician from Charlie Parker to the Marsalis brothers.

Anna Marie was an intelligent woman who had taken money Clarence won from gambling and bought rent houses. Anna Marie was not the typical cookie-baking grandmother. The most time Gail spent with her during the summer was when they went shopping for clothes for Gail. Otherwise, Anna Marie was always busy with her business.

Phillip had inherited his father's good looks and charm and his mother's business acumen. Gail had known these people all her life, but her father's insight into their relationship made her look at everyone differently. It was as if she were now seeing them through grown-up eyes.

Anna Marie asked Gail about her mother, Annette, and her family. Gail had talked to her mother earlier in the week.

"They're all doing fine," Gail said. She correctly guessed that this was just a warm-up question for Anna Marie.

"So, do you have any interesting suitors in your life right now?"

"I have a couple of friends, but I'm not focusing on a relationship at the moment."

"I've actually met one of Gail's friends. He's a doctor," Phillip said. Gail looked at her father in shock.

"Dad, Darien is just a friend. He goes to my church." She couldn't believe her father would even mention Darien.

"That makes him an even better candidate," Phillip said.

"When are we going to meet this doctor, Gail?" Anna Marie asked.

"He's very busy with his work, and we're not involved in that way."

"I hope you're not giving him a hard time. You don't want to end up like Cassie," Anna Marie said. Cassie was Ann Marie's youngest daughter, and she never married and never had children.

All eyes were on Gail and she wanted to sink through the floor. If she responded to the last comment, the conversation would never end. She wanted to change the subject before someone asked the question, "You do like men, don't you?" Lillian came to her rescue.

"Speaking of Cassie, where is she spending Thanksgiving?" Anna Marie then launched into a conversation about where all her children were spending the holiday.

"But for Christmas, everyone will be at our house." Anna Marie said. "Gail, I hope you can make it."

"I'll do my best to be there," Gail said.

Friday was a big shopping day for the women, and they had warned Gail to get plenty of rest Thursday night. They showered Gail with gifts of clothes and shoes, and she was glad that neither Lisa nor Leslie had shown up. To Gail's delight, Anna Marie was too involved in shopping to ask her any more questions about relationships.

On Sunday, Gail went to church with her parents and enjoyed the wonderful fellowship at the full gospel Baptist church they attended. The church was not as large as The Word, but it was growing so fast they were planning to build a larger sanctuary. After church, Gail's father was unusually quiet. When they got home, he asked to speak to her privately.

She followed him to his study feeling like she was about seven years old. She stared at his back, trying to decipher the meaning of his square shoulders and purposeful stride. Gail settled on a plush suede love seat and Phillip sat on a matching chair. He leaned forward with his elbows on his knees and his hands clasped.

"I didn't want to ruin the holiday, so I put off this conversation until now," Phillip said.

"If this is about what I went through in the hospital, you don't have anything to worry about," Gail said.

"Oh, I have plenty to worry about, Gail. It looks like the cycle is repeating itself. Listen, I don't need to know the details. I've lived different scenarios so many times myself, and I've brought shame on my entire family as a result. I can't tell you how to live your life, but I pray that you'll listen to what I have to say."

Gail relaxed as her father's tone softened.

"Adultery is one of the top Ten Commandments for a reason. We may enjoy the intrigue and temporary gratification from an illicit affair, but it speaks very little about the characters of the people involved. When I was running around, cheating on your mother, I was sowing seeds of betrayal that have now developed into dissension, lack of trust and total turmoil in my relationships with my other children. Lisa and Leslie have not forgiven me for cheating on their mother, and the boys have not forgiven me for not being in their lives. My mis-guided attempts at reconciliation have been met with everything from indiffer-ence to contempt. You are the only child that I have been able to begin to build a real relationship with, and now I find out you're involved with a married man. This relationship could devastate your life."

It already has, Gail thought. "But it's over between me and Mario," she said.

"Well, when he comes back around, I hope you're strong enough to stay away from him. I know what kind of man Mario is. I used to be like that. Trust what I'm saying because I know all the tricks and schemes. He'll string you along, telling you he's going to leave his wife, but he never will. And even if he did and married you, he would cheat on you with someone else."

Gail was exasperated at Phillip's assessment.

"I need you to understand the spiritual problems with adultery. You have to understand that it is wrong according to God's word. You've got to have a desire to please God rather than please your flesh. I'm not going to tell you that I didn't enjoy myself when I was out there running wild, and I can't say I slowed down when I got older. If anything, I was more determined to prove that I could keep up. The only thing that made me stop was a real encounter with the Lord. I was like Paul on the road to Damascus, and when the blinders fell off I was able to see my life in a totally different light. I stopped being unfaithful because I realized that God had called me to be a man of honor, integrity and faithfulness, and He provided a way for me to live for Him through His Son. Do you know how many years I lived for myself and my own pleasures? I was so grateful to hear that God could and would forgive me! My main regret is that it took me so long to really hear the message of the cross and allow God to change my life."

Gail had begun to cry silently somewhere in the middle of her father's speech.

"I do want to please God, Dad," she said, her voice cracking. "I got saved, but God didn't get me out of this relationship."

"Sweetheart, God is not going to physically remove you from situations in most cases. You still have the freedom to choose. You still have to struggle through internal and external battles."

Phillip sat next to Gail and held her hand.

"Gail, I want you to know that I take full responsibility for the results of my not being in your life. If I had been the kind of father I should have been, you may not have even ended up in this mess. Forgive me for being so distant, and allow me to build a relationship with you now."

"Oh, Daddy, I've already forgiven you. You're right. I've made some bad choices, but in spite of it all, I've been growing in the Lord."

Phillip explained that he believed there was a generational curse in their family. Adultery was passed on from one generation to the next, and he was determined to break the curse. They prayed together, and Gail's admiration for her father grew as she listened to him pray and speak the word of the Lord over her life and others in their family.

Gail returned to Austin Sunday night and to work on Monday, resuming her regular work schedule. Sara welcomed her, and they were almost back to normal in their friendship. Gail didn't even mind Sara's constant invitations to church. It was just like old times.

True to his word, Mario called Monday night. She avoided his calls until Tuesday when she forgot to let the answering machine pick up.

"I'm in town, I'll be over in a few minutes."

"No, Mario. This is not happening tonight. You absolutely cannot come over here."

"Okay, that's fine, Gail," he said. "Meet me at the Omni at seven. I just want to talk to you. Even if you want to end the whole thing, you can at least meet me there so we can talk like civilized adults."

"Whatever you have to say to me, you'll have to do it right now on the phone. I am not meeting you at the Omni. Do you think I'm stupid?"

"No, I don't think you're stupid, but you've confirmed one thing for me. You can't resist me."

"I just did, but you refuse to flee. Now what do you want to talk to me about."

"Okay, have it your way," Mario sighed into the phone. "You drive me crazy sometimes, Gail. I love you so much, and I want you so much, I don't know what to do."

Gail rolled her eyes, and didn't respond.

"I want you to understand that I'll be as available as I can, but things have changed somewhat," Mario said.

"Changed how? Besides the fact that this relationship is over?"

"Well, it looks like Nina's pregnant now."

Gail sank into the couch and tears welled in her eyes.

"So now that Nina's pregnant, you want to be with her? Is that it? Is that what you called to tell me?"

"I wanted to talk to you about this in person, Gail. You're the one who has me on the phone telling you this. I love you, Gail. I've just gotten myself caught up in this mess of a marriage, and now she's pregnant. I still want to leave, but I just don't know what to do. I want to be with you."

"I can make this very easy for you, Mario. You just take care of your family and forget about me."

"I've tried that already, Gail. I can't live without you," Mario said. "Please work with me on this. I hoped you would understand what I'm going through."

"Who do you think I am?"

"You're my woman, Gail. You're the woman I love."

"Well, who is Nina to you Mario?"

"Right now, she's carrying my baby, and I can't just leave her."

"I have never asked you to leave Nina."

"So why are you having such a problem, now? Look, let's meet in Corpus Christi again. We had such a wonderful time."

"Mario why do you think this is okay? Why do you think you can have both me and Nina?"

"I've explained this to you before. I shouldn't have gotten married. When you came along, you helped me realize that. Please work with me on this. We can get through this thing together, Gail. I love you, and the last time I checked, you loved me, too."

"If you love me so much and you don't want to be with Nina, when did you have time to get her pregnant? Did she just force herself on you, Mario?"

"Well, I am married. That's just part of it."

"You're full of crap. Let me tell you one thing right now. I am no longer part of it. I'll tell you one thing, though. You really had me. I fell for you, hook, line and sinker. Even after you raped me, I came back for more."

"Wait a minute. I did not rape you. You wanted it as much or probably more than I did. You came to my home looking like a fashion model, and then you flirted with me the whole time you were there. You knew what you were doing."

"Well, let this be your notice. This relationship is over. Don't call me anymore. Don't send me flowers or gifts."

"I hear what you're saying, but this is what I'm going to do. I'm going to put a ticket in the mail, and I'll be at the airport in Corpus Christi to pick you up. We'll just see how much resolve you have to resist me. I know you're upset right now. You've had a horrible miscarriage and you probably feel like I abandoned you. But, I know you can't forget how good I make you feel, and nobody will ever be able to treat you like I do. December eleventh. That's the day I'll see you in Corpus Christi."

"If you send me a ticket or anything else, I'll tear it up as soon as I get it."

"That's fine. Tear it up if you want to, but when you come to your senses, just go to the airport in Austin and give them your name. You can fly without the ticket. I know you, Gail. Eventually, you're going to need me. Your body is going to yearn for me to the point that you ache. I'm the only one who can satisfy that ache, baby."

"Lord, help!" Gail yelled after slamming the phone down. Although she was outraged over his sheer gall, she was also frustrated with the small part of her that was actually aroused, even now, by Mario. This man knew exactly how to appeal to her flesh. This was the final test and she was determined to pass.

The best way to avoid the temptation to take Mario up on his offer was to simply be out of town already. She called her father and asked if she could visit on the weekend of December eleventh. When the ticket arrived in the mail, as Gail promised, she tore it up and threw it in the trash near her mailbox. On Friday, she left work early and drove to Dallas.

CHAPTER 33

Gail woke up Saturday morning feeling triumphant. She had successfully avoided the last temptation, and now she looked forward to her reward, which was another shopping spree with Lillian. Although she could pay full price for the best designer clothes, Lillian had a gift for finding good deals.

After a quick breakfast with Phillip and Lillian, Gail watched as the two of them hugged and kissed before they said good-bye. Phillip was going to play golf for the morning.

"We're meeting for lunch, aren't we?" Gail said playfully. "You would think you're not going to see each other for weeks."

"You just make sure Lillian doesn't spend all my money. Remember that every dime you spend decreases your inheritance," Phillip said to Gail, winking.

After shopping, lunch with Phillip and a little more shopping, the women returned home exhausted. Later that evening, Gail was napping in the guest room when there was a knock on the door.

"Gail, there's someone here to see you," Lillian said. "It's Mario."

Gail jumped up, angry. How did he even find her in Dallas? Gail paused when she saw the suspicious look on Lillian's face, but she continued past her and marched downstairs without washing her face or fixing her hair. Mario was in the sitting room off the grand entrance of the house.

When she stormed into the room, he held out his hands toward her and said, "If this doesn't prove I love you, I don't know what will."

"How did you know where I was? Did Sara tell you I was here?" Gail's mind was racing. She had told Sara about the ticket, and they both agreed that going to Dallas was a good idea to keep Gail's mind off Mario's last proposition.

"It really doesn't matter how I found out, but this should tell you how serious I am about us."

"This tells me that you're crazy," Gail said with venom in her voice.

"Yeah, I'm crazy for you, Gail. Look, I haven't seen you since I left you at the hospital. I was really worried about you, but I had to get Nina situated that day. She was acting completely out of her mind at the hospital. Darien assured me that he would take care of you, so I got Nina out of there as quickly as I could. We both lost something that day, and I've never had a chance to mourn with you. That little life that slipped away was a result of our union of love, Gail. That is a serious thing to me, and I'm sorry I couldn't be there for you the way I should have been."

"Okay, but that's over now." Gail fought back the tears and emotions stirred by his words. Darien had been there for her that day, but she had really wanted Mario there for all the reasons he just named. Nevertheless, she had resolved to end things with Mario. "I'm over it. You just have to get over it as well."

"You don't get over a miscarriage just like that. You're just trying to be strong for some strange reason. Come here and let me hold you. I'm the only one who really knows what you went through."

"I don't need you to hold me. I'm fine." She felt the first tear slip down her cheek.

"Look at you. I know I've put you through hell. Let me make it up to you." Mario crossed the few steps between them, and gingerly took Gail into his arms. "I don't want you to be unhappy. Just tell me what you want and I'll do it."

Just then, a knock on the frame of the open door startled Gail. She turned to see her father at the door.

"Oh, Dad, this is Mario Lewis," Gail said wiping her tears.

"Mr. Adams, I'm delighted to meet you," Mario said, turning on his charm full throttle. Gail watched as they shook hands. Mario clasped her father's hand in both of his, and in that instant, Phillip looked down and grabbed Mario's left hand and looked at his wedding ring. Seeing the angry look on Phillip's face, Gail didn't know what to expect from her father.

"Where's your wife, Mario?"

"Well, uh, sir, we're separated right now."

"Is that right?" He glanced at Gail. She saw that he didn't believe a word of it. You can't play a player, she thought.

"How long have you been separated?"

Mario pulled his shoulders back in defiance. The men stared at each other, and the tension in the room became so thick, Gail began to feel claustrophobic. They were like two lions circling each other before battle. Phillip's face had a menacing glare. Mario responded with his own battle stance, letting Phillip know he was ready for a fight, even if it came down to getting physical.

"Daddy, Mario was just leaving," Gail said.

"Excuse me, sweetheart," Phillip said looking at her briefly. His voice softened when he spoke to her, but the look on his face silenced her and made her more nervous. "I need to talk to Mario in private. Would you come into my study with me, Mario?"

Mario didn't answer and didn't move when Phillip turned to walk out of the room. "I won't take up much of your time," Phillip said over his shoulder.

"With all due respect, sir," Mario said, barely maintaining a respectful tone. "I came here for one purpose only, and that was to see the woman I love."

Phillip spun on his heel and walked back into the room, right up to Mario. He was about three inches taller than Mario, and his larger frame was clearly dominant.

"I don't know what kind of games you're playing, but you won't be playing them with my daughter."

"You don't know anything about me, Mr. Adams. I don't know what Gail has told you, but I have every intention of—"

"Of what?"

Just then, Lillian walked into the room.

"What is going on in here?" she asked, surveying the scene. Phillip took a step back from Mario but still maintained a threatening stance.

"Mario was just leaving, wasn't he, Gail?" Phillip said.

"Listen, Gail, just come with me so we can talk about this," Mario pleaded. "When I found out that you didn't board the plane, I immediately came down here. All I'm asking is that we just go somewhere so we can talk."

"Well, maybe we could talk here," Gail said, looking to Lillian for some kind of support.

"I don't think that is necessary, Gail," Phillip said sternly.

"Dad, why are you acting like this? You don't even know Mario."

"I know more than enough," Phillip said. He glared at Mario, and continued, "This man is married and he's probably filling your mind with lies about how he's going to leave his wife."

"I was going to get a divorce before I found out—"

"Mario, please!" Gail yelled.

He looked at her, surprised.

"Before you found out what?" Phillip asked. Mario turned to him, but refused to answer his question. Phillip turned to Gail. "Trust me, Gail. This relationship will devastate your life if you continue on with it."

"But look at you and Lillian, Dad," Gail said. "You cheated on my mother with her, and now you two are happily married!"

"What?" Mario said throwing up both his hands. "I can't believe this! And you're trying to tell me how to run my life?"

"You're right about one thing, Gail," Phillip said, ignoring Mario. "I cheated on your mother. But I cheated on Lillian, too. We have only been 'happily' married in recent months."

"If I were married to Gail, I would never cheat on her," Mario said, tipping the scale of Phillip's anger. Before Gail and Lillian could respond, Phillip had pushed Mario against the wall and pinned him there with his forearm across his throat.

"I was going to let you get away with this mess, but I'll just let you know right now that I know about your other two children." Phillip spoke directly into Mario's face as Mario squirmed, trying to free himself. Phillip leaned into Mario's throat, causing him to gasp for air. "Gail probably doesn't even know about them, does she? Do you think the child support you pay is going to be enough to make up for you not being there? How often do you actually visit them in Corpus Christi?"

Gail sat down, shocked and drained of all emotion.

"Phillip, just let the man go," Lillian said, placing her hand gently on her husband's back.

"I'm not finished with him, just yet," Phillip said, still staring into Mario's face. "I used to be just like you. I know all the tricks and schemes. You may be able to fool the women, but you can't fool me. You need to realize that there is a price for the way you're living."

Phillip must have relaxed his grip. Gail watched as Mario somehow got enough leverage to push her father away from him. Phillip's body fell into Lillian who was still standing behind him. She fell backwards and her head landed on the coffee table and bounced onto the floor. Gail screamed and Phillip bent over his wife, "Lillian are you all right?"

When he saw that she was unconscious, he turned around looking for Mario who was inching his way toward the door. Even as he ran toward Mario, he had the presence of mind to yell at Gail, "Call an ambulance!"

Phillip tackled Mario and they landed out on the marble floor of the grand entry. Gail ran toward the phone as the men fought in the foyer.

While she was giving the 911 operator information, Lillian came to. "She's conscious now!" Gail told the operator.

"Are you okay, Lillian?" Gail yelled frantically. The only response she got was a groan, and Lillian seemed to have a hard time moving. "Please hurry," Gail yelled into the phone and hung up.

Gail heard a crash in the foyer and was torn between tending to Lillian and trying to break up the fight.

"Oh my God," Lillian groaned. "Don't let Phillip kill that boy." Gail ran into the foyer and saw Phillip straddling Mario. Phillip had a fist in the air, preparing to deliver another blow to Mario's already bloody face.

"Daddy, please don't!" Gail yelled. Instead of hitting Mario, Phillip grabbed his collar with both hands.

"When I release you, I want you to walk out of this house. I don't want to ever see you again in my life. Do you understand?"

Mario just stared up at Phillip, but when released he walked directly to the door. Once he was outside, he began yelling at the top of his voice. "I love you, Gail. Don't ever forget that! I love you!"

After slamming the door, Phillip ran to Lillian.

"Oh, baby, I'm so sorry. Where are you hurt?"

"My head is throbbing," she said rubbing the back of her head." Phillip got a pillow from the couch and gently propped her head up.

"I'm not going to move you, okay, honey," he said softly. "We'll just wait right here for the ambulance."

"They're on the way," Gail said feeling stupid.

The ambulance arrived within minutes and the paramedics took Lillian's vital signs. The fall didn't break the skin on the back of her head, but there was an ugly swelling, and they were apparently concerned about her neck because they stabilized her head before placing her on a stretcher.

Phillip told Gail to follow the ambulance to the hospital in his car.

Although the doctor wanted to keep Lillian for a few hours for observation, he assured Phillip that she would be fine. The most humiliating thing for Gail was talking to the police about the entire incident. They insisted on talking to them all separately, and Gail felt intimidated by the questioning. Thankfully, she told the plain truth and the police seemed satisfied with everyone's story.

"I should have pressed charges against that fool," Phillip said after the police had left. He got a private room for Lillian. Even if they were only going to be there a few hours, Phillip refused to have Lillian in a common room full of other patients.

Gail was impressed with the attentiveness her father showed toward his wife. He stayed close to her bedside, holding her hand and talking softly to her.

"Phil, I'm really okay. I just have a headache."

"Baby, I'm so sorry this happened."

"I'm sorry, too, Lillian," Gail said. "Dad, I don't know how he found your address. I'm really sorry."

"It's okay, Gail. I don't blame you for what he did today."

Gail sighed in relief. She shivered at the thought that things could have been so much worse.

"Dad, what is this business about Mario having two other children?"

"I wasn't sure if you knew about them or not," Phillip said, moving to sit in a chair next to Gail. "I did some investigating on Mario Lewis when I got that hysterical call from his wife at the hospital. I found out that he has two children by a woman in Corpus Christi. He does pay child support, but he has a hard time getting to see the children. You didn't know anything about that did you?"

"I didn't know. I wonder why Mario didn't tell me about them."

"Because he only gives you information that works to his advantage. Don't you see, Gail? Mario is not such an honest man. I should know. I used to be just like him not so long ago."

"It was very painful to have a miscarriage, but I guess it's a good thing that I didn't have his child."

"God is in control, Gail. It was never meant for you to have Mario's child. God just used the situation to get your attention."

"He certainly has my attention now."

CHAPTER 34

Monday morning at work, Gail asked Sara if she would join her for lunch.

"I just want to thank you for trying to warn me about Mario," Gail began. She went on to tell her what happened over the weekend.

"I can't believe that! Your father beat Mario up?" Sara's eyes were wide and she looked as if she were suppressing a grin.

"I guess he did. Mario had a bloody nose, and my father didn't even have a scratch on him."

"I'm glad your stepmother is okay. Thank the Lord. That could have been totally disastrous."

"Did everyone know about Mario's children but me?"

"It's apparently a very painful thing for him. Their mother tries to keep him from seeing them. Every once in a while their grandmother arranges for Mario to see them. If he ever goes to Corpus Christi, it's probably to see his children. I started to tell you, but I thought he would have let you know at some point."

"Well, he didn't, and I even met him in Corpus one weekend," Gail said. "I know I shouldn't care, but what happened to the relationship with his children's mother?"

"After all you've been through with him, do you really have to ask? It was the same song, different verse," Sara said. "Would it have made a difference if you had known about his children?"

"I don't know. I'm just glad it's over now."

"Is it really over?"

"Of course it is," Gail said. "I wasn't impressed with him coming all the way to Dallas and demanding that I leave with him. It just showed me how selfish he is and how much he wants things to go his way. He's not concerned with what's best for me or anyone else."

Christmas in Dallas was full of festivities and good food. Again, none of Gail's siblings showed up, but Phillip, Lillian and Gail filled their time visiting friends and family. On Christmas Day they gathered at Clarence and Anna Marie's house. Gail enjoyed seeing all her aunts, uncles and cousins but quickly got tired of answering questions about whether she was dating or engaged yet.

Gail drove back to Austin a few days after Christmas because Sara insisted that she attend the New Years service at The Word. The church was decorated throughout with balloons and streamers, and there was a festive buffet banquet before the service started. Gail sat with Sara and Anthony at the party and avoided socializing. The service proved extremely healing for Gail. She felt like Pastor Kline's message was just for her.

"The things that hindered you this year are not going to hinder you next year. When the clock strikes twelve, I want you to know that your time has come. You have the power to speak to that mountain and tell it to be removed. Don't drag all the things that kept you from serving the Lord into next year. Leave it all here at this altar and walk in the mighty power of God."

When he started his message, Pastor Kline had instructed the congregation to write down all the things that hindered them in the past year. Anytime in the service when they felt ready, they were to take the piece of paper and place it on the steps of the altar. During the sermon, people randomly went to the altar to lay down their burdens.

"Those that know their God shall do mighty exploits. You are here on this earth to worship the Lord and carry out His mission for your life. Don't let anything hinder you. Don't let money problems keep you from giving and progressing. Don't let relationship problems keep you from fellowship with the saints. Don't let the cares of this world keep you from living your life devoted to God. Lay down all the things that will keep you from moving forward. Tonight you are empowered to do the wonderful works God has planned for your life."

Gail had one thing she knew of that had hindered her, and that was an unhealthy desire for a relationship at any cost. She didn't blame Mario for seducing her into a relationship. She knew her own desire led her down a destructive path. She thanked God that He showed her honorable men like Jason and Darien who refused to take advantage of her. When she felt a release from the shackles that bound her to the fantasy of a relationship with Mario, it was like a well-spring bubbled up inside of her. She jumped from her seat and joined others in the aisles taking their issues to the altar even as Pastor Kline continued to encourage them in the word.

The possibilities in her life included working with her father in his business. He had asked her to be his chief financial officer and travel all over the world with him and Lillian, but she would have to be based in Dallas. She didn't know if she would take him up on his job offer, but it was an exciting possibility.

After the service was over, Jason approached her.

"Hey Gail. We're going to IHOP for breakfast if you would like to join us."

"Actually, Jason, I think I'm going home. I want to spend some time pondering the message."

"I can understand that. This has been some year for you, hasn't it?"

"It has, but I've learned so much."

"You've also grown stronger. You know, Gail, you are a wonderful woman. One day you're going to be somebody's good thing. You know the Bible says that when a man finds a wife, he finds a good thing," Jason said with a smile.

"I have a long way to go before I'm wife material, but I appreciate the compliment."

"It may not be as long as you think," Jason said quietly.

"Well, in any event, our next bride is Sara."

"I was disappointed to hear that you're not going to be in the wedding. Why did you back out?"

"Mainly because it's time for me to be honest with myself. One of the reasons I liked being in weddings is because of the fairy tale atmosphere. Weddings, small and large, are really quite wonderful. But because of where I was in my mind, it was always a big fantasy for me. Each wedding just fed into my fairy tale view of love and marriage. I would often pretend I was the bride when I walked down the aisle. Instead of a bridesmaids dress, I would imagine that I had on a designer wedding dress. That's over for me. I need to concentrate on being the best person I can be so that one day, if I do walk down that aisle, I'll be prepared for life after the ceremony."

"So you're not going to be in any more weddings unless it's your own?"

"That's right. And I'm in no rush."

0-595-32067-8

Printed in the United States
128148LV00004B/6/A